5/97

SANTA MARIA PUBLIC LIBRARY

D0034770

Discarded by
Santa Maria Library

FIC M
Reed, Philip (Philip C.)
Bird dog /
c1997.

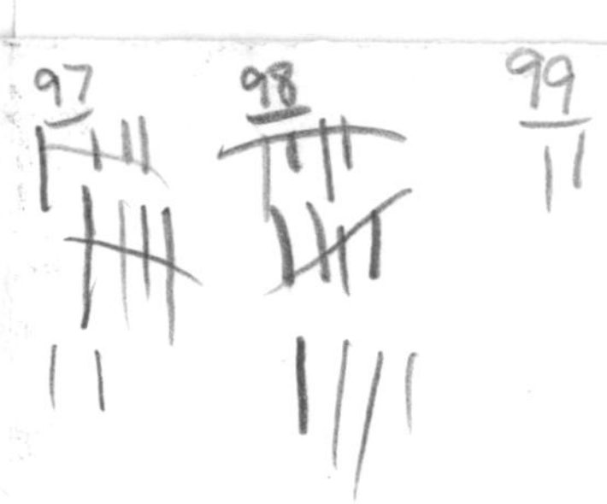

JUL 97

GAYLORD MG

6/97

Bird Dog

Bird Dog

Philip Reed

POCKET BOOKS
New York London Toronto Sydney Tokyo Singapore

This book is a work of fiction. Names, characters, places and incidents are products of the author's imagination or are used fictitiously. Any resemblance to actual events or locales or persons, living or dead, is entirely coincidental.

POCKET BOOKS, a division of Simon & Schuster Inc.
1230 Avenue of the Americas, New York, NY 10020

Copyright © 1997 by Philip Reed

All rights reserved, including the right to reproduce this book or portions thereof in any form whatsoever. For information address Pocket Books, 1230 Avenue of the Americas, New York, NY 10020

ISBN: 0-671-00163-9

First Pocket Books hardcover printing June 1997

10 9 8 7 6 5 4 3 2 1

POCKET and colophon are registered trademarks of Simon & Schuster Inc.

Printed in the U.S.A.

To Vivian Blackwell

Acknowledgments

I want to extend my sincere thanks to John Hawkins for his expert handling of *Bird Dog* and for being everything I always hoped an agent would be. Warren Frazier and Luis Rios also have my thanks for their help and support. On the other coast, I would like to express my gratitude to Irv Schwartz, at Renaissance, for his intelligence and commitment to the book.

At Pocket Books I am extremely grateful to my editor, Dudley Fraiser, for asking all the right questions, encouraging me to rework the ending and doing it all in such a wonderful way. I would also like to express my gratitude to Emily Bestler and Amelia Sheldon at Pocket Books for their care and skill in publishing this book.

My friend Mark Stevens and my brother Kevin Reed read the book at a critical time and their enthusiasm helped me to move forward. Other friends who helped me greatly by reading, critiquing, and responding were Matt Wagner, Bob Sykes, Kirby Hall, and Bruce Perry. My parents and the rest of my family and friends have also given me years of encouragement and support, and for that I am deeply indebted to them all.

Bird Dog

El Jefe and his crew were selling two cars a minute at the LA Auto Auction when Harold looked up and saw her coming toward him, knifing her way through the crowd, her eyes dark with anger. Guys stepped aside, then checked her out from behind, shaking their heads and smiling at the short skirt and killer legs propped on spike heels.

Trouble was, Harold had his eye on an '86 Maxima inching its way toward the sign that said, "This Car Being Sold Now." It was a real cream puff, and Harold knew he could slap a hundred-dollar detail job on it and make a grand easy in a week. Nice piece of change for a little hustle.

But now here she was, arriving in front of him, squinting in the blazing October sun and saying, "They told me I'd find you here."

Just like that. He'd never met her before—officially. But he knew she was Marianna Perado and she worked across the hall from him in Requisitions. He watched her walk back and forth across the office every day, the sight taking his mind all sorts of places it shouldn't go.

"They told me you come here on your lunch hour," she said, her voice cutting through the auctioneer's drone.

"They?"

"Your secretary. I heard you know something about car buying."

"I used to sell cars," he said, glancing toward the Maxima.

It was on the block, and El Jefe was about to start the bidding. "Before I got a real job."

She didn't laugh. Instead she paused, breathing hard, and said, "The son of a bitch lied to me."

Harold saw her cheeks were flushed, eyes shot with hatred. Raven hair pulled back. A red gash of lipstick surrounded flashing teeth.

He slipped his hand into his pocket, unconsciously seeking his therapy ball. He used a Hacky Sack ball, kneaded it all day, mashing the beads between his thumb and forefinger. He was on his second therapy ball this month and that wasn't good. The seams had split and the beads were leaking out into his hand. Stress. It was a noose around his neck, squeezing the life out of him.

"You get ripped off or something?" Harold asked. He felt puny beside this woman with her volcanic anger.

"I just wanted a good reliable car. . . ." Marianna began. Then the memory of what happened overwhelmed her. "Fuck," she said, the word hissing from her mouth.

Harold thought of the women he'd seen on the streets of Santiago with a history of violence and death in their eyes. He thought of the night, lying in bed, he'd mentioned his ex-wife to Carmen and had seen the jealousy flooding her face. He had assumed Marianna was Mexican. Maybe he was wrong. But she's from down there somewhere, that's for sure.

The hell with the Maxima, Harold thought, realizing it had always been women and cars—in that order.

Harold steered the tray toward Marianna across the cafeteria, slow now in the afternoon. As he passed two women talking he caught that word again—"layoffs." All through the eighties Aerodyne was going gangbusters. Now, overnight, everyone was saying that as soon as 1990 began, so would the layoffs and cutbacks throughout the aerospace industry in Southern California.

"So tell me the gory details," he said, handing Marianna her coffee. She took it black, just like him.

"I feel so stupid!" She suddenly laughed, but not because it was funny. She clenched her hand, driving red nails into her palms.

"Everyone gets taken once. No big deal."

"Three grand! No big deal?"

"Place I worked, they wouldn't even brag about that. They'd take four, five thou easy, on a single deal."

She paused and looked at him as if seeing him for the first time.

"You really do know about these things?"

"I sold cars once, yeah."

"They said you wrote a book. . . ."

"I—yeah, well. Hired a guy to write it." He took a copy of his book, *How to Buy a Cream Puff*, from his briefcase and handed it to her. She turned it over in her hands, amazed. Her finger traced his name on the cover as she said it.

"Harold Dodge." She looked up at him, matching name to face. "That's you. I didn't know you were a *writer*."

"I'm not, really. Like I said, I hired a guy to write it. I was the subject expert. I sold Fords for Joe Covo down in Torrance years ago. Before he got the Matsura dealership. Was a closer too."

Her eyes widened. She touched his wrist.

"That's where I went! Joe Covo Matsura!"

She sat back and folded her arms across her white translucent blouse. He saw lace underneath. The place she touched on his wrist was glowing.

"Good old Joe," Harold chuckled. "Lotta the salesmen

down there were from the old school. Pinky rings, white shoes."

She giggled. "Soooo obvious."

"He used to have the salesman get your keys, you know, to check your trade-in. Then he'd throw them up on the roof."

"What? So—"

"Right. You couldn't leave. You had to make a deal. So that's rule number seven in my book—always bring a spare set of keys. So they can't hold you hostage."

She threw her head back and laughed. Her exposed throat flashed white.

"How funny!" Marianna looked at him with that look—he had answers. He didn't just understand. He had answers.

She leaned forward and touched his arm, higher up now.

"I'd never have gone there, but it said in the ad 'five hundred dollars below wholesale.' "

Harold smiled but kept silent. She caught the smile.

"What?"

"Nothing. Go on."

"No, you were going to say something." Leaning forward, looking at his lips, waiting for more answers.

"They say five hundred below retail—ah—wholesale,"—he was getting flustered now, calm down—"then they get you in the selling rooms and push the protection plans, the detailing contracts, the extended warranties. Everyone knows those things aren't worth the . . ." He saw her face tighten. "You didn't—"

The blood rose in her face again.

"He said he'd throw it in for free. When I saw it in the contract he said, 'Hey, I said it was free, didn't I? Don't worry about it.' "

Harold picked up the documents she offered and pretended to be reviewing the figures. But he was looking for something else. Ah, here it was on her credit ap: "Age: 28 . . .

Marital status: Single." His stomach tightened. He touched the therapy ball in his pocket.

"I just want my trade-in back," she was saying when he calmed down enough to listen again. "I want to dump that Japanese piece of shit I got and just get my old car back again."

"You want to unwind the deal."

"Yes!" He put things in a way that showed he could control them. *Unwind the deal.* That's exactly what she wanted. "Can you do it? I'll pay you or—"

"Or—" He raised his eyebrows insinuating, then laughed. "Okay, let's not get into that." She laughed, too, then was serious, searching his face.

"The salesman I had, what a slime. But you know how these bastards operate. Don't you? I mean, you wrote a book."

"I hired a guy to write it for me. . . ." He hid his indecision behind a sip of coffee. "But car dealers—they're not like other businesses. Once you sign on the dotted line, you're locked in. But, tell you what, if you want, after work, we'll go down to Covo's, raise hell, see what we can do."

Her face flooded with relief. "Thank you, Harold."

Then she touched his arm again, and he knew he would think of her that night as he fell asleep in his pathetic little room. And he'd think of her the moment he woke up the next morning.

Harold was having trouble with his gate pass. The plastic card was frayed and wouldn't fit into the slot. He was leaning out of the window of his GMC C2500 pickup with Marianna sitting beside him trying not to watch his awkwardness.

"Thing's an antique," he said, showing it to her as the gate finally opened and they drove through and out onto the street. "It wears out, they lay you off. Figure it's cheaper than replacing it." He hesitated, then laughed, ah-ah-ah in descending notes. She smiled at his laugh—it was like he talked his laugh.

"You think the layoffs are coming like they say?" she asked.

"I keep hearing that. You never know."

"What'll you do if you get laid off?"

"Go to Chile."

Said for effect. Silence, driving sounds.

"Chile?"

"It's a great country. They know how to deal with their problems down there. Drug dealers, man, Pinochet rounded them up, put them on a boat out in the ocean, then torpedoed the damn thing."

"Stop it."

"Seriously." Pause. "Where you from?"

"Sherman Oaks."

He smiled. She was playing with him.

"You know what I meant."

"Guatemala." Staccato, her accent coming out.

"Ah." It was how he acknowledged answers. "Beautiful country. But I've got this thing about Chile. They've got great beer down there. It's so good you can even drink it warm. And the women—I dated Pinochet's daughter if you can believe that."

"I can't."

He shot a look at her, surprised, then the laugh again, "Ah-ah-ah."

"Are you a bullshitter, Harold?"

"Aren't we all?"

"Yeah, but it's been a while since I heard a line like that. Pinochet's daughter? Give me a break."

She relaxed into the seat and let the city slide by, heading over the La Cienega Pass with the South Bay in front of them. She liked not driving, not worrying about the little stuff, letting her mind wander and just watching things around her—the October-brown hills studded with oil rigs, a jet low overhead, heading into LAX.

And after they got through at the dealership, then what? Last week she'd told Kathy, "I've had it! Men are such pigs!" That was because of David. He'd shown up the night before, gave her a quickie, borrowed some money, then split. As she watched him leave she noticed he'd parked in the half-hour parking space out front. Pig.

"Just give me some rich older guy, and leave me alone," she'd told Kathy. Here he was. Strange how sometimes life gave you exactly what you asked for. And how, when you got it, you weren't sure you really wanted it after all.

She closed her eyes and leaned her head back, feeling the truck cab throb around her. The sleep juices began to rise up into her brain, narcotic-like, and broken images appeared in her mind: Pancho jumping on her bed that morning, licking her face . . . David pulling his pants on, grinning, proud of himself . . . the files she'd been sorting that afternoon . . . the new Matsura Accell back in Lot C . . .

Then for a moment, she went to a place she'd never been before, dark and warm, letting herself go and not asking questions, not demanding to know where she was going and who she was with.

The truck stopped. She woke up.

Harold was signaling for a left into the dealership. Across the street, the salesmen in their white shirts and ties leaned on the hoods of cars, shooting the breeze, waiting for some sucker to walk onto the lot—some sucker like her. She looked at Harold, who was touching something in his coat pocket, waiting for traffic to clear so he could make the turn.

Vito Fiorre was closing a librarian from Long Beach when he saw them walk on the lot. He could see past the librarian to the demos in the showroom where the floor whores were hustling walk-ins and be-backs. It was great to finally have the new 1990 models on the lot; 1990—that sounded weird.

Vito saw she had a guy with her this time. Stocky, graying hair and beard, mid-forties, business suit. Who the hell was he?

"If you're including it for free, why does it have to be in the contract?" the librarian was asking. Her finger shook as she pointed to the number on the paper in front of her.

"Ruth," he said, teacher now. "How can I make it any clearer? It doesn't matter what I put here—nine ninety-five or two million dollars—we took care of you on the back end. So don't worry about it. Okay?"

They were in the showroom now, the suit bending down to Joe's secretary, speaking, smiling. The PA popped to life, "Vito Fiorre, customer on the floor."

"I want you to take the warranty out of the contract and retotal it," the librarian was saying.

"Sure, and then we'll be here all night. Look, Ruth, I go into the boss again, I'll look like the backside of a horse going north." He waited for her to laugh. She didn't. "I'd like to come down but there's just no room. We dropped our pants on the first pass. Tell you what, I'll get you a protection plan—gratis—not even list it on the contract."

"I don't want a protection plan. I want the car without any—"

"Ruth, please, you're not gonna find these models on any other lot. That's why they're going for two grand over sticker." He couldn't take it anymore. He suddenly shoved back from the desk. "Excuse me one second. Okay?"

On the phone in an empty salesroom. He fingered the gold chain on his wrist, waiting for Sharon to pick up. Come on. Come on. Come on. She was so friggin' slow. The suit was looking in the window of a new Integra now, talking, laughing. Sharon picked up.

"Who's the guy with her?"

"Didn't say. Just a friend, I think."

"You *think*. Great. I think he's a DMV investigator. What's she want?"

"She has a question about her contract."

"Like what?"

"She didn't say. Just asked for you and—"

"Okay! Okay?" He put down the phone. He considered rewriting the librarian's contract. But this was one for the book. He pictured his initials next to the final price in the little leather book in Joe's desk drawer. It was how they kept track of the amount over sticker they sold cars for. Besides, Joe had posted an extra two bills to anyone who moved the last Integra, 'cause then he could call Cincinnati and order up another dozen or two. Maybe he'd just let Madame Librarian think it over while he handled the suit.

"Vito Fiorre," he said, hand extended, friendly but ready for anything. He shook hands with the girl, like he remembered, overripe but still hot. He turned to the suit, shook his hand, thick fingers hard to close around, and the eyes a cold gray. Cheap suit, Aerodyne badge clipped to his shirt pocket. Who was this guy?

"Okay, so you love the Matsura and you brought your friend in here to buy one too." Vito followed it with a laugh.

She didn't join him. In fact, he saw something happen to her eyes.

"Not exactly," she said slowly.

"Okay. I'm out of guesses. What's up?"

"You said you'd give me five thousand for my Escort if I traded in," she said.

"Sounds right . . . I can't remember what we actually wound up giving you."

"Well, I'll help you remember. You actually wound up giving me two thousand. When I asked you about it you said you were going to take care of me on the back end."

"If I said that, I did."

"No you didn't."

"Wait a minute. What are you saying here?"

"I'm saying you lied to me, and ripped me off for three grand."

Vito paused, as if trying to formulate an answer to such an outrageous accusation. A picture of her in bed flashed into his mind. A cat—she was probably a real fighter in the sheets. Why was he going for a slut that was ten pounds overweight? Because she was hot, that's why.

"Marianna, you've caught me completely off guard. I don't know what to say here. I mean, in good faith I helped you purchase the car you said you wanted. Now you're accusing me of—of—I really think you owe me an apology."

Vito looked back and forth between the faces. The suit still wasn't talking. Just watching with those gray eyes.

"Bullshit!" she spat at him.

"Now look here. If you have a complaint, I want to hear it. If you just want to insult me—"

Harold finally spoke: "She wants you to unwind the deal is what she wants."

Vito turned to him, "Who're you? Her father?"

"It doesn't matter who I am."

"If I'm dealing with you it damn well matters who you are."

"A friend, okay?" Pause. "Marianna described the whole thing to me and it's clear what you're doing. For the most part, that's your business. But you ripped her off to the tune of about three grand. So unwind the deal and we disappear—no questions asked."

Vito was nodding, a little amazed at this guy—this suit from Aerodyne. His eyes didn't blink when he spoke. He was a pro. Definitely a pro. Vito felt real anger rising. He pictured himself taking the ashtray on the table and pushing those gray eyes back into the guy's head.

Instead he matched the delivery, sitting back, forcing himself to appear relaxed.

"I'm curious. What do you think we're doing?"

The suit looked away, then back. She was watching him now, getting off on it. Power was a turn-on for women.

"You got a major TO operation here—prospect won't buy you turn him over to the next salesman . . . and the next, till you break him down. Right?"

Vito shrugged, uninterested, so Harold kept rolling.

"The front-liners make water, over there you hide it in bogus service warranties, protection plans—" Harold paused and pointed to the computer guys pounding out contracts in one corner of the office. "You promise a price, then the contract comes you take two to three grand extra per deal. Not bad for a little fast talk and a few lies."

The guy had this way of talking, he'd open his thick hands, palms up, as if it were all so very obvious. Vito glanced at the ashtray—a heavy old glass one. It'd feel nice in his hand. He let the silence grow. That drove most people bananas. They hate it when you don't say anything.

"You're from the DMV."

"I'm just a friend helping a friend."

"Everything you say is strictly bullshit. Okay? We sell cars—we make a profit. We're in business. Am I supposed to apologize for that? Of course we use computers. Everyone does these days."

"Unwind the deal."

"I'm not through."

The guy looked away, as if to say, go ahead and talk, but I'm not going to listen.

"We have a reputation to uphold here. Okay? It's the principle of the thing. I'm not saying we ripped anyone off. I did what she said she wanted—gave her a sweet car at a super-low price, and took a piece-of-shit trade-in off her hands."

"My Escort's *not* a piece of shit!" she hissed. A real cat, he thought.

"But since we have a reputation to uphold here, I'm going to do something I ought never to do. I'm going to sell you your trade-in back to you. You want, you can sell it on the street, see what you get for it there."

The guy thought about it, then said to her, "It'll be a hassle—but you'll get a fair price for it."

Everyone relaxed. Vito let the new mood settle on the threesome, then added, as if it was no big deal, "I'll have them bring your Escort back over from the warehouse. You want to stop by tomorrow morning with a check, you can take possession of it then."

They all shook hands again. Christ, the guy's hand was big. But he probably wouldn't be with her when she came back tomorrow.

He turned back down the hall and headed for the librarian from Long Beach. A voice boomed out of an open office door.

"Vito!"

Vito's stomach tightened. It was Joe Covo, the dealership's owner. He stepped into Covo's office and stood on the huge Oriental rug. He kept it dark in here, sun barely coming through venetian blinds. Music barely audible.

"Who's the guy?"

"What guy?"

"What guy? The guy and the girl. He looked familiar."

Covo was six feet of steel poured into a thousand-dollar suit. He was one of those guys that would look exactly the same way for about another two decades. And he could generate silence worse than any closer on the lot. Just sat there and looked at you till you wanted to slit your wrists.

"Were they prospects?"

"No. He was some nobody. Came in with the girl 'cause she had a question on her contract."

"What question?"

"Joe, I handled it. Okay? What's the problem?"

Joe finally looked away, saying, "LaBounty called. He's coming out tomorrow night."

"Party time," Vito said, a big smile growing on his face.

Joe cut him off. "N*ot exactly*."

"Why not?"

"He's bringing Parker and Bales with him."

"So?"

"So I don't like it." Pause. "I'm hearing things."

"Like what things?"

"Like it's all over. Like it got too big. Like someone got pissed and they're gonna shut us down."

"No way, Joe. They can't do that."

"That's what I heard. And now I get this call from La-Bounty. He's comin' with Parker and Bales. What am I supposed to think?"

Vito waited, then timed it just right, hoping to get Joe out of his funk.

"Hey, I got one for the book—a librarian wants to buy that silver Integra. I'm closing her right now."

Joe looked up at Vito. "You close her. Understand?"

"Okay, Joe."

"Close her. And when LaBounty gets here I'll hit him up for another shipment of Integras."

"I'll close her. Okay?"

Harold started as a Bird Dog for Joe Covo fifteen years ago. He was working his way through night school, getting his degree in chemical engineering when he needed some extra bucks. Joe slipped him a crisp hundred-dollar bill for every sucker he flushed out of the bushes, sent down to the dealership like pigeons to be shot out of the sky.

Joe gave him a loaner with the lot paint still on it: SUPER CLEAN it said across the windshield in big white letters. LOW MILES. That was a good conversation starter. He'd run into another student in the parking lot at City College, or strike up a conversation with someone at the store. *Was it really clean*? they wanted to know. Not a scratch on it, he'd say. *Didn't they turn the odometer back sometimes*? Maybe at some places, but not at Joe Covo's. Look at all that rubber on the brake pedal, that's how you tell. *But car salesmen are so damn pushy*. Not at Joe's they're not. You ought to check it out. Tell 'em I sent you. They'll take care of you.

So the Bird Dog sent the pigeons in, one by one, and the salesmen shot them right out of the sky. They could always spot a pigeon when one showed up and said, "I'm a friend of Abe's." That's what the Bird Dog called himself then. And the salesmen took it from there. And the Bird Dog pocketed a hundred-dollar bill. Not bad for a little fast talk and a few white lies.

Soon Joe gave the Bird Dog a job on the lot, and his nickname stuck. And the Bird Dog told bigger lies, and made larger bills, and put his college plans on hold. He began to acquire a taste for gold, and for paying in cash, and for bragging about his lies. The Bird Dog was so good that Joe made him a closer in the F & I room. Customers were led down the hall to Finance & Insurance, where Harold was waiting for them behind a big desk. He was famous for hitting home runs—loading contracts with everything from cheap alarm systems to detailing contracts no one ever used. And the customer always signed. Sure, they signed. It was the fastest way to get the hell out of there.

But one day the Bird Dog looked up from a contract and saw the sweet face of his grandmother. It wasn't his grandmother, because she had died a dozen years before. But it was enough like her so that he read the numbers on the contract and began to think what they would do to her. Then he looked at the "Super Clean!" "Low Miles!" car she was about to drive away in. And he decided he didn't want his gramma—or anyone's gramma—driving around in that piece of shit. At that price.

And the Bird Dog helped the pigeon fly away.

Harold took gramma down the road to Don Kott's Chevrolet, picked out a nice runner for her, and wrestled the salesmen for it. And she drove away happy. When he returned to the dealership Joe was waiting for him. Joe called all the salesmen together outside under the perfect California sky, the sunlight glinting off their gold watches and white shirts and oiled hair, and he told them what the Bird Dog had done. The Bird Dog went soft, he said, and everyone laughed. The Bird Dog let a pigeon go, he said, and everyone laughed.

The Bird Dog was a sucker, he said, and laughed. And then he fired Harold right there in front of them all as an example.

The Bird Dog knew he would be punished or fired. But he hadn't allowed for the power of public humiliation, for twenty five guys looking at him and snickering and saying to each other, "Weak asshole." And so he turned to Joe Covo and said only one thing before he left: "You shouldn't have done that."

Harold sold his gold watch and rings and picked up his former plans to become a chemical engineer. But he never forgot what happened on the car lot that afternoon, never forgot how it felt to be told "you're fired" in public. It made him mad. So mad he couldn't think about it directly. The only way to lose the anger was to think of gramma out there somewhere, driving a cream puff at a grand under wholesale.

Harold sat at the table in Denny's as if he were preparing for surgery. He inspected the silverware, straightened the napkin, aligned the menu, and, after the waitress took his order for the skillet omelet, said, "I want two glasses: one with ice only, and one with water. Salsa on the side and extra napkins."

Marianna watched everything he did, half amused. He hadn't even looked at the menu. He was a regular here, this Denny's with LAX-bound jets practically landing on the roof. A regular at Denny's, for Christ's sake.

"I travel a lot, for my books," he was saying, still straightening things on the table, preparing for the meal. "I spend a lot of time in greasy spoons."

She nodded. "What's water?"

His face showed bewilderment, then understanding, remembering what he'd said at the dealership.

"Car salesman talk."

"But old Vito almost wet his pants when you said it."

"Wasn't that something? I made a guess, got lucky."

"You were bullshitting again."

He just laughed: ah-ah-ah. "I remembered how they work things there. The rest was just a guess."

"But it did the trick. You got me my Escort back."

"Yeah, well . . ."

"No, really. Thanks. Thanks, you're sweet."

She thought he was blushing. How could a guy so cool in the dealership turn into a marshmallow an hour later?

The water glasses arrived and Harold began some sort of ritual, pouring small amounts of water over the ice, stirring it. He jumped, surprised, then took the beeper off his hip and read the number.

"Sorry, gotta return this call," he said, sliding out of the booth. "I'm selling a couple of cars."

"A couple?"

"I buy them at auctions, put a hundred-dollar detail job on them, and turn 'em around."

Marianna nodded, then watched as Harold went to a pay phone in the corner. She could hear him talking to someone on the phone, saying, "No, it's got the twin side-draft Webers. They started using them in '84," and lost interest. She looked around the restaurant, dreamy. There were two cops in a corner booth, a salesman by himself, a black guy with a white woman having a fight. This was Harold's hangout.

"So what's water?" she asked him as he eased himself back into the booth, glancing at notes he'd written on a three-by-five index card.

"What you told me, the way they quoted high upfront figures, used the computer to generate contracts. They were creating water. They inflate the early figures they give you verbally—DMV fees, transport fees. Then they hide the profit in legitimate items like service warranties—i.e., they launder the monies."

"I.e., they're ripping off suckers like me," she said, waiting to see how he took it. He smiled.

"I talk funny, don't I?"

"Yes, Harold. But you're sweet, so don't worry about it."

"I think I like that."

She saw the waitress picking up their food from under the heat lamps, then timed it just right, covering his thick hand with hers and squeezing.

"Are you married, Harold? 'Cause if you're not I want you. If you are we're going to have an affair."

Kim saw him as soon as she stepped out onstage, building his house out of five-dollar bills on the runner. The hotter the dance, the bigger the house got, till there was fifteen, twenty bucks there—a big tip for a short dance. When the girls saw Harold on the runner, they gave it everything, then danced over and collected it in their G-string.

She hadn't seen him in here for a while. Must have been on the wagon again, or tied up in one of his damn books. He got busy he didn't come around much. And she missed him. Missed his money, missed the loopy talks they had.

She was doing it to "Brown Sugar," her favorite, the twinkle lights throwing shards of color on her breasts and hips as they glistened from her work. She danced it just for him, right over him, giving him everything from the deep wild place where all the good dancing and the good sex came from. She didn't know how to get to the deep wild place all the time, but when she did, she let it pour through her like a river.

Her body was on fire now and everyone in the place knew it. Broken-down old guys in dark corner booths looked away from the other girls. Steve behind the bar glanced over while drawing a beer, and a pair of vice cops stopped watching their mark. Everyone knew Kim was the best.

She was still beautifully flushed when she sat down beside Harold. Her breasts were glowing with a fine moisture, her breath heavy. She tossed her hair like a mane.

Harold's thick finger pointed to his house of bills. "You won the house," Harold said. "The whole damn house. You practically burned it down. Want it now or later?"

"Now." She stood up and offered herself.

Harold gathered up his bills and put them in her G-string. His hand lingered, brushing her pubic hair, feeling the swell of her vagina opening up somewhere out of reach of his fingers. He pulled out while he still could.

She sat down again. His face was flushed. He was so cute when he was like this. She thought of their times in bed; he touched her with respect and love and strength. He knew women.

"Got a favor," Kim said.

"Right now, you can have any damn thing you want from me," he said, wiping his forehead.

"It's Pam. She's been on the street the last three nights. Help me find her, would ya?"

"Pam." He said it not as a question, but to stall.

"Don't say you don't remember her. The redhead."

"Redhead. Oh-oh."

"What?"

"Linda, my ex-wife, was a redhead. Just when I got used to the color, she left me. Swore I'd never touch another redhead."

"So don't touch her. Just help her. Steve's got her a place. But it's not open till Friday. Till then he said she could sleep in the back."

Harold thought about it. Then, as if to explain his hesitation he said, "I met someone today."

"Then what're you doing here, tongue hangin' out on the runner?"

"I just met her is all. She's petite, like I like them. Black hair, a little heavy maybe but—"

Kim slapped him, harder than just playful. "Be an angel. Help me get Pam."

Harold's truck headlights found Pam in the parking lot of the Oceanview Motel on El Segundo, some black guy hitting on her, offering her some free coke if she'd step into his car and give him a little curbside service. Oceanview—shit. No one had ever seen the ocean from here. No one who stayed here had ever even been to the ocean.

Pam's frizzy red hair shot out above thin little-girl shoulders. Light blue dress hugging her growing breasts and falling down on her hips so nice.

Harold angled the truck up next to them and hit the power window.

"Pam!"

Maybe he could scoop her up and get the hell out of here. What was he doing here anyway? One minute he's minding his own business in a strip joint, the next he's rescuing hookers.

"Pam! Get in here!"

She looked over, eyes not focusing on him—just another guy in another car yelling *get in*! Right now she was warming to the idea of some free coke.

"Sorry, honey, I'm busy." She turned back to the black guy, skinny and tall, turquoise bracelet falling loose on his long arm.

"Go get her," Kim said, pushing Harold.

"You get her."

"She won't listen to me. Go get her."

Harold leaned out the window. "Pam! It's me, Harold! Get in here!"

She started for the cab.

"The fuck you goin'?" The black guy yanked her back by the arm.

Kim pushed Harold again.

"Go get her."

"All right!" he said, and got out of the truck, came around into the headlights thinking, this guy sticks me, I'll wind up with my head in a puddle. *Engineer Slain in Motel Tiff*. Fitting end to a shitty life. And just when I found someone I like.

"Hey you. Lemme talk to you," Harold said to the guy.

"Got nothin' to say to you, man," the guy whined, falsetto. "I'm being with my lady right now."

"We can talk here, we can talk at the station. Have a nice long chat there," Harold heard himself say. He pulled his wallet, flipped it open to his Aerodyne ID. Just flashed it. Just for the effect.

"County juvenile investigator," he was saying, almost laughing inside, laughing until he imagined the guy pulling a knife or a sneaky little gun from his boot. "You don't want to get mixed up in this."

"You try and take her," the guy said, jabbing a finger at Harold. "I'm gonna mess you up, motherfucker."

"Easy," Harold said, taking one step back and reaching

behind, up under his coat, as if for a gun in his waistband, a move he learned as an MP in South Carolina. He spent the whole time fighting rednecks who thought Californians were soft-brained beach boys. Harold hated the water. Always had.

"Get in the car, Pam." She was staring, surprised. "Get in the fucking car! *Now!*" She started moving. The guy stood there, telling Harold all the things he was going to do to him. But he didn't come for Harold. That was all that mattered.

The door opened on Harold's stuffy little one-bedroom, the heat of the day trapped stale inside. It was a low duplex on one of those streets where everyone fixed their cars out front, throwing the empty oil cans in the gutter. Cheap new condos on one side, a trailer court on the other. Eight lanes of the 405 somewhere up above, traffic moving through the night.

Kim stood in the cramped living room and looked around. Shelves everywhere, packed with books, paper, envelopes, a postage machine. Sheets over the sofa and chairs. Then the noise hit her—ticking. Lots of ticking. There were clocks all over the place. Ticking.

"I do these insurance losses," Harold said to explain all the clocks. "Pick up some nice things every once in a while. Got a big buy tomorrow. Radiators."

He opened the refrigerator. "Want something? I could make some eggs or something. They're good with salsa."

Harold took off his jacket and hung it on the back of a chair.

"You don't have a gun," Kim said, looking at his broad back, empty above the waistband.

He laughed. "I hate guns. Scare the shit out of me."

She giggled. "You're such a liar, Harold."

He was facing her now, smiling, arm up in the kitchen archway. "I'm a bad boy, aren't I?"

"I don't know. Are you?" She began unbuttoning her dress.

"You don't have to," he said, watching her.

"What if I want to?" She kept popping loose the buttons, still in that fake flirty talk she used in the bar.

"It was just a favor. I do favors for people, I don't expect nothing in return."

"Harold, honey, it's awful hot in here." She let the dress fall down around her and stood there naked. Naked on stage, with eighty other guys ogling her, was one thing. Naked here in his apartment all alone with her was another.

He was amazed how tight his voice sounded when he said, "Does that mean you don't want any eggs?"

Later in bed he told Kim, "This girl I met today—I got a good feeling about her."

She murmured and snuggled up to his chest. He stroked her shoulder, her skin still baby smooth.

"I know what you're saying, 'You're always meeting someone.' But this is different. Gut-level I feel she's different. She's got everything—i.e., she's pretty, smart, tough. And she loves to flirt. I like girls that flirt with me, tease me, turn me upside down."

Traffic on the 405 was still light—just an occasional truck thundering by in the night. The clocks began chiming in the other room. And the world stood still for a moment. One little moment of peace. Harold even felt for a second that everything was really going to be all right.

"I did a favor for her. She got taken by some car dealer. I straightened it out for her. Impressed the hell out of her. I think things are gonna change now. I hope they are. I've been down a long time."

Kim shuddered and woke up. Then, in a voice that came from somewhere far away but carried truth, she said, "We're lost Harold, you and me. We're lost and they ain't never gonna find us."

She turned away from him and went back to sleep.

"Where's Dad-boy?" Vito asked as they crossed the lot to the used-car section to pick up her trade-in.

"You know he's not my father," Marianna said, trying not to show anger, since that was exactly what he wanted. Just get the car and get the hell out of here.

"Oh, that's right, 'just a friend helping out a friend.' You know what I think?"

"Vito, I'm not the least bit interested in what you think." Halfway across the lot now, her patience as brittle as cut glass after waiting a half hour in customer service, drinking battery-acid coffee, reading back issues of *Car and Driver*.

Vito kept on anyway. "I think you got a little sugar-daddy action going. Guy that old, that's the only reason to be with 'em. See that Mercedes over there? The 560 SEL with the gold kit? Tonight, you and me, cruise Sunset, dinner at Le Dome, or the restaurant of your choice. And you don't have to put up with some old bastard, belly falling over his belt. What time shall I pick you up?"

It was like he was closing her for a late-model superclean cream puff. She wondered if his performance in the sack was covered by a bumper-to-bumper warranty.

"Vito, when you get me my car, I'm going to get in it and drive away and never come back, never see you again. So let's just get this over with."

He wouldn't give up. "Hey, money's a turn-on. Try it. You'll see."

"At this point, just seeing my car again would be a super turn-on."

"The Escort? Why're you so hung up on that thing?"

"Because it's mine."

They crossed under the electronic signboard now, rising up so commuters on the southbound 405 could read it. Today it was flashing two messages. First:

INTEGRITY
WILL
EMPOWER
U

Then:

'85 HONDA
LOADED, $2995

It was Vito's idea—something more than just car talk. Something inspirational. Joe didn't go for it right off. But he gave it a try. When he saw another dealer copied the idea on his sign it became a permanent fixture. And Vito picked up two bills from Joe for the brainstorm.

They ducked into the used-car section now, a low-rent counterpart of the new-car showroom across the lot.

"Have a seat. I'll have someone bring it up."

She sat in a plastic-formed chair on the edge of a big room and looked around: computers, desks, phones. Papers, books, contracts everywhere. Salesmen hanging around in white shirts and ties, drinking coffee, yawning, faces still puffy from sleep. Aftershave hanging heavy in the air, mixing with sports talk and shock-jock one-liners.

Vito crossed to a guy at a desk across the room. The guy looked up at Vito, then leaned back, laughing.

"Look at you, man."

"What?"

"Lookin' sharp today. What'd you do? Get detailed?"

"Thanks, man," Vito said laughing. "Here's the twenty I owe you."

Vito reminded Marianna of the Laker's coach. What was his name? Hair combed straight back and oiled down. When she watched the play-offs with David they called him the Lizard.

The Lizard. She imagined Vito's head on a reptile's body, slithering out from behind a car on the showroom floor saying, "If I gave you a super price on this car, will you buy it today?" Then flicking his tongue over his lips as he waited for an answer.

The Lizard and the other guy were still talking, laughing. The other guy glanced over at her for a second, then laughed some more, as if checking the size of her breasts or the extra five pounds that clung to her thighs with a death grip.

Sure, take your time, Marianna thought. You're already at work. She was two hours late and the clock was ticking. This might get her on the layoff list, if there was such a thing. But she wanted her car. And she didn't want to lose her temper. Problem was, she couldn't get half mad. She wasn't any good at that. It was an all-or-nothing proposition with her.

The Lizard's friend picked up a clipboard now, checked something. Vito dialed a phone, talked to someone on the other end of the line. About her car? He looked over at Marianna, then back to the list. He hung up, then crossed the showroom and stood in front of her.

"Little problem," Vito said, popping his knuckles.

"My car's not here yet?"

"Worse than that. It was already sold. Sold yesterday."

All sorts of chemicals were suddenly dumped into her bloodstream making her feel anger, hate, incredible strength. She felt she could pick Vito up and throw him into the southbound 405, see him splattered by a truck, then a car . . . then another car.

The Lizard stood there waiting for her answer, tongue flicking across his thin lips, an in-your-face smile that she wanted to tear off along with his face.

"You knew that last night."

"Marianna, be serious. If I'd known this last night, why would I get you down here this morning?"

"To get rid of him."

"Who? Dad-boy?" He laughed.

"You didn't have the guts to face him. So you get me back here, I take three hours off from work. And you knew it was already sold."

Her voice was rising. "Didn't you? Just tell me you did, didn't you?"

Vito looked around the showroom. It was early still, no customers, just guys in white shirts starting to watch the scene, amused. Vito decided to go for it.

"Yeah, I knew your car was sold. But I didn't tell you last night because I wanted you to come down here again. 'Cause you need to learn something."

"I already knew what a shitbag you are."

The other salesmen *oooohhh*-ed. This was better than a sitcom.

"Sweetie, maybe you can wag your tail at Dad-boy and get him to eat out of your hand. Down here it's the real world. You sign a contract, it's a done deal. You ain't never gonna see your money or your shitbox trade-in again. Now get your little tail out the door and don't come back with Dad-boy or we'll have to teach you both a lesson."

The salesmen were out of their offices now, leaning in doorframes, watching the fun. One of them muttered, "Tell the bitch, Vito."

Marianna was in a different place now where it was nice and quiet and she could think very clearly. She wasn't half mad or even just mad. This had gone beyond, way beyond.

"You can only go so far on your glands, Vito. You just jumped in over your head. I'll be back, I'll get my car, and I'll take your balls with me when I go."

She turned to the rest of the room. "Then you shitheads will really have something to laugh at."

She had something extra behind the words, something they didn't expect. So she left them silent as she went out the door, and when their laughter and hooting came, it was hollow and distant and didn't touch her.

And as she passed Vito's Mercedes 560 SEL with the gold kit she could imagine her spike heel slicing through the German metal on the driver's-side door, and could see Vito shelling out two grand for a little unexpected bodywork. But she wasn't ready to do that yet. She'd put her spike heel into the Lizard's face first.

"I'm confused now," Harold said. He had a new therapy ball in his hand and he was fingering it openly as his big arm lay on his desk. "Which do you want to do, hurt the guy or just get your car back?"

"Both."

He glanced toward the door.

"I'm sorry," she said, rising. "You don't have time for this."

"No." He hoped he hadn't said it too quickly. "I'm going to be called into a meeting in a second. Till then, go ahead."

She settled back in. He mashed the therapy ball, thinking how Jerry would be here any minute, with a million questions about the cutting oil, questions he couldn't answer yet. The emulsion they cooled the lathes and drills with was getting impossible to unload. State EPA was playing havoc with them. So they shipped it to Texas for a little midnight dumping. That was getting so expensive Aerodyne was considering moving out of state. Get away from the state regs. But if they could separate it out—back to just water and just oil—they could . . .

Marianna was waiting for him to speak. He refocused.

"Okay, we could hurt him, maybe, i.e., get the DMV involved. But your car, it's gone."

"You mean it's dropped off the face of the earth? I don't think so. It's somewhere. And Vito could get it if he really, really wanted to."

"But he doesn't want to."

"That's where we come in."

"*We*?"

"I saw you handle him yesterday. You got off on it."

He chuckled. "Still . . . it's just a shitty little Escort. I don't see why you want it back."

"Because it's mine."

There was that look—hatred settling in her dark eyes like a death sentence. No tears this time. Just a craving for vengeance, as big as a storm wave off the Pacific covering everything in its path. Christ, what was it about Latin women that turned him on? He knew he better not stand up now. His lap was too big.

"Besides—I shouldn't tell you this, but—no"—she looked away—"I better not."

"What?"

"It's not fair."

"It's not fair not to tell me."

"When he was flaming me, he said some things about you, too."

"Like what?" his voice tightening. He knew this was going to hurt him, hurt bad. The fact that she knew this and said it anyway was also in his mind.

"Stupid stuff. You're old, you're fat. I'm just hanging with you 'cause of the money."

He punished the therapy ball. This one wouldn't last two days. He tossed it aside and grabbed a pen. He began doodling—jotting down phrases—bullet lists like the ones he created for his book. He scribbled 1) *Where he lives*, 2) *Where he works*, 3) *What he has*, 4) *What he loves*.

"Why'd you leave Guatemala?" he asked, still working on the list.

"Not to change the subject."

He paused, waiting, then added: "I heard you left in the middle of the night."

"Better to leave in the middle of the night than to disappear forever. There was a war on then, remember?"

"Your whole family come up here?"

She didn't answer that, her mind wandering back in time for a moment. Then she returned to the present, asking, "Why'd you go to Chile?"

"Question is, why'd I come back?" Pause, smile, everything coming out in the open now. "Maybe we could go there together sometime."

"Maybe so. After we get Vito."

"Yeah, well . . . I'm going to be called into this meeting in a few minutes, so . . ."

He pushed the list across to her. As she read it she saw he had circled 4) *What he loves*.

"Thing about trying to hurt someone is, you need to know

more about them. What they do, what they like—or love, really—where they live, what they own. Then you know how to put it to them. What do you know about Vito?"

"Not a lot."

"That's a problem."

She thought about it a moment. "But I know a way to change that."

Harold saw her eyes come alive with excitement at the thought, then saw Jerry's face behind her in his office door.

"Ready to get started, Harold?"

Traffic was a bitch. Harold was between two semis on the westbound 91, elevated in Tustin somewhere. Postwar California cracker boxes to the horizon. Pick any house, it could be the one he grew up in.

He rolled his thick wrist over to reveal his watch. Ten minutes till they opened the bids. If I'm not there the deal's off. Five hundred down the drain. Another brilliant move by Harold. Like the ones Linda divorced him for. All the money he lost making that video on car buying. Then there was that shipment of voice keys he picked up at cost. Say the word and the lock opens, just for you. Pretty slick. But at $500 a pop he didn't sell a one. What a fiasco. But he didn't learn. No. Here he was trying to make a quick score on junked radiators.

In theory it sounded great. Buy on Monday for two grand, sell on Thursday for four. Double your money for taking a little risk. Not bad if all connections were made and Jerry didn't notice him missing all the time. What did it matter? The defense industry was going in the toilet anyway now that peace had broken out. Ten thousand people waiting for pink slips.

Then Marianna waltzed into his office and hung him up (not that he minded). And the goddamned meeting! Jerry must have known he was about to do his disappearing act. He dragged the meeting out just to grind his gears.

The semi in front of him lurched forward. He saw his opening and went for it. Time to take to the side streets. With a little luck and some fancy driving he could still be there on time.

He pulled into the breakdown lane and gunned it, down the ramp and onto Euclid Street. Now he was really moving. After sitting on the freeway, he felt like he'd just broken out of jail. Euclid wound through the hills, sage and tumbleweeds mottling the slopes around him. He and Randy used to ride their dirt bikes here, BB guns slung over their shoulders, Randy three years younger and trying hard to keep up with his big brother. That was before Randy discovered that he could stick a needle in his arm and then he didn't need to catch up anymore, didn't need to do anything except sit in the back room and watch TV all day. Every day.

Harold came up fast behind two old beaters, side by side blocking both lanes. A van and a Taurus. The lady in the Taurus was totally oblivious. Didn't even check her mirror. He flashed his lights. Nothing. Horned her. Nothing.

Only three miles away now. He'd come down out of the hills and shoot across on Imperial. He could make it. If only he could get around granny in the Taurus.

Straight road. Clear ahead. Pedal to the metal, across the double yellow. The big V-8 kicked down, reared up, and he started around the Taurus. But now she was braking, starting a left turn right in front of him! Christ!

Fishtailing now, back into the lane, his rear end swinging

toward the van. Fighting the wheel. Okay so far. He cleared the van. Straightened out. The cab came around in front of the van. Missed that, too! He was going to be okay! He was going to be—

B*oom*! From behind. A third car smashed into his right rear panel. Shit.

He pulled onto the shoulder and ran back to the car that hit him. An '82 Tercel with an old guy in it, mouth hanging open, chest heaving.

"You okay?" Harold called through the window. The guy just sat there. No blood. Hissing radiator with a bumper pushed into it. He looked for the Taurus. It was heading off up a side road. She didn't even see what happened! Totally oblivious.

He checked his watch. Still had five minutes.

"I've got to be somewhere or I'll lose a lot of money," Harold called into the old guy, still sitting there stunned. "I'll be right back. Okay?"

Harold jotted down the old guy's license number and took off.

Twenty minutes later Harold came back down the road in the other direction and saw the Mars lights. Two patrol cars and a paramedic van. Paramedics? That old guy wasn't hurt. Harold slowed and pulled onto the shoulder, the lights sending panic through his system. He'd have to call Jerry, tell him he was out playing hooky. Third time this month he'd be busted for that.

Maybe there was another way to do this. He could call the cops later, explain he had an emergency and had to leave. The cops were so overworked these days anyway they'd probably be glad he saved them the hassle.

As he pulled a U-turn he began thinking what he'd do with the two grand he was gonna make. Maybe he'd ask Marianna to fly to Chile with him. Maybe he'd get his truck fixed. He knew a guy in Compton who did it cheap, out of his garage.

He made it back to Aerodyne and slid in behind his desk before Jerry even came back from lunch.

"I was surprised to hear from you," Vito said to Marianna. "To put it mildly. I mean, after that little scene in the showroom I thought you'd go postal—you know, come back with an assault rifle, light the place up."

He sat at the table in Le Dome like a Mafia chieftain. Hands spread out on the table, pinky ring catching the sun setting out over the Pacific. Silk suit and blindingly white shirt. Cigarettes and gold lighter laid out next to his cellular phone and little leather purse thing. He'd already taken two calls and jotted notes on the starched tablecloth with his thin gold pen, his attitude saying, *So bill me for it.*

"I got to thinking about what you said," Marianna began.

"About what?"

"Money."

"That it's a turn-on. Sure."

"Thought I'd put it to the test."

Marianna was in full battle dress. Tight red top, plunging low in front, a slit in her skirt cut high on her leg. Hair pulled straight back and clipped behind her head. Thick mask of makeup to hide her lies. Not that she needed a cover. She knew how to lie and when. The only thing she didn't know was when to stop.

The waiter appeared. She started to order her standard, a Seven and Seven. Then she changed her mind.

"Something tells me this is a champagne night."

"I'll bring a wine list."

Vito jumped in before the waiter could leave. "Forget that. What's your best?"

"Dom Perignon or Veuve Clicquot."

"Yeah, yeah, yeah. Bring us a bottle of that."

"Which?"

"The second one you said."

"Veuve Clicquot."

"Si, si. Pronto. Pronto."

Trouble with these places, Vito thought, you had to talk that froufrou shit just to get what you wanted. And the waiters tried to push you around, make you feel small. Truth of the matter was, he was dying for a long-necked beer, something he could take down in one, two swigs. It hadn't been a good day. Joe was edgy, definitely edgy. They got a tip there was an undercover cop on the lot. Vito handled the guy, wasting an hour, doing everything by the book. Probably cost him a bill or two in sales. But Joe didn't forget favors like that.

"You speak Italian?"

"A little, maybe, when all the Fiorres get together at my dad's."

"Where's that?"

"Eastside." He didn't want to talk about it. She guessed Boyle Heights. Somewhere he never went back to without a gun, never parked his 560 SEL on the street.

"Homeboy makes good, huh?"

"What do you mean?"

"You grow up on the eastside, now you drive a Mercedes, live—where?—in Bel Air?"

"Come on . . . Beverly Hills." A slight pause, then he added. "Adjacent."

She laughed inside. Beverly Hills *adjacent*. How adjacent? Two miles would put him in gang territory. Low riders with thumpers that blew you out of your easy chair when they cruised by.

"And where might you be from?" he asked, covering her hand with his, the pinky ring biting into her as he squeezed.

"Chile," she said before she could stop herself. "Santiago. My father was a brewer—best beer in the city. People always said his beer was so good you could drink it warm."

"Really?" Vito leaned back, looked around, as if saying to someone, *Who would have guessed*? He wagged a finger at her. "Chile, huh? I thought there was something different about you."

The waiter arrived with the champagne and went into his routine, untwisting the wire, blowing the cork out, pouring two glasses.

Marianna looked around the restaurant, filling up now. Out the wall of windows the sun was sinking into the ocean, the LA Basin was a bed of coals coming alive in the dark, spreading south to Palos Verdes, west to the San Bernadino Mountains.

"Nice place," she said.

"Wait till later. We'll probably see some stars. I was here one night with a young lady, I hear, 'Hey, Vito, you guinea son-of-a-bitch!' I turn around, it's Tony Danza. You know, from—"

"*Who's the Boss*? Sure."

"Sold him a Porsche when I was at Beverly Hills BMW. Impressed the hell out of the girl, I'll tell you that. Power, that's another turn-on. Sluts dig it." He caught himself, pretending to be sorry. "Oh. I hope that didn't offend you."

She forced herself not to react, thinking, I'll just put it on the list with all the rest.

"I've never been with someone really powerful," she said instead, delivering a body blow to Vito's ego, then pulling it out by saying, "Until now."

"Me? Powerful? I'm just the manager of a dealership. That's all."

You're a fucking car salesman, is what you are, Marianna thought.

"But I'm movin' up," Vito said. "That's what I feel good about. I came on board, one, one and a half years ago and I was just a greeter. That's where everyone starts. Then they made me deskman, then closer. Now assistant general manager."

"Deskman. What's that?"

"You work the numbers. Draw up the contracts."

"I thought the salesmen worked up the numbers."

He was a little cautious now, probably remembering her Escort, her little outburst in the used-car salesroom.

"Tell you something, when you're selling a car, the numbers are meaningless."

"Come on, Vito. Everyone buys on price."

"They *think* they buy on price. What counts is what's going on up here," he said, tapping his temple. "I can sell a car just by looking someone in the eye *if* I have it together right up here. Sales is a head game. A very big head game." A huge Lizard smile split his face. "Speaking of head games"—he looked her over, seeming to lick his lips—"let's get back to my favorite subject."

"I can't guess what that is."

"We both know why we're here. Where we'll be at the end of this night. Let's get it started now. What turns you on?"

She remembered this morning when she went beyond any anger she'd ever known, back to that place she'd been only once before, long ago. Calm, very calm, not knowing what she'd do or say next, but not the least bit worried about it.

Vito's phone rang.

"Phonus interruptus," he said, picking up the phone like he was going to have sex with it. He flipped it open. "Yeah." His expression changed. This call was different. "How bad? What kids?" Long pause. "Why weren't you there to stop her?" He listened, frowning, becoming a different person. "I'll stop by . . . I don't know. Soon. Okay. Okay?"

He set the phone down, threw down his champagne, then looked at Marianna with a *who-the-hell're-you*? expression. Then he refocused.

"Tell me something really nasty. Something that blows me right out of my socks."

Harold pulled the truck into the lot off Vista Del Mar overlooking the beach in El Segundo. Behind them, the stacks of the power plant loomed silent and powerful. He opened the paper bag, took out a six-pack, and handed a beer to Kim.

"It's from Chile," he said. "Hard to find. But it's real good. The best in the world. You can even serve it warm." But this six-pack wasn't warm. In fact, he'd never even tasted it warm before. Someone told him that once and it sounded good.

Harold hit the power windows, and the ocean air blew through the cab. After the freeway ride the sudden silence of the cab made him self-conscious.

They had been talking about love, of all things. What was true love? Him an engineer and her a stripper, what did they know about love?

"I don't know how we even got onto this subject," Harold said, levering off the cap with a Swiss army knife.

"That's just what I was thinking!"

"I'll be damned. Maybe we're psychotic."

"You mean psychic." They laughed. "Psychotic means you're nutso."

"Oh. Right."

Then she said it again, serious. "Psychic. Maybe we are."

"Maybe we're in love or something. Who the hell knows?" He laughed, nervous using that word.

"No. I don't think we're in love. But I think we love each other."

"That's nice," Harold sighed, the beer working pleasantly in his system. He pulled off his tie, laid it across his suit jacket in the jump seat behind the cab. His Aerodyne ID still dangled from his shirt pocket.

"One day Linda says to me, 'Harold, I just realized, I don't love you. In fact, I despise you.' After fifteen years of marriage and all: 'I despise you.' After that I thought, I'll never take anything for granted."

"Bitch."

"All my little deals drove her nuts."

"Was she on the streets?"

"Hell no. We had a nice place, down in Garden Grove. Did the church thing every Sunday. Even tithed, if you can believe that shit."

"Tithed?"

"Give a percent of your income to the church."

"Oh, like with our tips. Give something to the bartender."

"'I despise you.' You believe that?"

"I'd never say that to you. Not if we had a little house in Gardena. I always wanted my own place."

"Garden Grove."

"Huh?"

"It was in Garden Grove. Not Gardena."

A bank of ragged clouds appeared over the ocean, turning a dirty yellow as the sun went down. Gulls climbed and dove against the clouds like flying ash off a trash fire. Was he buzzed on just one beer? Or was it something about being together? Harold looked at Kim; this light was kind to a face that shouldn't age.

Fat. Old. Harold thought of the words that shithead car salesman called him. It had burned in his gut all afternoon. He'd shove it away but it would come back, aching to be touched, examined, used against him. Okay, he had a few extra pounds, and he was looking down the barrel of fifty. But he knew the game better than that shithead. And if he saw a way he'd get him. That was what Marianna wanted, too. Where is she right now? Harold wondered.

"You think I'm getting old?"

It took Kim a moment to return. She'd been somewhere else, down in Garden Grove, maybe.

"I love you, Harold. I can say that right now. No promises for the future or any of that bullshit. But right now I love you."

"Thank you. That's nice." He sighed, reaching down and lowering the seat with a whine from the electric motor. He was comfortable again, thinking how glad he was he popped for that extra.

"Sometimes . . . ," he started, opening another beer. He chuckled as he thought of how it would sound out loud, then lost his nerve and stopped.

"What?"

"These things come into my head, I don't know what to do with them."

"What is it?"

"I can't."

"Go on."

"Love. Real love is—"

"Yeah."

"Keeping each other clean when you're too old to do it for yourself."

She was quiet after that. He grew ashamed and turned to his beer.

"I don't know where the hell that came from."

"Don't apologize. You said it and it's real. But it scares me."

She slid over against him and he put his arm around her and they drank their beers and watched the clouds and the gulls.

Sometime later he said, "I tell you I racked up the truck today?"

Apparently Vito's old buddy Tony Danza wasn't here tonight. They'd finished their dinners (if you called the dinky salad and pasta "dinner") without a single point in the stargazing column. Now she was heading for the ladies' room, past the blur of faces, women made up like witches, their men with cannibalistic leering faces, overly tanned, even in the pseudocandlelight. Not a real well-adjusted crowd, she thought, shoving into the ladies' room and getting blasted by cruel fluorescent light.

She had to do this quickly to leave time for the other, so she skipped the makeup check and slid into a stall, bolting the door after her. While all that expensive champagne tinkled into the water below her, she opened her purse and took out the small plastic bottle she bought in the hardware store that afternoon.

Directions: Apply thick coating of gel to desired area. Let paint bubble, then scrape to remove. Covers approximately 20 square feet.

She wondered how many square feet the 560 SEL was, then chuckled as she imagined Vito's face seeing it for the first time. Pure Lizard rage. She only wished she could be there the next morning, too, when his buddies in the used-car section heard about it.

In the parking garage she found his car on the lowest level next to a concrete pillar. Not a good place to be in an earthquake. She looked around. Nobody. She popped open the cap and reached out over the gleaming Mercedes hood, enjoying the feeling, like holding an ice pick above Vito's eyeball.

Squealing tires echoed in the subterranean garage. Marianna stepped back behind the pillar as a Mazda Miata flew past, a blond valet at the wheel. That's the way they drive them down here; then they baby it up to the owner. The Mazda pulled into an empty space and the valet passed a few feet from her, his ponytail bouncing, tossing the keys into the air and singing something off the radio.

She turned back to the Mercedes.

Vito was wagging his finger at her as she returned to the table looking like Mickey Rourke in one of his lesser roles.

"You was gone awhile," he said, flicking his cigarette ash toward the ashtray but missing it. With his scribblings and the ashes the tablecloth was a disaster. "I know what you was up to."

"Aren't you a clever boy." She felt a little excitement, thinking he did know, but knowing at the same time that he couldn't. She slid in across from him and found a fresh glass of champagne waiting for her.

"Gettin' a little protection. No?"

"There's no protection against you, Vito."

"What's worse than interrupting foreplay to go wrestle with a little rubber yarmulke, all slippery and shit?"

"Yarmulke?" she giggled. "You think it's a yarmulke, try putting it on your head."

He leaned closer, smiling suggestively. "Which one?"

"The one you think with," she said over the rim of the champagne flute.

"Zing-go, you got me," he said, aiming a forefinger like a pistol and squeezing off a round. He stuffed cigarettes, lighter, and cellular into the purse thing. "Got to make a quick stop. Then we'll engage in a little boy-girl fun. Let's roll."

She drained her champagne. Mmmmm. She could get used to that stuff in a hurry.

"What's keepin' that beach-boy son of a bitch," Vito said, looking toward the parking garage and peeling a fiver off his gold-clipped wad. They were standing outside the restaurant under the canopy, night air swirling smells of jacaranda and garlic and exhaust around them. Sunset Boulevard was a time-exposure photo of taillights and frozen billboards advertising the latest beauty product and cop buddy-flick. Above the strip, the Chateau Marmont frowned on the traffic and late-night antics, as Marianna thought, *Isn't that where they found Belushi dead?*

"Probably parked it in some alley," Marianna said. "Count the hubcaps when it comes back."

"There's one scratch on that car, I'll tear his fuckin' face off," Vito said, stuffing the five back in his suit-coat pocket.

Marianna felt a pleasant sense of anticipation, a delicious tightening.

Headlights climbed the ramp out of the garage and came toward them. The Mercedes 560 SEL slid in under the canopy lights, its hood gleaming smoothly, the car as detail-perfect as when he drove it off the lot.

At the last moment she had changed her mind. Sure, it

would have been fun to see his face and watch him try to fire everyone at the restaurant, and maybe even accuse her. But there was more to be gained here than a laugh at a cheap act of vandalism. She had to get her car back, and standing there over his Mercedes, she realized that there was a way to do that. His briefcase was in the trunk. She could get it and find out where her car was; then Harold would help her find a way to reel it back in. *Unwind the deal*, isn't that what Harold called it?

"Have a nice vacation?" Vito was saying to the valet.

"What do you mean?" the kid said. Eighteen, good-looking—real good-looking—and he worked out. Probably waiting to be discovered.

"Need to run a few errands or something? I mean, we're in no hurry here."

The kid was getting the drift; he nervously checked the ponytail. "Hey, sorry, man. It was on the level D. I ran all the way."

"Run after this, asshole." Vito flicked the rolled-up fiver like a cigarette butt across the sidewalk and into the gutter. It uncurled and started blowing down the street.

Vito jumped into the car. Marianna slid in the other door, the leather creaking as it accepted her. Vito stomped the accelerator and they shot out into traffic. He studied the rearview mirror as they left the restaurant behind. His laughter filled the car like hot oil.

"Little shit's gonna kill himself trying to get the thing."

She knew he wanted her to acknowledge the encounter, maybe to protest it. She clamped her mouth shut on the urge to speak.

Vito was still glued to the rearview when the back end of a delivery truck filled the windshield.

"Vito!"

He cut the wheel, missed the truck, and they dropped over the sharp ridge and barreled down La Cienega and into the Basin again. He laughed, proud of himself. The evening was a little out of control.

"Where we headed?" she asked after a moment.

"The state of bliss," he said, glancing toward her. "Ever been there?" She saw his face stroboscopically in the passing streetlights. His teeth were exposed.

"Thought you had a stop to make?"

"Shit, yeah," he said, remembering. He spat the next words out: "My *ex*."

"You really should make those alimony payments."

She felt his mood darken. Let's see how sensitive this nerve is, she thought.

"They lock up deadbeat dads now."

"Got nothin' to do with that," he growled. "If anything, I'm too generous. I really got a very big heart. Ask anybody."

"Like the valet back there?"

"He deserved it. But anybody else, my friends, family, even my ex—"

"You have kids?"

"A girl. Scratch that—a *teenager*."

Somehow that took her by surprise.

"Something wrong with that?"

"No. Just—"

They tooled along in silence for a few moments. Then, for some reason, he said, "You make one mistake, one goddamn mistake, you pay your whole life."

He turned to her, thinking she understood or would at least sympathize in theory. She gave him her best smile and said, "I wouldn't know, Vito."

He hovered on the verge of anger for a moment, then threw out an explosive laugh.

"You play that tough-chick role all the way, don't you?" He wagged a finger at her. "I like that. Like it a lot. I got a mind to take a detour here, go to my place first. . . ." He let it hang there in the air as they swept along under yellow lights and palm fronds. And if they did, Marianna thought. What then? Would she get under the sheets with him just to find a way to get her car back? Like everything else that happened recently, she thought she'd work it out when she got there.

His hand found her thigh, his fingers sliding between her legs. He let it lie there, testing. She was surprised at her reaction to his touch. A distant thrill stirred in her system.

"No. I'll take care of business first, then we have the whole night."

Vito slid his hand higher now, pushing her skirt back, the back of his hand touching her panties, but still just testing. Her feelings came closer now and she glanced at them briefly, like signs flashing by on a freeway at night. Excitement, lust, danger, and, yes, here comes understanding. She knew this man, his ego coming out, exposed, looking for her approval even though he tried to maintain that "fuck-you" attitude. But he could be vulnerable, he would bleed if I cut him, Marianna thought.

Another wave of excitement crept over Marianna as she realized that Vito was coming into range, walking into her sights, and if she played it just right she could have anything she wanted. Who would have guessed this yesterday, when he was just an obnoxious salesman she had to deal with? Strange how you could pass anyone in the street and look at their face and know nothing about them. People looked so ordinary on the surface, but open their lives and what would crawl out?

Vito's hand began to nuzzle into her now, brushing silk,

seeking her fluid warmth. She covered his hand, not removing it really, and said, "What kind of a girl do you think I am?"

"I guess we're going to find out."

Harold felt the music before he heard it, thumping bass like someone kicking him in the stomach. He had pulled his truck into the garage behind his father's place and it seemed the walls were moving, like a sounding board for the stereo in the house. He killed the ignition and started to get out. The sound was incredible.

"Why don't you wait in the truck," he was shouting, but Kim was already hopping from the cab.

"Oooo. A party." Kim started moving to the beat in the cramped, dark garage.

Harold left her there as he headed across the small backyard toward the house, a rotted avocado slippery underfoot, and the smell of marijuana drifting from the house. In some corner of his brain he noticed the marine layer had slid back in over the area, the low, dirty, ocean-blown clouds lit by the dull orange light of the vast LA sprawl.

He knew this yard. Every inch of it—now clumped weeds and bare dirt—was a separate island of adventure where he and Randy had played. First trucks and racing cars, then soldiers and tanks. Then they made a little trip down to T.J. and got a gross of cherry bombs. In one day they'd blown up every model car they owned, but, God, it was fun. Finally they had left the yard forever, riding dirt bikes and rebuilding Chevy V-8s to drag race on Harbor Boulevard. And the little yard was empty again.

Harold never came back except to see his little old father,

his lungs failing along with his eyes and his memory and his will to live. But Randy never really left. He did a stretch in Chowchilla for possession and came back. Worked a year in Dago—was fired and came back. Went on the road and came back. Crashed with friends and came back. Now Randy was back, and he brought his friends, and their friends and their dogs. And they were taking the place over. Sleeping on the foldout in the living room, eating his father's food, searching for money and spending anything they found. All the while the old man hid in his room in the back until he couldn't take it anymore and he reached for the phone.

Harold's beeper vibrated an hour ago as they sat in the pickup downing beers. When Harold saw his father's number he knew what it was. Another disaster was what it was, thought Harold as he sobered quickly, his stomach tightening and his hand searching out the therapy ball, only to discover a pile of beads in the corner of his coat pocket.

At the back door now. Harold paused, looking out over the rooftops. From here he could see down the street to his grandfather's house. Of all the childhood memories this was the only real treasure. The old man had owned the whole area and held on to it as wave after wave of bulldozers turned Garden Grove into tract houses and shopping strips. They offered him what seemed then like a fortune for the farmland, and he refused, hanging on to the land and tending his strawberries, his tomato plants, and avocado trees.

Harold stopped in to see him on his way home from school each day, and grandpa greeted him with: "Got another hole in my pocket, Harry." Without a word Harold ran out the door and searched among the tomato plants where he'd sometimes find as much as eighty-five cents lying on the dark soil. It was his to keep, and all through the rest of his life, his marriage, night school graduation, landing the job at Aerodyne, he could never remember being as happy as when he heard his grandpa say, "Got another hole in my pocket, Harry."

Harold shoved in through the screened back door, and the music and smoke hit him head-on. Someone was in the kitchen, a woman with hair hanging around her face as she drank from the tap above a sink full of dirty dishes. She straightened, and he saw the scabs on her cheeks. His brother had them too. T*weakers*, his brother called them. As a chemist he called them methamphetamines.

The woman was taking in his white shirt and Aerodyne ID clipped to the breast pocket and said, "You got the wrong party, man."

And Harold turning on her said, "I don't, but you definitely do."

"Whoa, hostile."

"You get a head start," Harold told her. "I come back and find you here, your ass'll be airborne over the fence."

He was rolling now, determined to get this done and done fast. He headed down the dark hallway toward the living room as he heard the woman behind him say, "Flow, man."

Harold kicked someone's shoes in the hallway and stumbled. Hadn't these people ever heard of lights? He remembered a study where two groups of rats were given all the alcohol they wanted—in a lighted room and in a dark room. The dark room rats drank twice as much. Now he knew what happened to those rats after the experiment.

Dark shapes filled the living room, sprawled on sofas and chairs and lying on the floor. As he entered a lighter flared, showing a gaunt face caving in around a pipe. And then he smelled the chemicals. Christ, they'd set up a lab here. They were making this shit right here—right in his father's house.

Kim appeared at Harold's elbow and held his arm, unsteadily, adjusting to the gloom as the music hammered their ears.

Harold's eyes swept the group and found his brother, propped against a wall next to a girl who couldn't have been more than sixteen. They were sharing a bottle and smoking. Harold advanced on him.

"Outside, let's go," Harold said, bending over Randy and trying to raise him by his arm.

"Harr!" Randy said, realizing for the first time he was there.

"Outside. *Now*." Harold found the nerve in Randy's shoulder and squeezed—a move a paramedic showed him once. Like an electric cattle prod, he'd said. The pain stabbed through Randy's drug haze and he said, "Ow! Shit, man. Okay."

In the front yard the streetlight illuminated the bumps on Randy's face and the spiderweb tattoo on his forearm as he motor-mouthed, stringy hair swaying around his face, saying, "Hey, Harr, it's just till Monday. We got a gig at the Bear in Lomita. We can crash in the bar while we play. So relax, man."

"You're leaving tonight. Now, get them out of here."

"Man, what's the big deal? Monday night we got—"

"Dad doesn't deserve this. Now get them out or I will."

Randy suddenly looked like he was going to cry. "Don't I deserve something? Huh? Dad never did nothin' for me. He shit on me, man."

"That ain't true," Harold said, falling back into brother-speech.

Whoops were coming from the house. Through the front window Harold saw Kim dancing around the living room, going through her routine. Shit, he couldn't let her get started or they'd never leave.

"Randy, look, it was *you*, not him, not me. You. Get that through your head. Now are you gonna get these assholes out of the house or do I have to throw them out?"

"Yeah, *right*. You try anything, they'll fuckin' kill you."

Harold looked at his little brother and felt the rage rising inside him and thought how many times his emotions had gone one degree past love and found hatred, a special hatred reserved only for a brother, one he'd helplessly watched fall down one step at a time.

Harold turned toward the door.

"Harr—hey! Don't do it, man!" But Harold was in the front door and moving around the living room turning on lights. And what he saw gave him unstoppable strength. No wonder they stayed in the dark. The room was strewn with beer bottles and pizza cartons and dirty clothes and pill bottles and cigarettes—all spilling together and being ground into the shag carpet until it was all one carpet of filth.

He charged on into the bathroom, the smell of chemicals almost overwhelming him. The counter was lined with bottles, burners, filters. He swept the whole mess into the bathtub, hearing the bottles and glass smash into a million pieces and mix in new deadly combinations. Probably blow the place up, he thought as he charged back into the living room.

Kim was reaching for the edges of her shirt top, about to pull it over her head when Harold grabbed the stereo cord. If she turned those loose all would be lost, Harold thought, yanking the plug from the wall. The spell was broken. Kim stopped dancing. Everyone turned to Harold, cursing and grunting like a caveful of bears stirring from hibernation, too sleepy to be dangerous, yet.

"Party's over!" Harold shouted, turning on the overhead light like they do in neighborhood bars to get the drunks out. There were about eight of them all told, guys and girls in jeans and T-shirts and tattoos. Heavy-metal rockers.

"Hey, man . . . ," a big guy said, struggling up out of the depths of the couch. Looks like they'd need a forklift to get him up.

"Everyone out! Get your stuff and get outta here!"

The big guy was still fighting the couch. "The fuck're you?" he growled.

"My big brother," Randy told him, smiling, perhaps imagining Harold flattened against the wall.

"Big brother needs to learn some manners," the big guy said, finding his feet and starting to rise.

If he gets up he'll kill me, Harold thought. And with the kind of desperation that borders on courage he nailed the guy on the chin, making a crack like a femur snapping. The big man dropped between coffee table and couch and Harold had his shrimp-tailed loafer on his neck bearing down perhaps a little harder than he needed to. Garbled words came out the guy's mouth but were mostly lost in the shag carpeting.

As Harold looked around at the faces he saw his father standing in the doorway. Smiling.

"Move it!" Harold said to the rest of them.

No one did. There was an ugly silence and mutterings from under his foot when they all realized a car was idling out front, the crackle of a police radio filling the neighborhood. Seconds later they heard two car doors banging and the room began to empty. The big guy got to his feet, much taller than Harold, but turning to see the cruiser outside said only, "We'll finish this later, pard."

"Anytime you want," Harold answered, now that he knew he was safe since the cops were practically at the door. Neighbors must have called them because of the music, he thought, crossing to let them in.

"Party's breaking up now," Harold told the two cops, neither one over twenty-five, one with a crew cut, the other a bodybuilder type. The cops looked puzzled.

"We're looking for an individual named Dodge. Harold

Dodge," the crew cut said. For a second Harold couldn't figure out why a cop would come here looking for him. Then he remembered that he listed this as his address. In most cases it prevented just this sort of unpleasant surprise.

Harold's mind whirled as he stalled with: "What's this about?"

"Are you Mr. Dodge?" the other cop said.

"I—yes," he said, realizing there was paper in one cop's hand. Warrant. What the hell for? His mind shuffled back through his recent indiscretions and quickly found that morning's accident. "But Harold's my brother."

"Is he here, sir?" the crew cut asked more insistently.

"Yes—well, that was him going out the back way. Want me to get him?"

"Yes, sir."

Harold turned to Kim and said, "Be right back." As he left he heard her saying, "Hi, fellas," and the cops saying, "Ma'am," as if she was a schoolteacher or something.

Classic rock-and-a-hard-place situation, Harold thought, looking out the back door, hoping brother and company had vanished. The coast was clear.

Moving across the backyard and into the garage he didn't really think the cops would be able to see his headlights pulling out of the garage. But just to make sure he waited till he hit the street before he flipped them on.

Marianna watched Vito move up the walkway into the bungalow before she began searching his car.

"You can listen to some tunes," he'd said, leaving the keys in the ignition turned to ACS. She tried to picture the guard at Gate C as she pulled in tomorrow morning driving fifty grand of precision German engineering, but then decided against it. It's not me, she thought. I'm more the Ford Escort type.

Things weren't going real well for Vito inside. Angry voices poured out across the yard and into this West LA neighborhood. Glancing toward the house she realized she'd have plenty of time to do what she had to do.

She reached forward and opened the glove compartment: maps, registration, instructions for the Blaupunkt stereo/CD player. Digging deeper now: Binaca, hand lotion for troubled skin, some golf tees, a key ring with two figures that would copulate if you moved it right (the boys in the used-car section must have gotten a kick out of that), and a condom. It was old, the packaging worn and faded, practically army issue. Shows how often he sees action.

Nothing interesting here, she thought. Let's move on. She leaned over and reached under the front seat and touched something cold and heavy. She took out and briefly examined a small handgun. A little car-jacking protection. She slid it back in place and kept groping around until she found the trunk release lever, pulled it, and felt the trunk lid bump open.

The night air was cool and moist as she climbed out and moved around to the rear of the car. She glanced toward the house again, a little stucco bungalow lit up, hedge rising halfway up across the front window. Through the vertical blinds she saw a figure pacing and heard Vito saying, ". . . we had a deal. You know what a deal is? It's when you learn to—"

A teenage girl's voice overlapped Vito, saying, "—everything's a deal with you! You think just because—"

And then another voice chiming in, saying, "Take it back! She doesn't want the damn thing, then take it back!"

The teenager again: "Go ahead! It'd be soooo typical . . ."

Then they all started shouting again as Marianna looked into the trunk lit by a single bulb on the trunk lid. Cases. Cases of what? she wondered, leaning closer and pulling open the cardboard flaps. Foil-topped champagne bottles. She slid a bottle out—it was the same stuff they'd had in the restaurant. She saw the bill and realized it was a hundred bucks a bottle in the restaurant. That made it maybe fifty in a liquor store. Expensive stuff, even by the case. And there were four of them here, so many it took her a moment to spot his briefcase.

"Enough, okay?" Vito was taking command of his little domestic situation now. "I said it was for you and I meant it. Now you take responsibility. If not, I'll take the keys and you can—"

The briefcase popped open despite the built-in combination lock. Contracts paper-clipped to yellow legal pages. In the dim light she saw the yellow pages had boxes drawn on them with figures in the boxes. She recognized them as what Vito had used in the salesroom. Down payment, trade-in, finance, sales price. He presented it to her as if a first-grader could understand it, but none of it had made sense. Now if she could only find hers . . .

Someone was crying inside. Vito's ex and the girl were hugging. Vito stood by awkwardly. Marianna watched the scene as if they were in a museum—distant, easy to analyze their emotions.

"Thank your father . . ."

"She doesn't have to."

"Go on . . ."

The girl hugged Vito, still crying.

I know it's in here, Marianna thought. What if it was? Maybe grab it, take it to Harold. Ask him to unwind it. But where was the damn thing? Running out of time now. He'd be coming out any second. She looked around for a place to hide the briefcase. Come back later and scoop it up.

Looking down the driveway she saw the garage door was open. Perfect. She took the briefcase and started toward the dark entrance. As she approached she saw a car inside, wondering idly if it was the one Vito had given his daughter and then thinking, *huh, an Escort, like mine.* Then thinking, *exactly like mine.* And finally putting it all together and saying to herself, *I'll be damned. It is mine.*

A quick look toward the house. There was still time if . . . yes! The magnetic Hide-A-Key box was still under the back bumper. She'd never used it before, but this made it all worthwhile. Opening the car door in the dark garage, she tossed Vito's briefcase on the passenger seat and softly closed the door.

It started right up. Maybe they tuned it at the dealership. Free tune-up. That would make up for all this aggravation she had to go through. She put it in reverse and started down the driveway.

Halfway to the street she heard a "Hey!" and saw Vito coming out the front door and running across the lawn waving his arms. The car bottomed out as she ramped down into the street. She moved the shift into D and stepped on it.

At the last moment the face and white shirt of a very determined Vito filled the car headlights. But by that time all 86 of Detroit's horses were accelerating the little car faster than ever before in its life. *And they called it a shitbox.* A muffled bump shook the car and Vito was momentarily on the hood, then gone as she continued down the street.

Sweet. Very sweet, she thought.

But before she was even to the end of the block she knew that the satisfaction would not last as long as the repercussions that were bound to follow. Still, for the moment, she had the satisfaction, and for the first time in the past few days, the need for revenge was not with her.

She reached for the radio and clicked it on, retuning the presets to her favorite stations.

"Cops still there?"

"Sure. I'll put them on." Kim paused, then: "Kidding."

"Sheeze. Don't do that to me. I'm traumatized."

"You don't sound too traumatized to me. Where are you?"

"So you can turn me in?" Harold heard himself laugh, ah-ah-ah—three notes in a descending scale. It was his first laugh since seeing those cops and hearing them use his name that way. He had a thing about other people using his name—particularly cops.

The recorded voice of the operator interrupted, and Harold dropped another quarter into the pay phone at the back of Denny's. Across the restaurant the waitress set his patty melt down at his empty booth, looking around for him.

Meanwhile, Kim was saying, "Your dad convinced the cops you were tailing Harold all over Garden Grove."

"Then what?"

"They got tired of waiting and left."

"Dad can spin a good yarn."

"Yeah. He's a sweetie."

In the background Harold could hear his father's voice. Kim relayed the information: "He says he liked seeing you punch out that fat bastard." Another pause. "He says thanks."

"Tell him to get his locks changed. I'll pay for it." Then Harold remembered the shipment of voice keys he was having trouble moving. "Actually, tell him to hold off, i.e., maybe I have something he can use."

More talking in the background.

"What's he saying now?"

"Just telling me where to rub."

"Rub? What the hell's going on over there?" Harold said, laughing and shifting around on the red tile floor.

"He has a lot of tension in his shoulders. I mean a lot."

"Kim, go easy on him. He's an old man."

"He's not *that* old."

"What's that mean?" He heard his father's laughter in the background.

"The flame's still there."

"Well, the flame may be there, but the wick can't take it." Harold had to laugh at his own joke. He was feeling better by the moment. Maybe this cop thing wasn't that serious. He'd get his attorney Zorich on it. The laughter finally died down on their end.

"Look, I feel like I'm interrupting something or something."

"You are." Kim gave a fake moan and started laughing again.

But Harold was looking out the window, watching a Ford Escort with one headlight pull into the parking lot and take the space next to his truck. It couldn't be. But it was. Marianna stepped out of the Escort and crossed the parking lot carrying a briefcase.

"I gotta go. Call you later."

Marianna was standing by his booth when he got there, looking very pleased with herself. It reminded Harold of an expression his mother used: *The cat that swallowed the canary.*

"I unwound the deal, Harold."

He gestured toward the open seat and they both slid into the booth. "Want to tell me about it?"

She eyed his patty melt hungrily. Now that revenge was not grinding in her stomach she realized she was famished. That fifty-dollar pasta and salad just didn't stick with her.

"Want some of this?" Harold said.

She giggled. "I thought you might let me order something all by myself."

Now he was flustered. She did that to him. Harold stopped a passing waitress, then gestured for Marianna to order.

"I'd like one of those," Marianna said, pointing at Harold's plate.

The waitress wanted to leave, but Harold added, "And I'd like some salsa on the side, one glass of just water and one with ice only, and extra napkins."

The waitress seemed stunned by this list of requests so calmly delivered. Eventually she just wandered away.

"Must be new," Harold said darkly.

"Please. Don't wait for me," Marianna said, sampling one of his fries. He wanted her to tell him why she was here, where she had been, and whose briefcase she was carrying. But she just gazed at him and smiled. It unnerved him to have her here, smiling at him, as ripe as a bursting pomegranate in her low-cut dress. He was a sucker for cleavage. And she had major cleavage. As he looked at her he knew just how he would touch her in bed. And how wonderful he could make her feel. What he didn't know was, would he ever get the chance?

Harold was afraid his thoughts were showing on his face, so he bent over the patty melt and began eating cautiously with his thick fingers.

Across the restaurant an obese cabdriver in a baseball hat was joking with the cashier in a loud voice. "Don't ever change!" he roared with laughter. "Don't you ever change."

The waitress arrived with Marianna's food and Harold's salsa, water glasses, and napkins.

"So you unwound the deal," Harold finally said.

She smiled knowingly. *The cat that swallowed the canary.*

Harold gestured toward the briefcase. "I have the feeling that has something to do with this."

"Correct." She lifted the briefcase up onto the table, snapped it open, and lifted the lid. Harold saw the contracts.

"I'm afraid to ask where you got it."

"I'm just borrowing it."

"Temporarily?"

"What other way is there to borrow something, Harold?" He laughed, flustered. She made him act this way.

Marianna patted his hand. "It belongs to our friend Vito. As soon as I find my contract I'll return it. Along with that shitbox Matsura he stuck me with."

"That your trade-in out there?"

"Yes."

"I'm surprised Vito released it, i.e., I've never heard of a dealer doing that."

"He took some convincing," Marianna said, suppressing a smile as she recalled the look on Vito's face as he briefly rode on her hood.

"Let me see if I've got this right. You now have two cars and Vito's briefcase."

"Correct."

"And what does he have?"

"Pardon?"

"It seems you've gotten something for nothing. Make that *everything* for nothing."

"Harold, I'm just following through on what we started. Unwinding the deal." She paused, chewing thoughtfully, then began: "Here's what happened. You said the best way to hurt someone was—" She stopped, noticing a certain expression spreading across Harold's face. "What?"

"I don't think I want to hear this."

Harold was on the phone with room service, having fun with the guy, saying, "What do you mean you didn't know they made beer in Chile? Everybody's drinking it these days."

"Tell him it's so good you can even drink it warm," Marianna called over from the bed.

"It's so good you can drink it warm," Harold said, trying to keep a smile out of his voice. "Yeah, well you do that. Then tell your boss to stock some here, okay?" He put the receiver down, chuckling. "Looks like we're stuck with the Heinie."

He pulled two green bottles of Heineken from the room's refrigerator and passed one to her, sitting on the bed with her bare legs tucked up under her. As soon as they walked into the room she ducked into the bathroom and removed her stockings. It drove him crazy to see her naked legs, so white and smooth, and he couldn't stop following them in his mind up under the skirt to their logical conclusion.

Now she was taking the contracts out of the briefcase and spreading the yellow legal pages around her on the king-sized bed like leaves in an autumn yard. After she described the way she'd recovered her car from Vito she asked if she could spend the night at his place. He was forced to admit he had his own little difficulty, and they compromised on an eleventh-floor room at the Airport Hilton. What the hell, he'd turn those radiators around in a few days and then he could cover this temporary cash shortfall.

"You never told me what's in Chile for you, Harold," she asked, looking for her contract.

"I don't know."

He sat on the edge of the bed, near her. He took a swallow

of beer, then watched it foam up the bottle neck. "I think I'd be happier there. It's a simple place, lots of families."

"You want a family?"

"Yeah," then he added, "I had one, once. But it didn't work out. Now I'm a basket case. Stress. Shit, some days I feel like one more thing and . . ."

"What?"

"I have bad thoughts sometimes."

"We all do."

"You stressed out too?"

"It's different for me. I feel like I'm drowning."

"Now?"

"No. I feel free now. But most of the time. Tomorrow morning probably, back at work—"

"Work. I'd almost forgotten about that somehow."

"A lot of weird things have been happening."

"Tell me about it."

She suddenly started giggling, rocking back and forth on the bed.

"What?"

"I just—ever since I met you—everything's been . . ."

"Yeah. Sorry." He knew what she meant. He looked down.

"No. I mean—"

"Linda. My ex-wife . . ."

She noticed he didn't say it like Vito had. *Ex,* like it was a poison, like it burned his mouth to say it. There was love in his voice somewhere. Disappointed love.

"Linda said, 'You've always got a storm around you.'"

"What'd she mean by that?"

"My aura, I guess. She could see auras. And mine was bad news."

"She really believed that?"

"Sure, I mean, she saw angels all the time, could hear their wings, you know, flying by."

"Oh, please." Then she looked at Harold and saw he wasn't laughing. "I mean, really. You don't believe that? Do you?"

"I don't know what I believe," he said, wondering whether he should tell her now and thinking, yes, this is probably the time. "You see, you're not dealing with an ordinary guy here."

"Harold, I already put that together."

He laughed and thought, maybe I'll regret this, but she has to understand. "Something happened to me, when I was a kid."

No wisecracks now. She wanted to hear it.

"I was in my backyard, maybe nine or ten. The kid next door, Jackie Tombeno, came over, I thought he wanted to play. He had this board in his hand, and he came up and he just hit me with it. What he didn't know was there was this nail in the end of the board. The nail went through my skull and into my brain. Right here, see the little scar."

She winced and covered her mouth, still listening.

"I went into a coma. Doctor said there was nothing they could do for me. They took me back home and they expected me to die."

Harold stood up and wandered to one end of the room where the drapes were pulled across the window. He pulled the curtains open and looked out at the orange sky and the lights far away on the mountains.

"I remember I was having like this dream. I was with my family, and we all looked up and in the sky I could see this face, of a man. And his hair spread out and filled the whole sky and it had every color in it. It was so beautiful I wanted to look at it forever—just stand there and look at it. And I realized that I was looking at God."

Harold was nervous about telling her the story, so he paused and looked at her. But she was serious, sitting there on the bed, not moving. Finally she said, "So what happened?"

"This man—God—said to me, 'Harold, I want you to come to me now.' And I wanted to go, but I was afraid—I didn't want to leave my family. I just stood there. And he said it again, 'Come on, Harold.' And finally I said, 'No. I don't want to go.' And I turned away from him and I woke up and I was in my bed. I remembered thinking I'd been asleep for just a few minutes. But when I stood up I almost collapsed, I was so weak. I couldn't figure it out. It turned out I'd been in a coma for five weeks.

"I walked down the hall. I remember I could hear my mother. She was in the living room with my aunt and they were crying 'cause they thought I was about to die. And then they looked up and—holy shit—there I was! They couldn't believe it. Just kept staring at me like I was a ghost. And finally I said, 'Why did Jimmy hit me?' "

Harold looked at Marianna and wondered what she was thinking. He began to feel self-conscious and think he shouldn't have told her. But it was out now, so he added, "Ever since then I've been waiting."

"For what?"

"Something bad to happen."

"Why? You were healed. It was a miracle."

"But I said no to God. He wanted me to come to him and I said no." He paused and added, "You don't say no to God. You just don't do it."

He could see that she suddenly realized what he meant and had absolutely no answer for him. She got off the bed and came across the room in her bare feet, silent on the carpet, and stood next to him at the window, and they both looked out. A jet was coming in over Century, disappearing behind high-rises and reappearing, heading in to LAX under the dirty orange night sky. He couldn't seem to get more than eight miles away from the airport at any one time.

He felt her at his side, short without her heels, and it gave him a special feeling. He wanted to take her hand, to wrap her up in his arms, touch her in a way that would make her feel that everything was going to be all right.

"I don't feel a storm around you, Harold."

"Not now maybe. But she's right."

"So you think the weather will be better in Chile?"

"Can't be any worse."

Their hands brushed, then found each other and they began holding hands but were still looking out the window almost like it wasn't happening. Their faces were ghosts looking back at them from the window, and Harold felt they were gliding down a long long slide toward warm darkness. And while he wanted to get there as quickly as possible he also wanted to stay on the slide. So they just held hands and watched another jet come in, disappearing behind buildings, reappearing, then finally sinking out of sight.

"All the tired daddies on that plane coming home from business trips," she said. "And Mommy is at home waiting in a nice warm bed with the kids asleep and everything safe."

"Yeah," was all he could say. His voice was very husky.

"And we're together in a strange hotel room, not knowing if the cops will get us, or if we'll have jobs tomorrow, or if a crazed car dealer will send someone after us to break our legs."

It made him a little uncomfortable to hear her say "us." But their hands were getting to know each other now and he felt a special energy flowing between them. So the problems of tomorrow were a long way off and the bed was very close. He knew he'd opt for the bed.

Harold had noticed that sometimes it happened quickly,

and clothes were torn away impatiently and it got to be a little like a wrestling match. And that was nice. But every once in a while it happened differently, in a magical way. The world went into slow motion, and you felt you had all the time in the world and you were just hanging there in your own special universe, not connected to this world by time or place or even gravity. You floated around the room, weightless, and you just let it happen to you both at the same time.

Her dress slid up and over her head with a shush of silk and he found her mostly naked underneath, only some white lace here and there, and that came off easily, Harold's big hands finding her and cupping her as she moaned lightly and arched back into his arms as he lowered her onto the bed. Her eyes half closed, lazily looking at him as she slid her feet under the sheets. Her hands were tugging his shirttails from his pants and unbuttoning him, eager to get underneath. He was opened down the front now and their bodies came together with nothing between them and there was no hurry again, just lots of discoveries to make with many wonderful surprises.

Marianna was smaller than he'd thought, almost delicate through her neck and shoulders. Her skin blushed under his fingers, as he kissed her neck and shoulders, moist and fragrant, smelling of her more than the perfume. He worked his way down to her breasts, which were round and white and generous in the dim light of the room. He cupped her left breast with his hand while his lips brushed her right nipple, feeling it spring back harder now, a shudder going through her body, aware of her special sounds, breathing musically as she found higher and higher notes. God, he was going to make her feel so good.

Later he realized everything had occurred in a trance state just south of sleep and a million miles from consciousness. He lost track of the borders of his own body as they merged and flowed into and through hers. No fears, no words, just the warm breath in their throats and a long gliding journey down that dark slide.

During the night sometime he was aware of her in his arms and couldn't really remember falling asleep. Her body was curved into his, head on his shoulder, delicate breath whispering her dream thoughts in his ear. In a distant corner of his unconscious mind he wished they could sleep this way for a month or so and wake up and find all their problems gone, or so far away they couldn't reach them. Maybe, if they slept long enough, they'd just wake up together in Chile. He smiled in his sleep as this thought occurred to him.

But then, much later, yet still before dawn, as the first flights for the East Coast and the Pacific Rim were thundering down the runways outside, he opened his eyes briefly and found her on the other side of the room, under a small light, the briefcase in her lap, leafing through a small black leather book.

The cane was a nice touch. It gave him a Continental air, like Ricardo Montalban when he did those old Volaré ads for Plymouth. Vito could feel the prospect sympathizing with him as he painfully followed her around the car lot. Sympathy was good. It softened them up for the sale. Maybe he'd keep the cane permanently.

Of course, the pain wasn't completely a put-on. Knee hurt like a son of a bitch. Nothing broken in the X ray, but all sorts of screwed-up tendons. On the spur of the moment he told the prospect a story about an attempted car-jacking, standing in the path of a moving vehicle to try to save a friend's car. The story led nicely into a pitch for the computerized ignition cutoff feature of the Integra she was eyeballing.

It wasn't the first story he'd had to invent to cover what happened last night. He told his daughter and ex he thought some Mexican must have tailed him from the dealership. But then why didn't they steal his Mercedes? they wanted to know. There was no telling what went on in their brains, he said—if they even had any.

The prospect accepted his offer to demo the Integra, and as she headed for the driver's door Vito checked her out from behind. Her face was kinda foxy, blond hair and some of that pale lipstick. But now that the big picture was revealed, he saw the rest didn't measure up. Thick ankles could really soft-boil a hard-on in a hurry.

Lucky thing, really, he thought, sliding into the passenger seat and dragging his leg in next to him. He had a lot to take care of today without stopping by the Econo Lodge with another prospect. Sometimes, on a demo with a real babe, he'd just suddenly say, "I've never done this before, but I have this incredible urge to make love to you. And I was just thinking that you must be feeling the same thing." Sometimes they went for it. Sometimes they told him to go fuck himself. That was just the nature of sales. If you couldn't take rejection, then get the hell out. One thing was for sure, you could never tell what a woman was going to do. Like last night.

He had thought Marianna was coming around. She even seemed hot for him. Next thing he knew, she tried to run him down and drove off in her old car. Correction: his daughter's car. Man, Cindi was a basket case. First she sees her old man picking himself up off the pavement, then she realizes her new car's gone. Had to promise her the world to get her calmed down.

As Vito drove back to his place in Beverly Hills (adjacent) from the hospital, he thought of a million ways to kill that bitch. But sitting in his leather recliner in front of some Zchannel action flick with Chuck Norris blowing away eighty million guys with an assault rifle, he realized there was another issue here. He was still hot for her. Hotter than ever. Thing was, a woman had never done that to him before, tried to run him down. And it hadn't been all bad. As he saw her bearing down on him, he felt something close to sexual anticipation. In some corner of his brain, just before impact, the thought formed: *Hey, I wonder what this is gonna be like?*

Then this morning, when he drove up to the dealership, he found Marianna's new Matsura blocking the gate. The contract was under the wiper with "Null and Void" scrawled across it and a little Post-it stuck on it saying, "I unwound the deal."

Unwound. At first he wondered how she knew words like that, the kind they used around the dealership. Then it hit him. Of course, Dad-boy was behind all this. He had underestimated the old guy, and now he was paying the price.

Things went downhill from there. As soon as Joe walked in he dragged Vito into his office.

"Where the hell's the book?" he asked.

"In my office," Vito told him.

"Well, get it for me. When LaBounty gets here, he's going to wanna settle up for that last shipment. We got to show 'em what we can get for those things."

Halfway to his office Vito stopped, remembering that the book—the little black book where they recorded all their under-the-counter profits—was in his briefcase along with all the work sheets he had meant to shred. And the briefcase was gone. Marianna had taken it while he was hassling with Cindi and his ex. He had to return to Joe and stand in front of him like some greeter who lost a hot prospect.

"Of all the fucked up things . . . ," Vito began, watching Joe's body language go from bad to worse.

"I left my briefcase over at my ex's," Vito heard himself say. "I went over there last night and I forgot the thing."

Joe stared at him a long time, deciding whether to believe him or not, before he said: "The hell was it doin' in your briefcase?"

"It got in with some other papers, I guess."

"You guess? What's the matter with you? I don't want that thing floatin' around."

"Nothin's gonna happen to it."

"What if your ex sees it?"

"She's too stupid to know what it is. Hey, it's no big deal. I'll run over and get it at lunch."

"Run over and get it. Now."

"She's not home. I just called. I'll get it at lunch."

"You leave the booze over there too?"

"No, Joe."

"Stuff's worth three grand."

"Worth three grand. But that ain't what you paid for it," Vito said, hoping to flatter him.

"It's still worth three grand," Joe said, coming forward in his chair a little. "And it's gonna help get us another dozen Integras out of Cincinnati. You know how hard it is to get those things?"

"I'm not stupid."

"You're not? Then why do you want them going over to Beverly Hills? Or Sherman Oaks? LaBounty could just as easy send 'em to one of the dealers up there. That'd cost me twenty grand."

"It'd cost me too, Joe. And I won't let it happen."

"That's for damn sure. Now I wanna see the book on my desk when I get back from lunch. Got that?"

Vito got it all right. And he scrambled for options all morning—until he remembered the LoJack tracking device he had them put on it before he gave the car to his daughter. Halfway through the demo, Vito felt the beeper on his hip throbbing and interrupted his sales pitch.

"Excuse me a second here, Sandy," he said, checking the number. Yes, it was LoJack. They must have found the Escort.

This changed everything, Vito thought, remaining uncharacteristically silent for the rest of the demo. After talking to Joe he'd thought he would have to find Marianna, make a deal with her on the trade-in to get the briefcase back. Just to put out the fire. But this changed everything. So why compromise? That's what most guys would do in my position. But compromising's for losers. I'm going for the class play on this—balls out all the way.

Vito watched the prospect ease the Integra back into the lot and cut the motor. She wasn't exactly eager to get out. Just sat there in her navy suit stroking the leather steering wheel, waiting for him to start his sales job. She knew the drill.

A lot of these people, they wanted the sales job, Vito thought. Then later they could say, "I had no idea what was happening. That bastard stuck me in it before I could say no." That was bullshit. Most of them wanted to be told what to do so they could escape the blame. You had to know the psychology of the situation if you wanted to succeed in sales. Vito thought how he'd have probably made a damn good shrink.

"Doesn't look like you enjoyed driving this car, Sandy," Vito said, smiling.

"Do me a favor," she said. "Tear my hands off the wheel."

"Doing a little bonding here, are we?"

"Yeah. But I'm still in shock over the price."

"Sandy, I told you before, sticker shock is strictly forbidden here."

"You'll see what I mean when you pull up my TRW."

"Been a bad girl, have we?"

"Very bad."

" 'Beat me, whip me, make me write bad checks,' " he said, quoting a bumper sticker he'd once seen. "Look, Sandy, the TRW's strictly academic, okay?"

"What do you mean?"

"Well, I've got this magic wand in my office."

"Is that right?"

"Yeah, it's called a pencil. I wave it around a little and make all that stuff go away."

"You'd need a huge magic wand to get rid of my credit history."

"Sandy, it's not the size of the wand, it's how you use it." They both laughed at that. "Listen, I'll tell you a little secret. These Integra's are hot. Red hot. Last week some guy came in and offered me two K *over* sticker. Now if you want an Integra, you ain't gonna find one on any lot except ours. They just aren't out there. So come on inside and we'll see what kind of magic I can work on your TRW. Okay?"

He patted her knee, then climbed out of the Integra and began walking toward the salesroom, leaning on the cane. She would follow him. He knew she would. And then he would sell her the car. That would look good when LaBounty saw the book. Probably say to Joe, "This Vito Fiorre must be a helluva salesman."

He was halfway to the showroom door when he heard the *clomp clomp* of the prospect's heels behind him. She wore those clunky heels like so many mini-execs these days. Going for that assertive look. He knew she'd come around. This day is turning around, he thought, considering just how he'd play her. He'd get her all softened up, then turn her over to the closer in F & I and go after his briefcase. Then he'd chalk up another win in the book. When he got it back.

The phone on Marianna's desk beeped. She picked it up and heard Harold say, "Anything on your end?"

"All quiet." She looked between desks and partitions and across the hallway. There was Harold in his office, working something in his hand.

"What's that thing you're touching?"

His voice blushed. "My therapy ball. Stress, you know?"

"Didn't I relax you enough last night, Harold?" She was back to this flirty talk again. After last night he wanted her to be real with him.

Looking out his office door he could see a group of workers milling around looking depressed. There had been an article in the *Times* that morning saying that the defense industry was going to take a big hit in the nineties. Everyone was talking about who was going to get the ax, who was going to survive.

Meanwhile, the line pounded away downstairs, generating that milky oil that had to be shipped out of state and dumped in Texas. What the hell could he do about that? Jerry wanted an answer yesterday and instead he'd snuck off to put in a bid on those radiators. That reminded him. He had to move those things fast. Where was that number . . . ?

Prioritize. Prioritize. Isn't that what the MBA assholes around here said? Take care of the big problems first. The biggest was getting the cops off his back. And Vito off Marianna's back. But now he was finding that he wasn't onto her. That was a problem in itself.

"Why hasn't he called?" Harold asked her, pushing the therapy ball out of reach and folding his hands.

"He's stupider than we thought?"

"No. He's thinking. Why's he doing that?"

"Because he wants a novel experience?"

"If he was a regular car salesman type, and someone took possession of their trade-in, he'd be all over you—i.e., the cops would have picked you up by now for car theft."

"The car is *mine*."

Harold was getting a little tired of that position. "But he's not doing that. Why?"

"Because he's into something and can't go to the cops. Harold, I told you that this morning. I saw the contracts. He's—what did you say?—making water."

They both laughed when they realized what she'd said. "He's watering the contracts. But all those bastards do that. It must be something more significant."

"Bigger?"

"Maybe."

"Then take a look at that little book in the briefcase. It shows what they sold all these Integras for. And they're way over dealer cost—way over MSRP."

Harold was a little unnerved to hear her so smoothly reel off the abbreviation for manufacturer's suggested retail price.

"How do you know that?"

"I learned from the best. I read your book. Appendix C."

At first he was flattered, then nervous. She'd gotten his book and was using it on him. Christ. He'd created a monster. His hand wandered across the desk and picked up the therapy ball again.

"When you touch it that way it makes me jealous."

He dropped the therapy ball in the desk drawer. He'd forgotten she could see him.

"Oh-oh. Harold, Jerry's coming."

"Okay, gotta go."

"I'm not going to let you."

"Don't do this to me."

"You can handle him. I just want you to promise to look at that book. You can figure out what it means."

Jerry appeared in Harold's office and stood there, shifting his weight. Harold saw the requisition he'd submitted in his hand.

"Okay, bring it over and I'll have a look at it," Harold said, trying to sound like it was official business.

"You already have it, dear."

"I do?" It was harder to stay official now.

"I put the briefcase in your truck. It's in the jump seat."

Jerry was impatient. He was saying something like, "Quick question . . . ?" as Harold held up his hand, thinking, *When'd she get into my truck*?

Her voice was still on the phone saying, "Don't waste your best moves on that stupid ball. I want some more of what I got last night."

"Right. Okay," Harold said as if he were getting the tolerances of a new tool-and-die rig. He hung up and tried to put his face back together before he looked up at Jerry.

"Where did you say you got this?" Paige Patton said, her face slowly looking up from the black leather book filled with vehicle identification numbers, dollar amounts, and salesmen's initials. It was the first time she'd really looked at Harold since he walked in a few minutes ago. Granted, she was an overworked DMV investigator, and Harold refused to give her his name—just another guy off the street with a conspiracy theory. Still, he expected better treatment, since he was definitely sticking out his neck to be here.

"Friend of mine's a greeter on the lot," Harold lied. "He

borrowed it from his boss's desk—i.e., he needs to get it back real fast. That's why I told you up front: For now it's just FYI. You want to do anything more than eyeball it we have to work something out."

"Work something out," she said, biting her cuticle. Her nails disappeared into the cuticles, which were shredded and bloody. Strange, Harold thought, she didn't seem tightly wound from the outside. But those nails—ouch.

Paige riffled her hand back over short-cut brown hair and settled her steady cop eyes on Harold. She was a big woman, as big as a man (maybe she *was* a man, Harold thought). But now she was curled up around the leather book in her hand, slouched in a plastic chair in this tiny cubicle. Across the office a phone rang, and Harold heard someone answer: "DMV, investigations."

Without taking her eyes off the book, Paige slowly picked up her phone and pressed one number. A voice answered on the other end and she said, "Ted. Want you to take a look at something. Yeah." She hung up.

Someone else was coming. Harold felt his control over the situation slipping away. This might be hard to stop.

"You said you're in car sales," she said, turning back to him.

"Used to be."

"Now you're—?"

"An engineer, actually. But I'm still involved, in a way."

"What way is that?" She tried not to seem too interested in Harold. But he knew she was trying to fit him into the picture, trying to figure what the hell was going on. It was getting awful warm in this shitty little office.

"I help friends buy cars sometimes," Harold answered.

"You're a broker."

"I.e., as a favor only," he quickly added. Taking money

meant he needed a license. "This friend of mine went in alone, which is unwise, got ripped off."

"They stole his car?"

"Hers. No, got her buried in a contract, got her trade-in for two grand under blue book."

"They didn't put a gun to her head and rob her then. They screwed her is what you're saying."

"They stole two grand, is what I'm saying." Why do the cops do this to you? he wondered. Even a mini-cop like this lady. I'm doing her a favor, she makes me feel like scum.

"Didn't do too well for your friend," she said, glancing down the hall now, looking for Ted.

"That was before I was involved. That's how I got involved. She wanted me to unwind the deal."

"And have you?"

"That's why I'm here. I told you that."

"But I don't see why you can't tell me who you are."

Harold sighed, disgusted. He realized she was trying to take him back over the same ground, see if she could trip him up.

"I only came in 'cause I thought there was something in the book you should know about."

"You came in 'cause you thought you could make a deal." She picked up the phone again and jabbed the same number. No one picked up. She pressed another number and said into the phone: "It's me. Bring me the American Matsura file."

Harold stood up. "Look, if you're not interested I'll—"

"I didn't say that. Sit down."

Harold waited, then sat.

"Your friend. What kind of trouble's he in?"

"She. And who said she was in trouble?"

"People usually want to make deals when they're in trouble."

Harold was about to explain about the car theft when his mind abruptly shifted to his own problems. He said, "She, actually, I believe she's got an outstanding warrant."

"Uh-huh."

Harold hated Paige at that moment, hated her superior tone, but he continued, since he saw a possible angle here. "It's nothing serious. Something like leaving the scene of an accident."

"Leaving the scene of an accident? I'd call that pretty serious. In fact, I'd call that hit-and-run."

Harold's spirits dropped. He shifted in the chair and heard it creak as if he weighed five hundred pounds.

"I have to be very honest with you. I don't like being here. In fact, I think I'm going to leave." He stood up, pretending he was a prospect in a sales office who didn't like the numbers. Paige quickly got to her feet and stood at the entrance to the partition.

"Don't get me wrong. We're not *un*interested, Mr. . . . In fact, there's an investigation in progress. Not ours, but we're assisting. That's why I want you to talk to my supervisor. He's around here somewhere." She picked up the leather book and began to leave.

"The book stays here," Harold said, hearing the tone in his voice.

She looked at him, startled, and he repeated it: "The book stays right here."

She set it back down on the desk. "I'll be right back." She left.

As soon as she was gone, Harold pocketed the book. Listening to the phones and the disembodied voices around him he wondered what the hell to do next. Leaving was a definite possibility. His famous disappearing act. He glanced at his watch. Only got a few more minutes, then a quick stop at the radiator shop on Katella to check on that buy he made yesterday. (Two grand at stake there.) Then back to the office. If traffic wasn't bad. Of course it always was. Shit, I don't have time for this.

But then he imagined himself returning with the good news to Marianna. *They're gonna help you unwind the deal in exchange for the book,* he'd say. Then she'd look at him like he was a hero. She'd realize what she was dealing with. A guy that could pull strings and make things happen. They could celebrate over dinner. Another night together . . . ? Yeah, that would be nice. And so would the fact that Vito would get the double shaft, lose the sale and get investigated for watering contracts. Or whatever else they were up to at Joe's. Maybe he should hang in here for a few more minutes.

The beeper on his hip moved. He looked down and saw his father's number. Shit. Brother and friends must be back. He kinda thought they would be. And it'd be harder to get them out this time.

A new face appeared at the partition opening, a secretary type, judging by the way she didn't have an attitude like the others around here. She was carrying a brown file sleeve, looking at Harold in his suit, the beeper still in his hand.

"You from Sacramento?"

Harold sensed it wouldn't hurt if he indicated that he was, so he nodded slightly.

"Where's Paige?"

"Went to get Ted."

"Oh," the woman said. She set the folder down on the desk and left.

Harold stared at the thick file filled with legal-sized papers. On the label it said "American Matsura Motor Co. Case FD 89Q1334." He moved to the partition entrance. If he looked to the right he saw the reception area he'd entered through.

A few plastic chairs, a receptionist behind her desk, public-service posters, a drinking fountain. To his left was a double door into an open courtyard area. Several people were standing out there, smoking and talking, arms folded across their chests.

Turning back to the reception area, Harold saw Paige, her back to him, bending over to the receptionist. They were looking at something out in the parking lot.

". . . it might have been that truck . . . red one over there . . . ," the receptionist was saying.

Paige said, "Can you read the tag?"

She's trying to get my license! Harold realized. *She wants to find out who* I *am*! That does it. Harold glanced back inside the cubicle to make sure he had the book and saw that the file folder was still lying there, right on Paige's desk.

The smokers in the courtyard outside thought nothing of seeing the stocky man in the brown suit leave the building. They assumed he was just another overworked investigator carrying a thick case file tucked under his arm. What did seem odd was how quickly he crossed the parking lot and pulled out in that brand-new pickup truck.

I'll be damned, Vito thought, here she comes in all her glory. Through the windshield, he could see Marianna approaching down the sidewalk. He was parked across the street under a tree that kept dropping gumballs on the hood of the car. Each one hit with a thud and left a puff of orange dust on the cranberry red paint job. Didn't matter, though. It wasn't his car. It was Marianna's, the Matsura she bought last Tuesday. And she was finally going to take possession of it.

He watched as Marianna opened the Escort door, sat

sidesaddle in the driver's seat, then swung those legs up out of sight, but not before spreading them slightly, the short red dress she'd worn last night opening to reveal the inside of her thigh and the darkness up inside, between her legs.

He kept watching as the Escort pulled a U-ie on the quiet side street, and Vito eased the Matsura out after her.

The Escort was right where LoJack told him he'd find it. They even sent a rig from Mr. Jay's Towing Service, assuming he wanted the thing picked up like most repos. But he told the kid just to pop it open and he'd take it from there. The kid studied him, reaching back and smoothing that long braided rope of hair that lay down his back. Cool. Vito wondered if it got him laid much. Long hair was a turn-on for most women. He could go for one, maybe a little ponytail, if it weren't for his job. He had to be middle-of-the-road. Hip if the prospect went that way. Corporate if some suit wandered in.

The kid just stood there, looking at Vito until he extended the bill. When the kid saw Benjamin Franklin, he popped the latch and took off, pronto. Problem was, the briefcase wasn't in the car, or the trunk. So he went back to the Matsura and thought up plan B.

Vito felt something hot and liquid stirring in his gut, something wild he'd never felt or even been able to *make* himself feel even with all his elaborately staged sex acts, artificial aids, and stimulants. This was pure animal passion, he thought, holding the sensation like a glowing ball and turning it around as he savored it. I'm finally going to get what I deserve, he told himself. And she's definitely going to get everything she deserves.

Now the Escort was signaling for a turn onto the ramp, heading north on the 405. Headin' home, Vito thought, pleased. Yes, plan B was bound to work. And it might turn out to be more fun. A whole lot more fun.

"You're gonna have to speak up," Harold shouted into the phone in the back of Cao Tran's shop in Artesia. They were sandblasting the radiators, and the air compressor sounded like the space shuttle taking off in his ear.

". . . I said that fat guy came by looking for you." Kim's voice finally penetrated the roar.

"What fat guy?"

"The one you stepped on his neck. Remember now?"

"Of course I do," Harold said, a knot forming in his stomach. He didn't like people looking for him, especially big fat guys who wanted to beat the shit out of him.

The air compressor suddenly shut off and Tran's guy (his brother maybe?) bent over the radiator. They were doing an assay to see how much tin it had in it. The more it had the less it was worth. Harold was sweating it out as he waited for an answer. But you couldn't rush Tran. He knew scrap metal. He salvaged most of Vietnam after the war. Made a fortune off all the junk left by the U.S. military. Now Tran was starting in on Southern California. There should be enough scrap metal here to keep him busy for quite a while.

"And he's got a couple of guys with him," Kim yelled.

"I'm okay now," Harold said. "I.e., you don't have to shout anymore."

"I just don't want you showing up unprepared," she said, quieter now. "They're scary lookin', tattoos and—"

"I get the picture." Harold heard her giggling. "What's funny about that?"

"I was just thinking. . . . The fat guy looked so geeky with the neck brace on. I heard him talking about how much it hurt."

Harold thought about it for a minute, then: "Randy and the rest of them back?"

"Yeah."

"How's Dad takin' it?"

"He went back into his room. I've been keeping him company, but I gotta get back to the club. I'm dancin' tomorrow night."

"Can you stay put for now, while I figure out what to do?"

"I guess so. . . . This ain't fair to Sammie."

"Sammie?"

"Your dad."

"I know what my dad's name is. I'm just not used to hearing him called that. Dad can take care of himself. Just go if you have to. Take a cab. I'll pay for it."

"Okay." She liked that, but then added, "Harold, watch out. I heard them talking, saying what they'd do if you show up."

"I'm not going to come over now. But I'm not gonna let them traumatize Dad neither. Now let me work something out."

Harold hung up, glanced at his watch. Marianna said she'd be at her house until twelve forty-five. Said she wanted to change and shower. He looked across the dark shop at Tran and the other guy bending over the radiator.

"Tran! What's the word?"

"Need time. Five minutes only!"

Harold rummaged in his briefcase for her number. He dialed, listening to it ring as he started glancing through the file he'd picked up at the DMV. He wouldn't have taken it except, that woman—what a bitch. He'd give the file the once-over, then send it back down there—i.e., anonymously. He didn't need any more reasons for the cops to be looking for him.

Marianna's answering machine picked up on the sixth ring

and he heard her voice, breathy and low. "We're not here now . . ." Who the hell was this *we?* ". . . but wait for the little beep and leave us a message." *Us?* Probably just trying to sound like the kind of a place you didn't want to break into. Still, it could mean she was living with someone. That wasn't good. It seemed everyone he got involved with had some sort of mitigating circumstance, some reason Harold couldn't be more than just another element of their lives. That wasn't what he wanted. He wanted to be the main feature. He wanted a woman he could give all of himself to—and get everything back in return. Like last night. Marianna didn't hold back last night. She was all there.

Harold's eyes were moving across the pages in the file as he set the receiver back in place. Depositions, motion for finding, affidavits. It didn't make much sense yet. But then he found a page labeled *Statement of Timothy Flynn.*

". . . alleged the owner, Joseph F. Covo, boasted of securing luxury models over quota through the practice of bribes and gifts to national office executives such as John J. LaBounty." Harold's eyes caught on the name. LaBounty . . . LaBounty . . . He remembered Covo, years ago, talking to LaBounty on the phone several times when he walked into his office. Doing what? Arranging car shipments?

Harold read on with a rising sense of excitement, the document in his hand suddenly seeming like a weapon: ". . . securing the franchise from the American Matsura Motor Co. through a system of bribery, gifts and favoritism in violation of federal antiracketeering laws."

Marianna was right. This's got nothing to do with watering contracts. It's a federal case. That means the FBI is handling it. No wonder Vito was jumpy when—

"We finish, Harold," Tran said, standing in front of him smiling and nodding, holding the metal sample. "Assay good. Not a much tin. Very low."

Hot damn, Harold thought. Something finally went right. "What're we talkin' here, then?" Harold was getting excited as he began to picture some cash flowing back into his pockets. Yes, Tran was the kind of guy you came to when you wanted something. Anything. He briefly recalled the other things he'd heard about Tran—that his name wasn't really Cao Tran at all, that he had fought the Khmer Rouge before changing his identity and escaping to California.

"I'm thinking that five grand might be a fair amount. Fair to both of us is what I mean," Harold added. Sometimes you had to really spell things out for Tran.

Tran nodded, smiling nervously. "I give you really good deal."

"Yeah, but, how much?"

"Don't worry, my friend. I give you really good deal."

"Look, Tran. I need something now, some cash."

"Sure. Sure."

"Like thirty-five hundred, then you get ten percent on the profit when you move it. That's more than fair."

"Three grand now . . . Then, I give you really good percentage. Come into office. I get you money."

Harold started after him, but hesitated. "I'll be right in. Got one more call to make." He punched in his card number. Marianna won't pick up the phone, he thought, but at least I can hear her voice again. That'll hold me till I get back to the office and give her the good news.

Was that the phone? Marianna wondered. It was always hard to tell when you were in the shower. Harold said he might call if he found anything interesting in that little black book in Vito's briefcase. But she wanted just a few more minutes under the hot water. A few more minutes to dissolve the sweat and memory of her evening with Vito. A few more minutes to be alone and pretend she was still in control.

She told her hands to shut off the water, but they wouldn't listen. There was work to go back to. Problems looming on all fronts. Layoffs, cops, cars, money. And Harold. With those steady eyes asking her to give in to him. To take him body and soul. She had taken him in body. And that was really something. Who would have thought he had it in him? Why wasn't her soul following? Maybe she'd stay in the shower all afternoon and figure that one out.

She felt a cold draft swirling in from the open door. The hot water was going to give out soon, so she rinsed her hair back once more, cut off the water, and threw open the curtain.

Sitting on the closed toilet lid, a huge grin on his face, was Vito, chin resting on the head of a cane. She forced herself to stare at him while he slowly surveyed her naked body, getting his jollies.

"I definitely underestimated you," he said. Was he licking his lips, or was it just her imagination? "A few extra pounds. But hey, it's all in the right places."

"Hand me a towel, would you, dear?"

"And have this vision of loveliness stolen from my sight? No way."

She stepped out of the shower and reached past him for the towel. His hand rose toward her breast as he said "Come to Daddy" and she slapped him good, smacking that Lizard grin right off his face. The crack was sharp and pure, echoing off the tile and chrome in the small space, and he stopped, startled, and looked at her. She wound herself up in the towel and stepped out into the small kitchen. He was right behind her, moving awkwardly on the leg, and faced her across the table she put between them.

"Didn't you get my note, Vito? The deal's unwound. I got my car back. You got your Japanese piece of shit back and we're through now."

He was breathing hard, leaning on the cane, his face reddening where she hit him. She didn't like the look in his eyes.

"It's not that simple." He seemed to be hissing, like a pot ready to boil over and make a mess on top of the stove. "You promised something else and you never delivered."

"Refresh my memory."

"You come on with that attitude, that hot babe stuff, then you slam the door on me."

"Actually, I ran you over."

"Yeah. But I'm back. And I'm gonna get what's coming to me."

"You're getting nothing from me, Vito. We're square."

"I'm afraid you're wrong, sweetheart."

"Next time, put it in the contract."

Vito lunged as if he was coming around the table after her. She didn't react. He's testing me, she thought, holding her ground. He wants me to run. He wants to feed off my fear. Her mind was clear and sharp as she realized that everything counted now, every word and action.

"You may be wondering about your briefcase," she said, pulling out a chair and sitting down, protecting herself, her attitude neutral. "I don't have it here. But maybe we can work something out. It's—"

" 'You may be wondering about your briefcase,' " he mimicked, laughing. "I love it. So cool. So calm. Yes, I'm wondering about my fucking briefcase. But that's just part of our agenda here today."

"Have a seat, Vito," she said. But he kept standing.

She got back to her feet. "I'm sorry. Where are my

manners? You want a beer? Something to eat?'' She moved for the refrigerator thinking, maybe there's a bottle in there, something I can use. Vito came around the table and stepped in front of her.

''Who do you think you're dealing with? Some putz like that old guy you're leading around by the balls? Uh-uh. You make an offer, you back it up. Understand?'' He grabbed her by the shoulders and held her while he pressed his mouth against hers, trying to open her lips, trying to force his tongue into her mouth. She pulled back.

''You're not stupid enough to do this, Vito.''

He pulled her to him again but she shoved him away, kicking the cane out from under him as she twisted away and ran around the table, heading for the bedroom. He turned and put his weight on the bad leg and roared in pain, then launched himself at her, his hand raking her neck and back as he fell and then finding the towel and stripping it off her. She made it to the bedroom and was slamming the door as he came through it on his hands and knees. The heavy door banged on his neck, then again on his shoulders as he forced his way into the room.

He's getting in, she thought, and I can't stop him.

Marianna tried to jump back, but he dove for her and caught an ankle. She went down, hard, head cracking a chair leg, her other leg trying to kick him free. But his hands were reeling her in like a slippery wet mermaid, hand over hand, his fingers cold steel on her skin. She was being dragged into the mouth of a monster. And there was nothing she could do about it.

Vito had his weight across her legs now, his head on her stomach, her knees pinned under him, unable to damage his muscled chest. His grunting filled the room and she heard her own breath, high-pitched and weak.

Take control. Take control, she thought. But how?

He was squeezing her breasts now, licking her, nipping her. Biting her as she fought him. He had her left nipple in his mouth as she tried to pull away and the pain stabbed through everything. A vision of his face flashed before her, and she saw the blood on his lips and knew it was hers.

His free hand was pulling his pants down and she felt his hot penis on her bare stomach. He was fumbling down there, trying to get it in. But she was fighting too much, legs kicking.

Vito put his free hand on her throat and pressed. She panicked. Out of control, she thought, way out of control. But she couldn't stop fighting him. She felt like she was being stuffed down into a dark room and they were trying to close the door on her and she kept pounding and pushing it open. *Don't lock me in here,* she screamed inside, don't lock me in.

The room was shrinking. Vito's bloodied face was receding above her and she realized she was being strangled. A little voice in some corner of her mind suddenly said, You will die soon unless . . . She saw herself dead on the bedroom floor and felt a distant sadness about that. Sadness, not anger. Where was her anger? Then more words formed in her mind. There was rape and then there was death. Rape was bad. Death was worse.

She stopped fighting and spread her legs. He entered her with a satisfied grunt, his hand still on her throat like a rider controlling a wild horse. His hips began thrusting as she let all of him in.

His hand on her throat eased.

And she drew a breath.

Vito removed his hand from her throat. He bent her legs up and rose to his knees, slamming himself into her. He took her buttocks in his hands and squeezed the flesh wildly, moving to her thighs and then her breasts, working her flesh as his thrusting intensified. He was rough now. But he wasn't killing her. She would live, if she kept it up.

"Oh, my God—" she gasped.

Her excitement triggered a final flurry from him and he suddenly shouted "Oh!" as if something was being torn from him and stopped dead for a split second, then thrusted again saying, "Oh! Oh! Oh" and collapsed on top of her.

She lay there looking at the ceiling and panting. She was vaguely aware that he got to his feet and began straightening his tie and tucking in his shirt. He brought over a blanket from the bed and covered her, crouching low and whispering, "Sorry it got kinda crazy. . . . But man, it was incredible." As if she would care.

She closed her eyes, and made a low "Mmmmmm."

Sometime later she heard the water running in the bathroom and then he was back, next to her. "I guess we understand each other now." He was stern again, a male who'd been forced to assert himself. "Your Matsura's outside. I'm taking the Escort. I'll call you later and come and pick up my briefcase."

Marianna waited as his footsteps left her apartment. She was sure now what she would do. But she hadn't decided how she would do it.

The 2.7-liter V-6 in Joe Covo's Accell easily handled the climb up Crenshaw into the Palos Verdes Hills. Sea level to fifteen hundred feet in two and a half miles. Cars and trucks flashed by silently in the right lane as Joe felt the turbo feeding the hungry power plant. There was still an effortlessness in the car that thrilled him, a power-in-reserve quality he sought in his own life. His foot wasn't even on the deck yet. If it was, Katie bar the door.

The road twisted around the mountainside and straightened for the last shot up to the crest. This section always reminded him of the straightaway near the top of the Pike's Peak climb where he had driven modified Jags up the treacherous dirt road. You had to adjust the carb for one altitude—about eleven thousand feet—and make your move then. The pit crew timed it for maximum performance on the straightaway. That's when he blew off the Porsches and MGs. Only thing that could match that power were the Vettes, and those pigs couldn't stay on the road.

Joe had come up through the ranks doing hill climbs and racing formula Fords on the Canadian circuit. He had guts that wouldn't quit—even after he saw his best friend decapitated in a spinout in Toronto. But driving wasn't where the big bucks were. So he parleyed his name into a high-level sales position in Beverly Hills. Pretty soon he was managing a Ford dealership and built it to a $3-million-a-year enterprise.

Then in the seventies he saw the handwriting on the wall: The Japs were coming on strong. He courted the execs from the national sales offices at Toyota, Subaru, and Matsura and finally snagged a franchise in the South Bay, right off the 405. He thought he could cut the cord once he had his own shop, but no. It took the same kind of ass-kissing to keep the premium models on the lot. If they weren't there you had nothing. The prospects could just as easily go to Beverly Hills or Sherman Oaks. Those dealers were working their own game up there and they were brutal. Cut your balls off in a second if they could.

So he built his business around favors, gifts, and bribes. Some of the national guys wanted cash under the counter. For the big guys like LaBounty, money wasn't enough. He expected the unexpected: jewelry, French champagne, hunting rifles. *Surprise me,* LaBounty said. Once Joe flew him to Paris with a new Visa Gold at his personal disposal. LaBounty and his girlfriend maxed the card out. Jesus, that cost him. But then he got twenty Maxus Coupe LSs over quota.

What LaBounty didn't know was it all went into the book. All the bribes and gifts and kickbacks. Right into the book along with the over-sticker prices he was getting on the LSs and the other premium models. The ones you couldn't get without sitting on a waiting list for six months. And who wanted to do that? So he played the game and got premiums over quota and turned them over to Vito to work. An extra two, three grand over sticker on each one. Yeah, it was worth it. It was definitely worth it.

Vito. The kid was hungry. Like he was when he started out. He needed a tiger like Vito on the floor. Problem was, a guy got that good and he started looking around. It was inevitable. Joe knew he was pocketing a few extra bills that didn't go into the book. He had made a few aftersale spot checks. Called the owner at home with a bogus excuse and found out what they paid over sticker. It was easy to verify. That's why he needed the book. You couldn't just fake these things. Money was money and someone found out sooner or later.

But now Vito was up to something else. He sensed that this morning in his office. Something moved behind his eyes when he asked him for the book. Just a flicker really, but Joe caught it. His gut told him not to trust Vito on this one. That's why he thought he'd buy some insurance, create a pleasant diversion for LaBounty and company when they touched down. That would get him a little extra time in case Vito didn't have the book when he got back from lunch.

Joe considered inventing some figures but rejected it. You couldn't bullshit a guy like LaBounty. He might verify the figures on him just like Joe had on Vito. Then it'd all be lost—the premiums over quota, the kickbacks, the franchise. LaBounty could pull the plug on the whole enchilada. No, you had to go by the book.

Ahead, a 300TD Mercedes was signaling for a lane change, coming up fast on a panel truck, some Mexican gardeners with shit blowing off the bed and all over the road. The Benz had seen Joe coming and wanted to pull out but was hanging back, signaling, undecided. He who hesitates is lost, Joe thought as he flashed his lights. He was passing the point of safe return now, the point at which he could still hit the brakes and pull it out. But why do that? He wasn't that kind of guy.

Joe put the pedal down all the way. Yes, all the way down. No power in reserve anymore. Just a call to the engine house for everything they had down there. And he got it all—in one throaty roar of high-tech 24-valve Japanese engineering. The LS reached deep and stretched out, covering the pavement in a streak of chrome and speed.

The Benz and truck went by in a dream on the right, the guy blasting his horn and flipping him off as Joe made the yellow at the top of the hill. And in the same moment he came over the top and saw the Pacific in front of him, so wide and beautiful and it all combined with the speed and victory over the asshole in the Benz and filled Joe with a sense that he could still do it all.

Joe was still glowing from all that speed as he hit the clicker and the gates in front of his house rolled back. He pulled up the driveway in front of the rambling brick-and-clapboard three-story on two acres and waited for the four-car garage door to open. He could see Vikki's restored Austin-Healey inside the garage and knew she was probably out back on the tennis court, built on a platform out over the mountainside, or working out in the gym he'd had installed for her in the basement.

As he pulled into the garage he could feel the tires rolling silently on the carpeting. It gave him a sense of security to know that he could afford carpeting, even in the garage, and that the cars he drove wouldn't leak even a drop of oil on it. If they did leak he'd fire his mechanic and replace the carpeting. Besides the Healey and the LS, he kept the Porsche and 300 SEL in here. The Ferrari was down at the dealership. In his business you never really knew what you'd need to drive. He liked to say he changed cars like other men changed suits.

The *whoosh whoosh* of the NordicTrack came down the hallway as he headed for his study. He looked in and saw the firm backside of his second wife, her powerful thighs and haunches thrusting the slats in the cross-country machine back and forth, her developed arms and shoulders pulling the cords. On the video screen were edited highlights of the Olympics, athletes crossing finishing lines, clearing high-jump bars, throwing javelins, then pumping fists of victory into the air.

Without turning Vikki said, "I know you're there and I know what you're looking at."

"Busted," Joe said, laughing.

"If you're getting ideas, I'll be done in ten minutes."

"I gotta get back," Joe said, continuing down the hallway.

Behind him he heard her voice: "That never stopped you before. I'll take a shower and be right up."

He climbed the stairs to his study. It was a sunny room, none of this dark wood-paneled shit that lawyers liked, and the picture window gave an unparalleled view of the ocean. Today, Catalina shimmered on the horizon of the Pacific. He wondered if LaBounty and the boys would like to cruise over there in his boat. With the twin Evenrudes cranked up they could cover the twenty-six miles in a half hour. That'd impress them. But we'll see how things go tonight, Joe thought. Hopefully, by then they won't need impressing.

The wall safe was behind a picture of Joe and his first wife leaning against his mangled Porsche in Baja. They'd been leading the pack in a road rally when he hit some gravel on a corner and lost it. Flipped twice but came up on his wheels. He'd finished third even with the oil pan leaking and the bearings starting to dry out. That was a day to remember.

The safe door swung open and Joe took out the bag of cash. He couldn't quite remember how much was in it, somewhere around twenty grand, from profits here and there. Tax-free, of course. That was the beauty of this system.

The money would be plenty to buy a first-rate party for LaBounty. In the Rolodex he found the name he'd recalled on the drive up the mountain. Dash. That was it. Dash Schaffner. He'd recently sold Joe some insurance. But he had an interesting little side hustle. He knew a lot of people and he liked to set up parties. Like that blowout for Tom Richie down in Newport. The one where those two girls got up on the table and put on that show. Unbelievable. How the hell'd they do that trick with the Ping-Pong ball? That's what he needed now. Something that would really knock the eyes out of LaBounty and his buddies.

Joe dialed the number and sat behind his desk, looking out at Catalina and noting with a rising sense of sexual expectation that the shower was running downstairs.

Harold was with Gus, running a few tests on the cutting oil, when he saw Marianna walk by outside. It was practically four-thirty and he'd been looking for her all afternoon, the uneasy feeling in his stomach growing, unable to concentrate on the tests or anything else.

Harold usually took great pleasure in solving problems like this. Any other day he'd be totally absorbed watching this new product turn the milky fluid clear again, separating out the oil and leaving the water almost up to EPA regs. If he got clean enough to dump locally, it'd be one less reason to move out of state. A major victory for Aerodyne, a real coup for Harold.

But today it all seemed futile to Harold, doomed for future destruction. The Feds would never approve it. Some VP would torpedo his recommendation at the last moment and he'd be back to square one. Nothing ever really got solved around here. No wonder the defense industry was headed for the toilet.

"Look, if it clears I'll be in my office," Harold said to Gus, and started to leave.

"Another minute or two and it'll be finished," he was saying, but Harold waved and kept moving across the floor and toward the courtyard where he'd seen Marianna. She must have just come back from lunch because she was headed in from the lot, still with her purse, wearing a loose skirt, blouse, and sweater, walking stiffly, like she'd been in a wreck or something. He knew something had happened. He could feel it all around her.

"You hit pay dirt," he said, moving up and falling into step beside her.

She turned and looked at him, focused, then recognized him, like she was coming back from a great distance. She smiled sadly.

"Hello, Harold. What's up?"

"That book, it's gonna ruin your friend Vito and his pals. All those crooks down there at Covo's."

"Oh, yeah?" She wasn't really interested somehow.

"You okay?"

"Fine."

"You seem—I don't know . . ."

They kept walking, on into the building and down a long hallway with windows on the right letting in the afternoon sun.

"I had a little chat with the DMV. The Feds are investigating Covo for racketeering—i.e., he's bribing guys at the national level to get high-end cars. Those quotas are strictly controlled by Uncle Sam."

They stopped in front of the elevator. She pressed two and then slowly turned to Harold.

"They told you all that?"

"Not exactly."

"How'd you find out?"

"You don't want to know."

"Harold." She said his name with tenderness, as if it was the best way to describe him, a complicated word filled with contradictions. "Harold," she repeated.

The elevator arrived and the doors rolled back. They stepped aboard.

"Okay," she said. "So what are you saying?"

"As long as you have that book you've got them by the—over a barrel."

"By the balls is what you were going to say." There was a spark of her real self. "I know those words, Harold. You don't have to protect me."

"I want to protect you."

"Why?"

"I—don't get me going here. I'll tell you after work. We need to go over the book. I'll show you what's going on."

"I'm busy tonight." Somehow he knew she would say that.

The elevator stopped and the doors opened. They stepped out and started walking again. He felt desperate.

"What's going on?"

"Everything's fine, Harold."

They were almost to their office. He saw Jerry coming out of a side door and pulled Marianna into the lunchroom. They stood next to a Coke machine that had a busted fan that kept going *ding ding ding* as it turned.

"Listen, you need this stuff. They could nail you for theft, for assault, anytime, easy. You got to be ready."

"Harold, it's gone beyond that."

"Why? The hell's happened?"

"You don't want to know," she echoed him.

He saw that her face was blotchy red. Her eyes were sleepy and hinted of ultimate destruction.

"Why can't you tell me?"

"I've gotten you involved way too much already."

"What if I want to get involved?"

"You'll get hurt."

"What if I want to get hurt?"

She smiled sweetly at him. "Things are getting out of hand."

"We unwound the deal. That means that—"

"The deal wound me up in itself."

"So—"

"So it has to play out, is all I'm saying. Then maybe we'll see where we stand."

"Me and you?"

"That's 'we,' isn't it?"

Harold felt all the happiness of the past few days rush out of him like a balloon deflating. At the same time he heard that familiar inner voice saying, *What'd you expect, asshole*?

"You're ignoring what happened last night."

She started to say something, then changed her mind and said, "Maybe I am."

"Do you know what I saw last night?"

"You're not going to go into that here," she said, kidding.

He kept going because he had to say it, now that he knew that time was short and he'd be alone again soon. "See, there are people, lots of people in this world. And we're all alone. All of us. But every once in a while there's a combination which is good. And that's rare. You and me, we were good together. You can't go against that."

"I can't?"

"See, there's what you think you are, and there's what you really are."

"That's deep, Harold," she said, then saw it hurt his feelings. "My problem, Harold, is that I think there are combinations of people that are bad. And when you get those combinations, you get sucked down—maybe you won't even come up again."

"I don't know about that," Harold said. "Because you're into something and you're not telling me. And that's okay. But I can tell you that last night was real and you can't take that away." He was going to leave now, he really was, while he had a little bit of himself left.

"I saw someone different than what I'm seeing now. And if you need my help, I'm still here."

He walked away thinking, you should have left sooner, you idiot. Now there's nothing left. You gave it all away again.

"You missed her again." Joe echoed Vito's words, keeping him frozen in that stare of his. He's using that repeating shit, Vito thought. That's a bad sign.

"Yeah, see, my ex figured she'd do me a favor, bring the briefcase down here. I'm not here. I'm over there trying to get it from her. So we miss each other. It's as simple as that."

"You miss each other," Joe said from behind his desk. It

was maybe five, five-thirty, and things were getting hot out there, prospects out the wazoo, the floor whores hustling in hyperdrive. But in here was quiet and dark, just Joe behind his huge clean desk, sitting there in his leather chair waiting for answers that Vito couldn't give.

"It's no biggie. She'll be reachable at maybe eight tonight. I can probably get it from her then."

"Probably."

"Did I say probably? No. Definitely. In fact, I'll practically guarantee it."

"You practically guaranteed it would be here after lunch and it wasn't here. Now you want me to stall LaBounty while you schlep all over LA to *probably* get it."

"I told you what happened, Joe. Hey, these things happen."

In the lengthening silence Vito could hear the intercom out in the showroom floor paging him.

"Hey, that's for me. Probably my ex. I'll take it in my office." He used the cane to push himself to his feet.

Joe picked up the phone and punched line two. He extended the receiver to Vito.

"I don't want to hang you up, Joe. I'll take it in—"

Joe was still extending the receiver. Vito slowly accepted it and stood uncomfortably beside the huge desk.

"Vito Fiorre."

"I think it's time we put an end to all this." It was Marianna.

"How do you mean?"

"I want to make a deal."

"What've you got in mind?"

"Your briefcase for my trade-in."

"Jesus Christ. We're back to that, are we?"

He looked nervously across the desk at Joe, sitting back in his leather chair, watching Vito, expressionless.

"You're really hung up on that thing."

"You seem a little hung up on your briefcase. What's in it you want so bad?"

"Never mind about that. Just bring it to me. Okay?"

"Bring me my car, I'll bring you the briefcase."

"Sounds fair."

"How about we meet halfway? I'll be coming from Culver City 'cause I'm working late tonight. I wound up taking a long lunch."

Vito chuckled. "Funny. So did I."

"So I was thinking maybe I could meet you at La Cienega and Stocker. There's a pulloff just north of the intersection on La Cienega. Meet you there at eight."

"And you'll have the briefcase?"

"If you have my Escort. Otherwise I'll just keep driving."

"I'll have it."

"Bye, Vito."

"Bye."

Vito reached across the desk and replaced the receiver.

"Done," he said to Joe. "I'll have it for you at eight-thirty."

Joe slowly rose and walked across the floor in his three-hundred-dollar Italian shoes. He closed the office door and just as slowly returned to his chair and then said, "I'm waiting."

"I told you, I'm getting it back at eight-thirty."

"That was your ex?"

"Yeah."

"What'd she say?"

"She's been out shopping, then she went to the gym and then—I don't know. You know how women are. I didn't even pay attention."

"Vito." Joe's voice was very soft. "You've been standing there all day telling me lies. Now I want you to take a deep breath and from here on in, I want you to tell me everything. No more bullshit."

"Joe, come on. I told you it's one of those—"

Joe rocketed out of his chair and got right up into Vito's face.

"You lying little cocksucker! What the fuck's going on!"

Vito sank back into his chair and looked out the window at the cars on the lot, breathing hard. He kept thinking something would come to him. But for the first time in a while his mind was a blank. He knew he couldn't look back at Joe—unless he was ready to tell the truth. And Joe would definitely not approve of some of his moves. Rock-and-a-hard-place time. Things were coming apart fast.

"I'm involved in a certain situation," Vito began, licking his lips.

"What situation is that?" Joe said, adopting a paternal tone now. He wanted a full confession.

"Couple days ago I sold a Matsura to a secretary at Aerodyne. She went home, read the contract, saw what she got for her trade-in. Decided she wanted her trade-in back."

"What'd she trade?"

"A piece-of-shit Escort."

"Why'd she want that back?"

"I can't figure it. Anyway, she came back with this guy, used to be a car salesman."

"And you told them . . . ?"

"To pound sand, basically. But they've been on me ever since. Last night, she followed me over to my ex's, got into my car and stole my briefcase."

"With the book in it?"

"Yeah."

"Is that how that happened?" he asked, pointing at the cane.

"Yeah, she's a psychopath."

"Who has it now? The guy or the secretary?"

"I don't know. But that was her, just now, she says she'll give it to me tonight."

"Where?"

"Stocker and La Cienega. The turnoff just north of the intersection there."

"Why there?"

"It's near where she works. At Aerodyne."

"The guy going to be with her?"

"Dunno."

Joe thought about all this for a moment. In the silence Vito heard the intercom in the salesroom, heard a trucker hitting his Jake Brake on the 405, heard a radio playing an oldie in someone's office.

"Why's this guy helping her?"

"Got the hots for her probably."

"She good-looking?"

"Not really. Kinda broad in the beam. But hey, you can't account for taste."

While Joe lapsed into silent thought Vito felt he had done the right thing. Now things were basically under control. He'd get the book, deliver it to Joe, and close the deal there. But then Joe asked:

"What's the guy's name? This guy who's helping?"

"Dodge. Harold Dodge. Used to be a—"

"I know who he is." Joe looked truly alarmed.

"You do?"

"Yeah. I fired his ass out of here about fifteen years ago. And he's been after me ever since."

John LaBounty felt the turbines spooling back, the engines whistling and coasting, and knew they were a half hour from touchdown at LAX. He leaned his massive body over the empty seat next to him. Looking out the window he saw black sections of the mountains cutting into the orange glow of San Bernadino. He set his *Forbes* down and turned to the sleeping man across the aisle in the first-class cabin.

"What do we do with Covo?"

Tom Bales opened his eyes and ran a hand through his thinning red hair.

"Settle up, I guess. Then shut him down."

"That'd piss him off," LaBounty said, shifting in the leather seat. "We don't want him pissed off. We do that and who knows what he'll do."

The man next to Bales strained forward to join the conversation.

"We have no obligation to let him know what's happening," Parker Harris said, pushing rimless glasses up on his sharp nose. "He willingly set up this arrangement to serve his needs. Besides, if he's forewarned he may take steps."

"Meaning?"

"He may not get rid of, you know, may decide not to shred certain things that should be destroyed."

Bales frowned. "Larry said they're gonna get someone. Isn't that what he said?"

LaBounty ignored the question, so Parker answered: "It wasn't Larry. It was his partner, Lou. He was over in the statehouse and heard the attorney general was 'getting pressure to produce indictments,' those were Lou's words, 'indictments.' "

"Right, exactly," Bales said. "So the fact of the matter is, if they get Covo this might not go any higher."

"What're you suggesting?" LaBounty asked.

There was a pause before Bales said, "What do you think I'm suggesting," and they all laughed. Then seriously, he said, "Let's give them Covo."

LaBounty sank back in the leather seat. "But we need to find out what ties him to us and make sure it's under our control. Then, as a favor, we tell him about the investigation."

"Two problems with that," Parker said, leaning across Bales. "How do we find out what exists and how do we verify that he really disposes of it?"

"I thought you might say that," LaBounty grunted. "He's got a guy down there, a salesman, a young Turk. Giuseppe or something like that."

"Vito."

"Vito. Anyway, he's moved these premiums for Joe for years. We need to find a way to get to him. He can tell us what we want to know."

Bales said, "That'd work."

Parker shook his head. "It's going to seem awfully suspect. The head office goes around the dealership president, to a salesman for Christ's sake, and asks for the boss's records? That's not gonna fly."

"You don't know this kid, this . . ."

"Vito."

"Vito, right. He's the type that'd cut his own throat to make a deal. You know how they are in LA. We know Joe's got some big thing planned for us tonight—some dinner or—and Tom gets this Vito aside and—"

"Me? Why me?"

"Why not you?"

"No reason. Just—"

"Tom gets this kid aside, for a drink or whatever, and tells him there're going to be some changes soon and they may affect him positively. If he looks hungry, then say, 'But keep it from your boss 'cause he's not gonna come out so good in all this. In fact, it seems he's got his tit in a ringer so you want to get a little distance on him.' "

"I still think it seems suspect for—"

"Tom can handle it. Can't you?"

"But what would Tom's motivation be to do that?"

" 'Cause Tom's a greedy bastard and wants to align himself with another money machine." They all laughed.

"Seriously, I don't think—"

"Look, I'm not asking you to do it, am I? Tom feels confident he can handle it. Don't you Tom?"

"Well . . ."

"So let's let him take care of it."

"It might backfire on us."

"And you might get your dick caught in your zipper. But you still have to take a leak, don't you?"

Parker gave up and sat back into his seat. Then he leaned forward again. "So what are we supposed to do in the meantime?"

"Relax, and go along with the program."

"What program's that?"

"Fun and games, Covo style."

"**Oh,** man. What's he up to now?" Clay was watching the red-and-white pickup in front of them, signaling for a right off Century into a parking lot.

Adrian laughed. "He should have one of those signs on the back, 'This vehicle makes frequent stops.' "

Since they spotted him up outside Aerodyne Lot C he'd gone to a PO box on Sepulveda, a liquor store on Washington, and a video store on Slauson. Any one of the places would have been okay, except there was always someone there. A car pulling in, people hanging out. It just wasn't right. But now it was dark, getting later. His luck couldn't hold.

Clay pulled to the curb near the parking lot, and they saw the big lit-up sign above the cinder-block building: LIVE LIVE NUDE NUDES. He let the Buick idle, smoothing his ponytail with his left hand.

"Oh, man. What's he doing now?" Adrian said.

"What do you think he's doing? Gonna watch some snatch jump around."

"Covo didn't say nothing about this."

"Covo hasn't seen the guy for years. He's got no idea what he does."

They scanned the parking lot as the headlights in the pickup died and the guy got out.

"See anyone?" Clay asked, his voice tightening.

"No. Let's—"

Adrian was reaching for the handle when the door with "No One Under 21 Admitted" on it pushed open and a foursome walked out. They crossed paths with the husky gray-haired man as he entered the building. Adrian saw the guy was a little bigger than he'd thought, maybe 210. That made them the same weight. But he had an inch or two on him. Plus Adrian knew he had the reach. His reach was always better than guys his height—even taller. That's how he went as far as he did. Stick that left in a guy's face all night there's not much he can do.

"Guy's lucky," Clay muttered.

"So far."

Clay killed the ignition and the car was suddenly quiet.

Adrian settled back, the vinyl seat creaking. Clay pulled out a pair of drumsticks and started rapping on the steering wheel, humming and rocking back and forth.

"When Joe called I thought it was another repo," Clay said.

"I wish it was," Adrian said.

"I had a guy today, paid me a hundred just to pop a car door. Sweet or what?"

Adrian didn't answer, so Clay drummed for a moment before suddenly stopping. "It bother you at all?"

"What?"

"To jack a guy like this."

"No." Then: "But it ain't easy. Lotta things can go wrong."

"Don't say that."

The door opened and they leaned forward. An Asian businessman walked out, unsteady as he climbed into a rental.

"Guy could be in there for hours," Clay said.

"If it was me, I'd be. I haven't had any for weeks."

"What happened to Kelly?"

"Went back to her old man."

"Who? Bones?"

"Who else?"

Clay slowly turned. "You beat her up again? Right?"

"No."

"You stupid jerk. When're you gonna learn?"

"I didn't touch her. It was Bones. She goes to the store, runs into him there. Next thing I know she's goin' to the store all the time."

"So when you found out, then you beat her up. Right?"

Adrian didn't answer.

"You big moron. When're you gonna learn?"

Adrian fell into a sullen silence, watching the door that the guy'd disappeared through. A paramedic van came screaming down Century, lights sparking off the glass on the buildings around them. A jet rumbled in the distance. Adrian's stomach was jumpy. He wished he hadn't had that extra coffee.

Adrian finally said, "Make sure you stop me this time, okay?"

"Okay."

"Last time, I couldn't open my hand for a week."

"I'll stop you."

"When you start, it's hard to stop. You can't tell when it's enough."

Clay thought about it for a while. "How do you do it? I mean, the guy means nothing to you."

"Pretend he's someone else. Someone I want to unload on. Then it's easy."

"Bones, right? You're thinkin' he's Bones."

Adrian didn't say anything so Clay got the sticks working again.

A short time later, as he watched the door, Adrian said, "Think he has this briefcase with him. The one Joe lost?"

"I guess we'll find out, won't we?"

Kim was with some computer guy down from San Francisco when she saw Harold come through the door and stand there waiting for her. It was bad timing. The computer guy was going to be worth a lot. He'd seen her dance and waved her over to his table. She put on her vest and panties and moved in on him, thinking she could probably work him for a twenty-dollar tip. But then Harold showed up looking like hell. She knew he wouldn't hang around long.

"Honey, I think you're all talk," Kim said to the computer guy, standing up and heading for Harold.

"Forget him," he said, grabbing her arm. Jesus he was

strong. These computer guys were supposed to be pencil-necked geeks. "I like a little talk first," he continued.

"What's to talk about?"

He pried opened his wallet as if he were performing surgery. She saw it was thick with bills. He wanted her to see it and be impressed, come on to him. She needed the bread, after playing live-in nurse for Harold's father. But she needed Harold more.

The computer guy saw her looking at Harold again and said, "Forget him," and waved a ten in front of her face.

She stood up, saying, "I don't have any pockets. Maybe you can find someplace safe to put it." He plunged his hand into her panties and she could feel the crisp bill crumpling next to her pubic hair. His fingertips began to search her, working their way down. At the last second she twisted away, ruffling his hair and saying, "Thanks, honey." She heard him say, "I got plenty more!" as she moved across to Harold.

When she reached Harold he looked hurt and pissed off, his thick fingers building a little house out of five-dollar bills. He threw down his shot and chased it, then went back to his construction.

"What's that for? You didn't catch my dance."

"Taking care of my dad."

"I didn't do much."

"Whatever you did, it was a lot for him." He tried to laugh, but it sounded strained. Kim sat down with him.

"I thought you met someone new."

"I did." By the way he said it she knew.

"You got dumped again, didn't you?"

"She's busy tonight. That's all."

"So am I. But I'm here with you. Guy over there had three hundred in his wallet and I left him for you."

"Really?" Harold looked genuinely pleased. He leaned

around her and smiled at the computer guy. The guy was very still, watching Harold closely.

"That wasn't real smart, Harold."

"I'm not a smart guy. I'm stupid. That's why I get hurt all the time." He stood up.

"Sit down, Harold."

"Why?"

"Just sit."

He sat down saying, "I've really got to go."

"You said she's busy tonight. Stay and watch me dance."

He sulked.

"I'm up next. I'll do it for you." He didn't react. "I'll come for you." That got his attention.

"You can do that? In front of all these people."

"If I really want someone, sure."

Harold looked over at the computer guy again and smiled, pointing at himself. "She likes me. Not you, asshole."

Kim glanced at the computer guy and saw he was close to going ballistic.

"Don't do this, Harold."

"What?"

"This self-destructive shit. It's not worth it."

"I'm just having some harmless fun with the guy."

"You have any more harmless fun, the guy will break you in half." She touched Harold's hand. It was a shocking gesture, so out of place in here.

"Go home. Come back at eleven and we'll go out for something to eat."

"Okay," he sighed.

The bartender yelled over, "Kim!" and she walked toward the stage, looking back at Harold and saying, "Please."

Halfway through her dance she saw Harold finish his boilermaker and head for the door.

Bad timing. Very bad timing indeed, Vito thought. His Rolex showed eight-fifteen and the girls had just arrived. They were setting up for the act now, rolling out a long strip of red carpet on the tabletop and cranking up a boom box, shoving hotel dinner plates out of the way and knocking over the bottles of French champagne Joe provided by the case.

Christ, they were beautiful. Magazine beautiful—airbrushed perfection. Except they were right here in front of him. One was blond and lanky like an Olympic sprinter. The other was short and dark. Mexican? Italian maybe. Maybe he'd just shine the meeting with Marianna, pick up the briefcase later.

Bales leaned over and slapped Vito's arm, his drink and cigarette in the same hand. "Look at Joe, tongue hanging out."

Vito looked over at Joe, climbing up on the table and reaching for the blonde. She let him cop a feel before shoving him back in his seat.

"Something else's gonna be hanging out in a few seconds here."

Bales laughed. "Who gets her first?"

"Whoever gets into the service bay first. Joe's got two rooms set up down the hall."

"Jesus. And I promised I'd be good on this trip."

The blonde pulled off her T-shirt and her breasts swung free. Vito took in the sight, then commented, "I'd like to stick one tit in each ear and listen to myself come."

Bales nodded, awed.

Joe was reaching for his drink on the other side of her cassette deck saying, "Mind if I move your boom box?" And she didn't miss a beat, saying, "You can boom my box later, honey." LaBounty roared with laughter.

If I don't leave now I never will, Vito thought. He pushed himself to his feet, leaning heavily on the cane as he pocketed his lighter and cigarettes.

Bales said in a different tone, "Joe's really got to learn to control himself."

"Joe?"

"He loses control, makes mistakes."

"Is that what LaBounty was talking to him about?"

"Maybe. I can't say too much yet."

Halfway through the dinner LaBounty and Joe had disappeared into the hall, then returned a few minutes later looking like they'd gone a few rounds. They seemed okay now, but Vito wondered what the hell was happening.

"Give me the heads up," Vito said, settling back into his chair, lighting a cigarette and blowing smoke toward the ceiling.

"You heard about the investigation, of course."

Vito said, "I think I'd remember if I heard anything about any investigation."

"I assumed you knew the FBI is onto Joe—that's why you're cooling it with him."

"Am I getting Alzheimer's or something? Why isn't this making sense?"

"I see you distancing yourself from Joe. I mean, why else would you be leaving before that?" Bales pointed at the blonde as she pulled an assortment of things out of her Nike bag: lotion, lightbulbs, a long rubber thing with two ends to it. Could it really be . . . ? LaBounty saw it and put his head down, pounding the table with his fist.

"I've got a meeting," Vito said. "I'll be back. You can fill me in then."

"Sure."

Vito stopped. "Okay. Give me the executive summary."

"This thing's gonna hurt Joe. When it does, you can pick up a dealership—if you're aligned right when it happens."

"What's that mean?"

"You can't do anything for Joe. But you could help us."

Was he passing out? Or were the lights going down? He looked around. The Mexican was dimming the lights, nodding to the blonde, who slipped a new tape in and punched play. "I Heard It Through the Grapevine." The Mexican danced her way across the room, then jumped up onto the table, shucking the T-shirt over her head, revealing breasts that made him weak and strong at the same time.

Screw it, Vito thought, I've got to see this.

"Cincinnati wants a favor from you, Vito." Bales was ignoring the girls, leaning close, ash from his cigarette flying everywhere as he gestured. "You do us a favor, maybe we can set you up. Get you out of this penny-ante sales crap and into some real money."

"I'm listening."

"If the FBI starts putting pressure on people, what does Joe have that can hurt us?"

Vito digested what Bales said, thinking of Marianna waiting for him with the briefcase and the book. She'll wait, he thought. She wants her damn Escort bad enough, she'll wait.

Bales was waiting.

"Joe had a book."

"A book?"

"Yeah. A little black book. Everything went in it—VIN numbers, amount over sticker, the gifts to LaBounty. Everything."

"Shit."

"Yeah. Shit is right. FBI gets that, you're fucked."

"So how can I get this book?"

Vito felt his smile growing so big he had to turn away—and found Joe staring at him. Joe pointed at his watch, then jerked his thumb toward the door. Yeah, I'll go, Vito thought. But not to save your sorry ass.

The traffic was finally thinning out on La Cienega, leaving periods of silence during which Marianna heard the creaking of the oil pumps scattered across the mountainside like prehistoric grasshoppers. Then another wave of traffic came over the pass and she began looking for headlights to separate from the pack and pull down the dirt road toward her.

It was against her nature to wait for a dirtbag like Vito. It was practically eight-thirty-five and here she was, a sitting duck for any roving carload of gangbangers in the shiny Honda, detailed to the max, as Vito might say.

Marianna turned her head to check for her purse on the seat next to her. Her neck was stiffening painfully and her throat was bruised where Vito had choked her. Her nipple still throbbed under a gauze pad, and her left arm could only bend halfway without screaming in pain. Thinking of her wounds brought back that claustrophobic feeling of Vito's hand on her throat, her life flickering, catching a glimpse of death and panicking like never before. Maybe she could wait a few extra minutes. Even for a dirtbag like Vito. Especially for Vito.

There are bad combinations of people, she remembered telling Harold, *and they pull you down.* Was Vito pulling her down? And was Harold such a wonderful thing to pass up? Something tugged her toward Harold, saying, *Come on, what's the problem*?

He's what you said you wanted. But she wasn't ready to be so pampered, so adored. She wasn't that great. Harold didn't realize that. She didn't deserve what he wanted to give her. Maybe she deserved Vito.

Another wave of cars came over the pass and she saw a turn signal flashing. She pulled her purse into her lap and waited, the headlights blinding her as she tried to see if . . . Yes. The right front headlight was out from when she'd run him down last night. The memory made her smile as the car rolled up and stopped beside her. She got out, her purse heavy in her left hand.

Vito struggled to his feet, pushing up on the cane and hopping around on his good leg as he got out of the Escort. He left the engine running and lights on and steadied himself, facing her as she said, "You're late. I was going to leave."

"You'd never leave." He spat the words out, disgusted. She felt her anger rise, and it helped her with what she was going to do.

"'Cause you want your beloved Escort."

Breathe easy and just wait, she thought.

"So where's my briefcase?"

"In the trunk," she said, noticing him teeter unsteadily, his weight on his good leg, holding himself up on the cane.

"What're you waiting for? Get it." Vito seemed different now, uninterested in her, no more of that flirty stuff he used to pull on her. This was how he treated women after he'd had sex with them. Once the package was open his curiosity was gone.

"Thought you'd want to check it out first," she said, popping the trunk lid and moving around to the rear of the Matsura, "Make sure I didn't rip off anything."

"You wouldn't dare."

"Vito, I'm like you—capable of anything."

Vito hobbled after her saying, "I don't have time for this." They were standing beside each other next to the trunk now.

"Then take it and go."

As he lifted the trunk lid she stepped back and reached into her purse, thinking this wasn't quite the way I thought it would be. Too much light from the Escort, and he's taller than I remembered.

The courtesy light in the trunk reflected up onto Vito's face as he started to reach for the briefcase. Then he stopped and set his cane on the bumper so he could use both hands. But the cane slid away and fell to the ground. He swore, bending on one leg and groping for it as Marianna's hand in her purse closed around the wooden handle and she pulled it out.

Wait till he straightens up, she thought. He must have found the cane because he was pulling himself up, leaning on the edge of the car trunk and panting. He straightened and faced her, hair falling in his face, his features blurred and annoyed.

"Vito, do you think we're a bad combination?" she asked, poised, looking for the right second.

He looked at her oddly, her right arm out of sight along her side. Something penetrated his alcoholic fog.

"*What*?"

"Are you pulling me down? Or am I just as bad as you are?"

"What the fuck're you talking about?"

"Forget it."

They looked at each other for what seemed like a long time in the strange reflected light, the Escort idling nearby, as he tried to focus on what she'd said. Finally he just said, "You're up to something."

"Am I?" She wasn't worried. She could do it anytime now. But it would be better if he was over the trunk.

He turned and bent toward the open trunk. Hold that pose, she thought, and swung the hammer. The blow was a little hurried and it caught the inside of the raised trunk lid with a *bwang* and then struck the side of his head, catching his ear and partially tearing it off.

He bellowed in pain and staggered to his right, stunned, raising his arm instinctively. She swung again and caught him on the forearm, doing no real damage.

"What—?" he yelled, then: "Wait a—" but she continued to swing the hammer again and again, trying to batter down his raised arm. He was backpedaling now, in the open space between the two cars, almost in the beam of the Escort's headlights. She was aware of something dark streaming down the side of his face. His breathing was loud and hoarse.

She moved around and attacked him from the other side, driving him back toward the open trunk. He was turning around slowly, arms in front of him, groping, saying something like, "BBBBITTTCCCH!" She wasn't hurting him enough, though, and he was shaking off that first good blow.

She turned the hammer in her hand and swung the claw end at him, ripping into the fabric of his coat sleeve. He screamed and drew his arm back and she swung again, the claw going in over his arm and finding skull above the hairline. His body shuddered and she moved in, getting him again, not solid but punishing. She felt something hot and wet on her face.

Vito was stumbling now, going down, so she shoved him toward the Matsura trunk and he fell back against it, trying to hold himself up. She didn't want him to fall there, so she dropped the hammer and grabbed his legs, lifting him up onto the edge of the trunk. His arms moved automatically, flailing at her, and as he went up and over his hand clamped onto her wrist. It was a lot stronger than she thought and she realized he was still very much alive. Christ, what else did she have to do?

Vito landed in the trunk with a heavy thump, rocking the car on its springs, still with the death grip on her wrist. She pried at his slippery fingers, panicking, just wanting to get the damn lid closed on him. But he was pulling himself up, half rising from the trunk, with his ghastly face straining toward her.

She threw her weight down on his arm, across the trunk edge, thinking, let it break, he's dead anyway, and sweeping the ground with her free hand for the hammer, finding first the claw end and working around to the wooden handle. She straightened and swung the hammer into the trunk and felt solid contact come up through the handle and into her shoulder. Vito's hand relaxed and he fell back, still.

Marianna backed away from the car, panting and sweaty. The hammer in her hand was sticky and wet. She turned and threw it into the darkness down the mountainside. She never heard it land.

After the chaos of the fight she was surprised to find the world unchanged, the sky still orange, the lights of the Basin still throbbing, the Escort idling nearby, and the creaking oil wells still drawing darkness from the earth. She had killed another human being, but the world was continuing as always. And her life would go on as before. Except this man who had wronged her had been punished. No one could say he didn't deserve it. No one.

Headlights stabbed into her eyes as a new wave of traffic came over the pass. She suddenly felt exposed and vulnerable with the open trunk. She ran toward the car but stepped on something, her ankle turning. She looked down and saw Vito's cane. She tossed it into the trunk and slammed the lid shut. That's better. Now if some highway patrolman stopped there would be nothing to show what she'd done. Just pulled off 'cause the car was acting weird but everything's all right so I'll be going now thanks. It was going to be all right. She'd drive her Escort home, then call a cab and get dropped off up at the intersection. Move the Matsura and—

Wait a second. Why do all that? The vision of Harold's injured face suddenly returned to her mind from that afternoon. She'd said she was busy and it hurt his feelings. She was busy. But not anymore. Maybe she could explain it all to Harold now that it was done. Sure, she'd drop by and explain the whole thing to him. Even get a ride back up here. He couldn't refuse to do that. There was no harm in giving a person a ride somewhere. None at all.

AS soon as the door to Nude Nudes closed behind Harold and he started across the parking lot, he knew he'd been a horse's ass again. For only about the one millionth time this week. It happened over and over in his life but he didn't seem to be able to stop it when it was happening. He'd been an asshole and he was going to feel bad about it the rest of the night.

He could feel the night coming on and knew just what it would be like: a steady progression of beers (1 to 1.4 six-packs), the VCR playing his favorite movie in his cramped apartment, the remaindered books and insurance claims reminding him of past dreams and present failures, long-distance calls to friends he wouldn't remember in the morning. All because he had been an idiot again.

Boom-boom. Two car doors slamming in quick succession. Danger, danger, Harold thought. Don't accept collect calls, don't sign for registered letters, and watch out when you hear two car doors slamming. It means they're coming to get you, pal.

While part of Harold was saying, *About time, you asshole*, another part, pure animal instinct, was processing information. Twenty feet to his truck, two figures closing in on him coming from a Buick on Century, one guy with a ponytail, the other swarthy looking with dull hatred in his eyes and fists at his sides. Coming for you, he thought. Well what do you expect when you make all these stupid mistakes?

As he thought these things he was still moving, no faster, but still getting closer to his truck, unlocking the doors with his remote. And all the time that calm section of his brain saying, *You won't make the truck* and a picture forming in his mind of himself on the ground, his face on the cement, where people walked and spit and vomited. And that calm section knew he might be in real trouble here.

But then he heard a blast of music as the "No One Under 21 Admitted." door opened and Mr. Silicon Valley called across the parking lot, "Hey bitch! Yeah, you! I'm talking to you."

Harold stopped and turned toward him saying, "Are you serious?" and then glanced toward the two guys who were hanging back now, confused. There was something funny about all this, even though he could be in real bad shape in a mere five seconds.

Harold looked over at the two guys and said, "Why's he calling me a bitch?"

"Maybe you pissed the man off," the dark guy said, hint of an accent.

"But what's this bitch stuff?"

The computer guy wasn't fazed. Too stupid for that. He just kept his talk going. "You start something you can't back up? I'm gonna wipe the parking lot with you, you little bitch." His chest was right up against Harold now and he noticed the guy was about half a head taller. That never stopped me from getting the shit beat out of me before, Harold thought, and was tempted to start it right there. I can take my choice, get my ass kicked by this big moron or the two other guys over there.

The big guy shoved him back toward his car and Harold stumbled, only a few feet now from just getting in and driving away. The two other guys took a step closer, looking around, like maybe we won't go away after all. Harold saw this and thought, I could get really hurt here. And after I'm down, then what? The other guys take their turn? Where'd they come from and what'd they want?

"You talk tough in there—big man—out here you're just another bitch. Come on, pussy, do it. Start it, bitch, and I'll fuckin' kill you."

He shoved Harold again, and this time he went into the truck and bounced off.

"Go on. Start it. I'll kick your bitch ass."

"You always spit when you talk?" Harold turned to the two other guys. "You got a paper towel or something? I'm getting soaked."

"Keep it up, bitch. Give me a reason."

The other guys were laughing now, waiting, thinking any second it's gonna happen.

"Maybe it's starting to rain," Harold said, and the guy shoved him hard. He hit the truck and caught his balance.

"That's it," Harold said, peeling off his coat, the aggressive precursor to combat from the male of the species. That's what they'd say on a PBS documentary, back at home in his cramped apartment. How many times had he done this before? Mouth off 'cause he couldn't stop himself, only to pick himself off the deck a few minutes later, blood all over his face, all the satisfaction of a good comeback gone. The trademark of the Dodge subspecies, the PBS narrator would say. Picks fights that he can't win.

"All right, asshole," Harold said, opening his truck and throwing his suit jacket across the front seat. Then, without hurrying he climbed into the cab, slammed the door, and started it up. The old disappearing act he used so effectively. Only this was a little more aggressive, he thought, putting it in reverse and backing up without knowing what was back there, getting the impression of people diving for cover and realizing, as he burned rubber out onto Century, that the two other guys were running for their car.

Where the hell was Vito? Joe downed the rest of his Seven and Seven and checked his watch again. Nine-forty. He'd been gone over an hour for a trip that should have taken a half hour, max.

The show was over—in here anyway. It had moved behind closed doors where LaBounty and Parker were taking full advantage of the girls now that they had seen such an effective demonstration of their options and features. Christ, what a show. The diversion had worked. He'd have to give Dash an extra C-note when he settled up. But Joe knew that once LaBounty was done he'd move on to other things. The ruthless executive. Ten o'clock? So what? Let's get business done, get this thing settled.

Bales had mysteriously disappeared without showing interest in getting a turn with the girls. (Was he gay or something?) Then, when Joe left the partied-out room and paced the hallway above the hotel atrium, he saw Bales down by the lobby bar, looking around like he was going to meet someone. Joe remembered the way he was talking to Vito before the show. What the hell were they up to?

Joe had a gut feeling that this whole thing was coming unglued. He had to find Vito and get that book. Then he'd be back in control, no more unpleasant bits of information flying around. He leaned over the railing to check on Bales once more and headed for the elevator.

Harold had been home for about three beers, maybe an hour and a quarter, when there was a confidential knock on the door. He knew it wasn't the cops. They didn't have this address—and they sure didn't knock that way. They knocked on the door like they owned you. Of course, he thought it could be those two assholes who were following him (who the hell were they?), but that knock didn't fit them either. That left only one other person who might possibly be dropping in unannounced at ten o'clock at night.

Harold moved slowly to the peephole, barely daring to hope. He looked through and, in the weird distortion of the fish-eye lens, saw her standing there smiling playfully at him, knowing he was looking out at her.

"Hello, Harold," she said when he opened the door, using that loaded tone of voice, walking back into his life and bringing with her a feeling that everything had changed. Before he swung the door shut he looked out into the night and saw the Escort parked at the curb. Marianna was completely different than this afternoon, when she seemed broken and distant. Now she was exhilarated, like she had seen the meaning of life.

Harold would have expected her to look around and check out the books stacked to the ceiling, his clocks, and the sheets covering his furniture, and then make some kind of smart remark. But she moved to the middle of the room and just stood there in her jeans and maroon turtleneck with something dark spilled down the front. It seemed she could have been anywhere. Her eyes were on him, full of meaning but not ready to talk, not sure what she was going to do. She was excited and frightened. Dangerous and vulnerable. He wanted to take her little body and fold it up in his arms. But he didn't want his affection lopped off again like this afternoon.

He tried to hide his nervousness by saying, "I'm not used to having visitors. Have a seat. You want a beer? I'm having one."

"Is it from Chile?" she asked, as if trying to get back to a place they'd been.

He let himself laugh a little—ah-ah-ah—but it was tight and guarded. "I'm afraid it's Bud. And it's cold too. That's the only way to drink American beer."

He jiggled the can in his hand—only the foam left—and moved into the kitchen for two fresh ones. When he got back she was still there, that frightened/excited look on her face, clutching her purse like it was a life preserver. He opened her beer and handed it to her. They sat on the couch. Not too close. Awkward. Jesus, she made him nervous.

"I want you to take me to Chile," she said.

"Why? What'd you do?"

She reacted, turning. "Why'd you say that?"

"You show up here, in a trance, you say you want to go to Chile. I figure there's got to be a pretty good reason."

"Maybe my life's just shit. You said yours was too. I hate LA. Let's get out of here."

His answer to that was just to sip his beer. Then he remembered the eggs. He'd been cooking when she walked in.

"Damn!" He jumped up and ran into the kitchen. They were okay. "Want some eggs? I got some good bread too. Little salsa on the side . . ."

He started to turn with the skillet in his hand and she was there.

"It's not that easy, you know," she said.

"What? The eggs."

"Screw the eggs, Harold."

"But I'm hungry."

"You won't be when I tell you this."

"What? What happened?"

"You really want to know?"

He looked at her for a moment, then tossed the pan of eggs onto the counter and shoved past her into the living room. Got to get back to that can of beer. He had it tipped up and was emptying it when she began talking behind him. He didn't turn.

"It's not easy, like you think it would be when you read about it in the newspaper," she was saying, and he felt he knew what was coming. "You get angry and you think, 'I'd like to kill that fucker,' but you don't really mean it. But one day someone does something to you that's so bad you say, 'I'm going to kill him' and you realize you really are going to do it."

As she talked he felt they were on that slide again, the one that took them down into bed and into that strange and beautiful world where they made love in a hotel in the middle of the night and knew each other completely. Now they were sliding again, sliding down toward something forbidden and exciting, something huge and black, something you are told you should never, never do.

"You're talking about him, aren't you?" Harold said. "The guy at the—"

"Vito, yes. He hurt me, Harold. This afternoon, when I went home for lunch. I stepped out of the shower and he was there."

He had to turn and look at her now, electricity shooting

through his body in every direction, the room expanding and contracting around him.

"What did you do?"

"I tried to fight. But he was too strong." She paused, breathed deeply, and said, "He had his hand on my neck and he almost"—she breathed again—"so I let him do it. And I let him think I liked him. Because I knew, even then, that I would—"

Harold felt that he might have blacked out for a second. But he was still on his feet, breathing hard, clenching his fists. The room around him was as tight as a sock.

She was pulling down the turtleneck collar now. "He did this to me, Harold." A ring of ugly black and blue around her neck. "And this, too," pulling up her shirt and unsnapping her bra in the middle to show him the gauze pad over her nipple, on her breasts, her beautiful breasts, which he worshiped only last night.

He figured he'd better sit down before he passed out or something. A few seconds later he heard her voice saying, "But it isn't that easy."

"Wait, wait, now," he said. "What exactly did you do?"

"You know, you read in the paper and you think, I could do that, but it's not like that, Harold. Not at all."

"You went to see him tonight?"

"Yes."

"And you—" He couldn't say it. "Where is he now?"

"In the car."

"*In the car*. In the car where?"

"At La Cienega and Stocker. That's why I'm here. I need your help."

Harold was still hanging on to what she told him. "Okay so he's in the car. So he's not—not dead."

"No," she said, finishing her beer. "That's the problem."

This must be the turnoff Vito was talking about, Joe thought as he eased his Maxus Coupe LS off La Cienega and onto the cement-hard dirt road. Slow now. Slow. Don't want to kick up any stones onto the rocker panels. His headlights bounced crazily as he inched down the rutted dirt road. Ahead of him, a parked Matsura appeared. He pulled up behind the car and looked around. The car was from his lot all right—there was the temporary plate with "Joe Covo Matsura" on it. But there was no sign of Vito. Or his Mercedes. No sign of anyone. Just the Matsura sitting there like it had a story to tell. Shit.

Joe circled back up to La Cienega, ready to head back to the hotel. He craned his neck, waiting for traffic to clear. He saw an opening . . . but hesitated and missed it. Something was working inside him. What the hell was going on here? What was the Matsura doing here? Something must have gone wrong. Either that or Vito was working a deal of his own. That was entirely possible.

Joe pulled onto the shoulder, killed the engine, and stepped out into the night. Out of habit he noticed he was locking his car, even though he wasn't sure where he was going, what he was going to do. He picked his way between trees and bushes, walking carefully on the loose dirt of the embankment. A dirty orange light throbbed down on him as he reached the dirt road. The air was cool and wet, the oil wells creaking nearby. As he approached the Matsura he noticed beads of moisture on the heavily waxed trunk lid. He stooped and looked into the dark interior. No one home. Door's unlocked, though. Worth a look around. Maybe the book's here somewhere.

Joe carefully opened the driver's-side door, not exactly

sure why he was being so cautious except that something about all this had him really spooked. Inside the Matsura it was still detail-perfect. He could smell the air freshener they used at the dealership. He'd always liked the smell of it. It made him think of money. But out here it seemed phony, like a lie he'd been telling for a long time.

The driver's seat was pulled forward. Someone with short legs. This Acrodyne secretary probably. He slid the seat back and sat behind the wheel looking around the car in the pale dome light. The interior was as sterile as when it rolled off the line. He glanced in the glove compartment. Courtesy maps, brochures, temporary registration. Nothing changed. He ran his hands under the seats. Nothing there either.

He reached down beside the seat and pulled the trunk release. There was a bump as the lid sprung loose. He got out and walked to the rear of the car and was about to open the trunk lid when the wind swirled up and he smelled it.

Eucalyptus.

The wind must have shifted, blowing up the canyon and bringing day-warm air from the grove of trees below. Whenever he smelled eucalyptus he always thought of that first time with Vikki, lying on a blanket along Highway 79 near Temecula, finishing two bottles of wine and then looking up at the stars together. What a night that was. After the hell he'd gone through in his divorce he felt like a kid again with her. No problems. No baggage. A fresh slate. Starting over. Yes, that's what eucalyptus made him think of. Starting over. What a great feeling.

Maybe it wasn't too late to start over again. Make LaBounty happy and keep the dealership. Straighten Vito out—or fire him if he had to. Get the DMV off his ass. Then they'd take a little jaunt down to Cabo. Just him and Vikki. Lie on the beach all day. Get that *starting-over* feeling back. Like the way he felt that night on the blanket, holding Vikki after they made love for the first time.

Joe stood there by the trunk letting these thoughts swirl around him with the smell of eucalyptus, taking him back, back in time to one of the few really happy moments in his life.

And then he raised the trunk lid.

Vito's dream had been filled with strange sounds. Someone was moaning in the weirdest way—like the way cats yowl in the night and you wake out of dead sleep and think, *What the hell was that*? It was semihuman. Like someone was trying to say something but couldn't. It was freaking him out so he woke up—and realized he was the one making those sounds.

It took him a while to realize where he was. And that he wasn't dead. It took more than a few bumps on the head with a dime-store hammer to kill a Fiorre. Granted, he wasn't in great shape. But he was alive and that was the main thing.

No, actually, the main thing was that he had a real surprise for Marianna when she came back. He had put it in his coat pocket before he left, in case Dad-boy showed up. He struggled to reach it, all balled up in here with no room to move. Just a matter of shifting around and—yes—this might work. He had more room to move than he first thought.

And look at this roomy trunk folks! I've got to tell you a funny story. This broad tried to kill me once. Why? That's a whole other story. The point is, I wound up in the trunk and I've got to tell you, it was much bigger than it looks. Not pleasant, mind you, but roomy. Big enough to—yes—reach around and—

His hand closed on the handle of the little .25 automatic he'd taken from under the seat of his Mercedes. He gradually worked it around into his right hand and held it pointing skyward. Then, when she opened the lid, he'd be ready for her. Sort of an in-your-face reply, he thought, lying back now and breathing hard after the exertion.

Then he remembered the courtesy light. It was almost right above his face. He touched the smooth plastic surface in the pitch black of the trunk. See? He couldn't be hurt too badly if he could remember to take care of details like that. He reached behind the tiny light, found the wires, and yanked them loose. There, no annoying light to show Marianna what was coming at her.

He must have passed out again for a while because when he heard the car pull up nearby he was stiff. Could hardly move. And the blood on his hair and face was hard, like a helmet. Every time his heart beat it was like something loose in his head pounded. But he still had the .25 in his hand and he was ready now.

Vito felt one of the car doors open and the Matsura rocked as someone sat in it. Whoa, she was heavier than she looked. Shit. This might mean she was going to drive him somewhere. He waited for the car to start but it didn't. Instead he heard her moving around, opening things.

Then the trunk lid released. He could feel fresh air leaking in around the edges and wanted to shove the lid up and get the hell out of here. But maybe Dad-boy was with her and he didn't feel up to taking them both on in his condition. Better to wait here and give her a good surprise.

Footsteps. She was coming to get him now. Dump him like a load of garbage and get rid of him. Or maybe she wanted to make sure he was dead. And if he wasn't—what? Hit him with that friggin' hammer again? No way was anyone gonna do that to him again. The footsteps stopped outside and he could sense her there, inches away . . . hear her breathing. *What the hell was she waiting for?*

Finally, he heard a sigh and the trunk lid came up. A face bent over him, an arm reaching out when the gun in his hand exploded, and, in the muzzle flash, he saw that he'd made a terrible mistake.

* * *

The hot gases in the cartridge rapidly expanded and .057 ounces of lead began moving upwards at 780 miles per hour. The bullet entered the left side of Joe's neck. It traveled four and a quarter inches through muscle and tissue, severing tendons and small blood vessels but missing any life-sustaining organs. Just as it seemed about to harmlessly exit the back of the neck, it struck the tip of the bone in the left wing of the fourth vertebra and veered off at a new angle, back and up toward the brain cavity.

Now the lead missile was seriously misshapen, wider and ragged, as it sliced through the aorta and esophagus. Blood from the huge artery began pouring into the windpipe and cranial cavity. No doubt Joe would have drowned in his own blood if there had been time. But the bullet continued upwards, tearing through the central motor cortex, which immediately stopped the heart from beating. The bullet then traveled through pink brain matter, blood vessels, and tissue. Finally it struck the inside of the skull where it stopped, flattening into its final shape.

Joe, who had been strong and healthy only a moment before, immediately began falling as if the strings that held him upright had been cut. He dropped down onto the edge of the trunk, smashing his face, then rolled sideways, hitting the protruding bumper and landing on the ground on his left side, his arm twisted back, his legs splayed out under the rear of the car, and his face in the dirt in a widening puddle of blood.

All these events took only .0627 seconds to complete. And, although death was what a coroner's report would have called "instantaneous," Joe was actually still capable of several million thoughts, even though sections of his brain were torn apart. For example, he was well aware that death was rapidly closing in on him. At first this brought a terror so complete it seemed all darkness in the universe had gathered to suffocate him. Then images of his life flickered past like scenes in a movie, each loaded with meaning, and as these images progressed, they brought an acceptance of death and an indescribable sense of calm.

It was at this point that death enveloped him. He had entered this life 19,516 days ago, and, as an only child, had been the source of unending pride and love from his mother and father. He had made love to many women, married twice, and had two daughters. He had been cruel to many people, had routinely lied and cheated men and women, but had occasionally been inexplicably kind to others. Throughout his life he had avoided thinking of death and God and had instead devoted all his energy to seizing material things. But despite all these accomplishments, as Joseph Francis Covo settled back in the dust on this lonely strip of dirt, in the middle of this vast city of millions, life was already weaving a new pattern that was infinitesimally different. And it was a pattern that no longer included him.

"Open the trunk," Marianna said. She was standing a good ten feet from the Matsura even though it was silent and still now, not bouncing on its springs like it had two hours ago when she first heard the noises and went flying out of here in the Escort.

"I'm not going to open the damn trunk," Harold said.

"Why not?"

"I'm just not going to do it."

"How else are you going to see if he's . . . ?"

"I don't know. Listen for him."

They were both silent for a few minutes. A wave of traffic came up over the pass, shooting splinters of light around them. Harold didn't like that feeling, of being so close to a car with a dead—or partially dead—body in it while cars with normal people in them were zooming past nearby. He wanted to leave, to do something to get out of this ridiculous situation. He tried to build a list of options but couldn't think of a damn thing. He had very little preparation for dealing with situations like this.

"How long are we going to wait?" She was on him again.

"Until we're sure."

"When will you be sure?"

"I don't know! Jesus, I don't know what to do! What do you think we should do?"

"Open the trunk."

"I'm not going to open the trunk. I just can't do it."

Harold looked up. One of the cars coming over the pass had its turn signal on. Harold froze. Marianna sensed his fear and looked up.

"What?"

The car was just changing lanes. It sped by the turnoff and continued down the pass.

"Have you got the keys?"

"The trunk release is by the seat."

"I'm not going to open the trunk."

"Then why do you want the keys?"

"You're going to drive it out of here. I'll follow in the truck."

"But what if he—he wakes up or something. Makes that noise again. I'd freak."

"I think he's gone."

"But what if he isn't?"

"All right. We'll go together."

"Where?"

"I don't know! Let's just get the hell out of here. I hate being here."

"Me too." It was the first agreeable thing she'd said for a while.

Harold climbed in behind the wheel and hitched the seat forward a few notches as Marianna climbed in next to him. He turned the key, and the engine caught on the first turn and idled smoothly, like it'd been running all along. He eased it into first and the clutch slipped and caught and they bumped back up the dirt road past his parked truck and the white Maxus Legend LS parked along La Cienega.

He drove in silence, trying not to think about what was in the trunk only five feet behind him.

"Thanks for doing this for me, Harold," she said, sounding as if he were giving her a ride home from work because her car was in the shop. He started to say "No problem," but it never did come out. They stopped at Centinella and listened to the engine idle as they waited for the light to change.

"What was that?" Harold said, fear shooting through his body.

She was quiet, listening, feeling, then said, "What was what?"

"Something moved. I felt the car move."

"I leaned forward to scratch my leg," she said, demonstrating for him.

The car behind them beeped. They both jumped and Harold saw the light had changed. He overrevved, then dumped the clutch and it stalled. Harold panicked, fumbling for the keys in the strange car saying, "Shit! Shit!" as the car behind them blasted the horn again, then roared around them and disappeared.

Harold got it going and pulled out, taking the ramp down to the 405 south. Slowly, his heart stopped pounding wildly and returned to a comparatively slow rate.

"I know a place," he said finally, "up in the mountains. Near Arrowhead."

She waited.

"I used to go there when I was a kid. Church owned it." The church. Shit, he hadn't thought of that. He didn't like the idea of dumping a dead body on church ground. Still, he hadn't killed anyone. God knew that. And it would be dark there. No one to come up on them unexpectedly. Then maybe he'd open the trunk. And if he wasn't dead? He'd deal with that at the time. Now he just wanted to get the hell out of LA so he could think straight.

But something was coming to the surface of his mind now, something that didn't fit. It was taking shape as a question and he turned to Marianna and said, "Who drove this car last?"

"Huh?" She was thinking her own thoughts. She didn't seem too worried about this whole thing now that she dumped it in his lap.

"Who drove this last?"

"Me. Why?"

"I had to move the seat *forward*."

As she paused he was aware of the smooth road beneath them, the easy reliable sound of the engine, and the breeze coming in through the vent when she turned toward him, her face showing amazement.

Then a horn sounded and he turned to see them in the lane next to him—the two guys from the strip-joint parking lot—pointing for him to pull over.

The headlights of the cars on La Cienega exploded in Vito's head like fireworks. They rose in his vision and hung there, searing into his retina, then blasted his brain into sparks of pain, leaving white trails across his vision. At times he couldn't take the pain and he'd close his eyes. But then he'd fall. And he knew one of these times he'd fall and he wouldn't get up. So he wanted to make sure he was where someone would see him when he hit the deck for good. Didn't want to lie there out in the bushes where the coyotes would get him.

There was something else he had to do before he fell again. And that was figure out how the hell to explain to the cops how he got banged up like this. How to explain getting his head smashed in, and the fact he had just tromped through two miles of dirt trails in the canyon in the middle of the friggin' night.

That wasn't easy to do because he could hardly remember it himself. There was the beating . . . Darkness . . . Lying in the trunk . . . More darkness . . . Then he remembered thinking she was coming back to finish him off and then—the worst part—Joe's face, surprised in the muzzle flash.

It had taken forever to get Joe into the trunk. He weighed a ton, and with Vito's bad leg, he could hardly lift him. And all the time he kept thinking to himself that Joe wasn't dead. I mean, how could a little bitty wound like that one in his neck kill him? But he was dead. That was for sure.

Then there was more darkness. And, when he came to, he saw headlights coming and dragged himself out of sight into the bushes. He lay there on his side, watching as Marianna and Dad-boy argued about opening the trunk to see if he was really dead. Man, that gave him a weird feeling. Like one of those out-of-body things he'd read about. It sure made him glad he wasn't the one who was lying in that trunk.

Vito was climbing the embankment to La Cienega as he recalled this. The dirt was loose and rocky. He was dragging his bad leg by this time, caught it on something and—down he went. He was exhausted and the ground felt comfortable. Bad sign, he thought. Still, he knew he was almost there, and he had to have answers ready for the questions they'd ask him in the hospital. But still, a game plan eluded him, the events of the night circled in his confused mind like torn bits of photographs he was trying to reassemble. How was he expected to think straight with a busted skull?

Then, suddenly, the answer was there. The old amnesia trick, he thought, struggling to his feet. *I don't know what happened, Officer. It's so confused. I was going to meet a friend, got hit on the head and—jeez, the rest just isn't there. But I'll get back to you when it comes together.*

Red and green lights mixed with the white of the headlights. He was staggering into an intersection somewhere. And he didn't give a damn what happened to him. Just had to get someone's attention somehow. He heard horns and squealing car tires, then felt the cool pavement under him and closed his eyes. He knew now that he wouldn't die out there in the bushes. He might die here, or in a hospital, but not out there where he'd rot for a while before they finally found him. That was a comforting thought.

Consciousness was hanging by a thread now as he heard voices around him, then a siren, then began riding somewhere in something. The thread was going to be cut now, any second, and it would drop him a long, long way. But some corner of his messed-up brain had something it desperately wanted him to know before he took that long fall.

The paramedic monitoring Vito's condition in the back of

the van saw a slight smile curl his patient's lips. This meant nothing to the paramedic. But if he could read minds he would have heard Vito thinking, *She thinks it's you in that trunk. They don't know you're alive.*

The smile grew a little larger as he thought, *Now that presents some very interesting possibilities.*

"There's our man," Clay said to Adrian, watching as the Matsura pulled out in front of them, the bearded guy at the wheel, some black-haired chick next to him. Clay looked around; there was the guy's pickup, parked on the dirt strip next to La Cienega. He'd switched cars, but not soon enough. They had him.

"Sweet," Adrian said, sitting up straighter and stowing the nip bottle in the glove compartment.

All they had to do was get turned around, catch up to the Matsura, and they were back in business again. Maybe they'd even have an answer for Joe by eleven like he wanted. If the guy stopped. Or if they stopped him.

After the guy ditched them at the strip joint, Clay was dreading the call to Joe, telling him they'd come up empty-handed. But then Clay got a page with a message from Joe: "Go to La Cienega and Stocker." And here was the reason why.

"It's almost eleven," Adrian was saying as they tailed the Matsura down the ramp and south on the 405.

"I'm aware of that," Clay said, smoothing his ponytail and checking the rearview mirror as he changed lanes. The guy was doing sixty-five on the nose—just what you'd expect from someone with a guilty conscience.

"We said we'd call Joe at eleven."

"So call him." Clay handed him the cell phone off the seat.

"What do I tell him?"

"Tell him you didn't take the guy when you had a chance."

"I tried to take him. Fuckhead in the parking lot screwed it up."

"Sure, Joe'll understand. Just explain that to him."

Adrian sighed and sat back as Clay followed the Matsura onto the 91 westbound. Traffic was light, so they hung back.

"Look," Clay said glancing around, "I know Joe and Joe wants action. You try to give him an excuse and he'll eat you alive. Let's give it another five minutes. So we call late? At least we got an answer for him."

Clay edged the Buick up behind the Matsura. He saw the guy's head turn, checking the mirror.

"You're up to something, aren't you?" Clay said to the Matsura. "Changing cars, picking up the slut. I ask you, is that normal behavior?"

Adrian looked around and saw the nearest car was a quarter mile back. His voice was suddenly hard as he said, "Jam him up."

Clay turned, "No way."

"Jam him."

"Fuck you."

"You think you can fuckin' push me around." Adrian popped him in the face with the back of his hand. The Buick swerved.

"Jesus! What're you doin'?"

"You little pussy," Adrian said. He popped him again. The Buick was all over the place. "I'm sick of this shit. Jam him up!"

"Okay!"

Clay edged up on the Matsura. Only a couple feet between their bumpers. The Matsura held steady.

"Cut him off," Adrian said. "Now. Put him in the ditch."

"Yeah. Okay." Clay put his foot down.

They pulled out into the middle lane until they were even with the Matsura. But the guy still wouldn't look over. Clay jabbed the horn, saying, "Hey! Over here, dipshit!"

The face at the wheel of the Matsura turned and the guy looked at them for the first time. Adrian shouted through the glass, "Pull over," and pointed to the shoulder.

The guy was shouting something back, his mouth working.

Adrian cranked the window down and shouted into the wind, "Pull over!"

The guy rolled his window down, and they could barely hear him against the roaring wind as he said something like, "What do you want?"

"We want to talk to you! Pull over!"

The glass slid back up and the guy turned back to the road. They could see him talking to the girl. The Matsura didn't slow down.

"Okay, asshole," Clay said. "Check this out." He moved the Buick into the lane ahead of the Matsura and hit the brakes.

The Matsura cut into the middle lane and passed them, putting on speed.

Clay stomped the gas and the Buick passed on the Matsura's right, moved up and around until it was straddling the middle and fast lanes. Clay hit the brakes and cut the wheel, blocking the Matsura toward an exit that was coming up.

"All right," Adrian said, looking back.

"What's he doing?" Clay asked, trying to find the Matsura in his mirror.

"He's—okay, yeah, he's stopping!"

"Where?"

"On the fuckin' shoulder. Pull over! Pull over!"

Clay swerved across three lanes and slid to a stop in the breakdown lane. Adrian had his hand on the doorknob as Clay put the Buick in reverse. The tires slipped and shuddered underneath the car as they sped backwards, coming up fast on the Matsura, Adrian jumping out. He was crossing in front of the Matsura when it pulled out again, back out into traffic, a semi blasting its horn and nearly rear-ending the Matsura, locking up its brakes. Thick blue tire smoke swept over the stopped Buick.

Adrian was back in the Buick, the car already moving when they saw the Matsura make the exit and drop out of sight down the ramp. A second later a cruiser flew past in front of them, lights on, chasing the Matsura. Clay took the exit, following at a distance, in time to see the cruiser fishtail at the bottom of the ramp and blast off, catching the Matsura after a light or two and getting right up behind, spotlights and flashers on it. The Matsura kept moving.

Then they heard the cop's voice over the speaker.

"Stop the car, *now*!"

The Matsura kept going. Not fast, but it was still rolling.

"Not too close," Adrian was saying.

But Clay just laughed, watching the cars ahead of him and saying, "Crazy asshole."

The voice over the loudspeaker was pissed now, breaking out of that official cop-talk. "Pull over *now*. You will be arrested unless you pull over *immediately*!"

The Matsura signaled for a left, then turned onto a side street. Clay saw the guy's face in the cop's searchlights. He was waving as if to say, "Okay, okay," and pointing to something ahead of them.

"Man, doesn't he know?" Clay said. "You don't fuck with cops."

"They're gonna lock his ass up," Adrian said. "It'll be weeks before we get another shot at him."

They saw the other cops coming now, two cruisers with their lights and sirens going.

"Go straight, go straight," Adrian said.

Clay slowed as the cruisers passed, then continued past the side street the Matsura had taken. He drove for another block, then made a left.

"So what're you gonna tell Joe?"

"Oh, we're back to that again, huh?"

"You're the muscle. And you didn't deliver. Maybe you can explain how that happened to Joe."

Adrian was silent until he said, "Circle around. Let's see what they're doing."

They cruised down the side street and saw the Matsura lit up in the glare of high beams and spots. The guy was getting out, hands up, and the cops were crouched behind their doors, guns drawn.

"Man, those cops're stoked!" Clay said. They both laughed, enjoying the scene for a moment, then pulling back onto the main street. A second later another pair of cruisers flew by, lights and sirens on.

"Must be a slow night," Clay said.

Adrian didn't answer. He had the cell phone in his hand and was dialing as he muttered, "Get this over with . . ."

He waited, phone to his ear. "Joe's gonna be so pissed." But then, after the phone rang a dozen times he disconnected. "It was supposed to be so important, then he doesn't answer. Where the hell is he?"

Harold couldn't make himself take his foot off the gas pedal. He needed just a second or two more to come up with a plan, anything, to keep the cops from popping the trunk, finding the body. That would be almost impossible to explain. He pictured himself saying: *You've got to believe me,* I *had no idea it was in there,* and felt sick to his stomach.

"Pull over now!" the cop's voice echoed through the dark neighborhood and filled the world with its authority. The Matsura interior was blazing with hot white light from the cop cars. Harold glanced over at Marianna and saw her hair backlit like a halo around her shadowed face.

"Ah, Harold, I really think you should stop," Marianna said, sinking into her seat.

"And how're we supposed to explain what's in the trunk?"

"Stop now and they won't search the car."

The voice came again, "Pull over *now*. You will be arrested unless you pull over *immediately*!"

Harold waved into the rearview mirror. "Okay, okay. I'm pulling over." But then he looked around and realized where they were—two blocks from his father's house. A plan was forming now, a way to take care of a couple of problems at the same time. He waved to the cops as he turned the corner, "Just two more blocks," he said, pointing, as if they could hear him.

"Harold, what are you doing?" Marianna said, her voice flat, all hope gone.

"Going to my dad's.

"Your dad can't help you now."

"If they arrest me there he can call my lawyer. Get him over there before the cops beat the shit out of me."

The voice came from behind again. "Stop now! You will be arrested!"

"If you don't stop soon, they're going to kill you."

Harold saw that three cop cars were behind him now, and a fourth joining in.

"Almost there," Harold said. Now he was fiddling with the trunk key, working it off the chain and locking the inside floor latch so the cops couldn't open the trunk. He'd always liked that feature, kept parking-lot attendants from getting in the trunk. *If you're a jewelry salesman, if you have samples in the trunk and you're taking a client out to lunch it comes in very handy,* he used to say to prospects on the car lot. Somehow, as he said that, he never imagined using it for this particular application.

The Matsura's interior was blazing, like the seats might catch fire. The light seemed to explode in his brain and dissolve his nerves. The key was slippery in his hand. If he could only get the trunk locked before—yes—there it was.

"Hide this." Harold handed the key across to Marianna, keeping his hand below sight level. "Stick it in the glove compartment or something."

She popped the glove compartment and stuck it deep in the spine of the owner's manual just as they rolled to a stop in front of his father's house.

Harold got out and stood in the street, trying to look back beyond the wall of lights from the cop cars. He saw the cruiser's doors were open and the cops crouching behind them, guns pointed at him. What the hell did they think he'd done?

"On the ground!" they shouted across at him.

"Family emergency!" he shouted back. "My father's in trouble! In there!" He pointed across the street.

"On the ground! N*ow*!"

Harold slowly got to his hands and knees feeling very stupid.

"F*lat on the ground*! C*ross your hands behind you*!" He did what they said, but he hated every demeaning second of it.

Then they came running at him. He felt a knee in his back, wrenching pain in his shoulders as his arms were twisted back and his wrists handcuffed.

"My father's in trouble," Harold said to the cops' ankles. "That's why I couldn't stop."

"So call the police," a lady cop said.

Hands were on him now, patting him down. He felt the bulge on his hip disappear as they lifted his wallet.

"I called the cops," Harold said, sensing this might distract them from the car. "You never do nothing. They could be murdering him right now. And you're out here—"

"Who's murdering him, sir?" the lady cop asked.

"Home invasion," Harold said. "Druggies moved in on him and I can't get them out. Go over there. You'll see."

Marianna suddenly appeared on the ground next to him.

"Harold, I told you you should have pulled over," she said. Amazing how composed she could look flat on her stomach in handcuffs.

A different voice said to Harold, "Sir, what's your father's address?"

Harold strained his neck and looked up at a beefy cop, blond, stripes on his shoulder, a sergeant. "Fifteen twenty-eight—across the street there."

The sergeant jerked his head and spoke to the lady cop: "Well, check it out."

"But—"

"Check it out. Take Rosa and check it out."

The lady cop and her partner ambled across the street. Other cop cars were still pulling up. The neighborhood looked like it was being invaded.

Harold craned his neck to see his father's house. He heard one cop yelling, "Get the back door!"

Dark shapes behind the curtains were moving rapidly. Then the cops started running, converging on the house. Everyone was running for the house—except the sergeant guarding him. He heard motorcycles blasting to life in the alley and pulling away. A pair of cops ran back to their cruiser and tore off after them. A moment later he saw a huge guy with a neck brace being led from the house in handcuffs. Harold smiled. At least that problem was taken care of. Now it was up to his dad to make the most of it. He really had to get him those voice keys.

"Can we get up?" Harold asked the sergeant's ankles.

Another cop came up to the sergeant and Harold heard him say, "Nothing in the car."

"Check the trunk?"

"Can't open it. It's got one of those inside locks."

The sergeant crouched next to Harold. "Sir, would you open the trunk for us?"

"I can't do anything down here."

The sergeant took Harold's arm and helped him up, almost lifting him to his feet. Christ, did all these guys work out? Harold read the sergeant's name tag: R. Polk.

"Her too," Harold added. They helped Marianna to her feet and positioned them both up against the cruiser.

"Now would you open the trunk, sir?" Polk repeated.

Harold was fumbling for words when he heard Marianna, just as calm as you please: "Lock's jammed. See, I just bought the car and it's got a lot of bugs."

"She bought it at Joe Covo Matsura," Harold added. "He's a crook. Don't ever go there."

"Where's the ignition key?" Polk asked Marianna. "That's supposed to open it."

"In the ignition," Harold said, wanting to add, "you dumb shit."

"Maybe you can make it work somehow," Marianna said. "It didn't work for me. I was going to bring it in first thing in the morning. But I've been back there several times."

"He's a crook," Harold said. "I should know. I write books about car buying."

Marianna said, "Harold, that's really not necessary now."

"I'm just establishing my credentials," Harold said.

The sergeant was at the Matsura's trunk now putting the key in the lock and—Harold waited, his heart jumping wildly in his chest, head swimming. He looked at Marianna. She winked at him. Shit. *Winked at him*, at a time like this.

Harold looked back at Polk. The sergeant was lifting up on the trunk lid. With his muscles Harold expected him to tear it right off the damn hinges. But it wouldn't budge. He tried the key again, lifted—the lock held.

Another cop approached Polk with Harold's driver's license in his hand. "Sir. Dispatch had an outstanding on him." Polk looked at the cop, then over to Harold.

"Him?"

"Yes, sir."

"For what?"

"Twenty-two eighty-seven."

The sergeant paused. "You free for a transport?" The other cop nodded. "Radio dispatch you're out of service and get going."

Harold's stomach dropped. He was being arrested. Panic. Blinding panic choked him.

"Sergeant, you can't—" He couldn't say any more.

"Leaving the scene of an accident," the sergeant said. "Serious offense."

"Let me call my lawyer. I'll call him from my dad's."

"Sorry, sir, you'll get a phone call after you're booked."

"But what about my father? He could be—"

"Your father's okay. Now please . . ." He took Harold's arm.

Arrest. Booking. Jail.

Panic, like a cloud of darkness, enveloped the world and choked all hope from Harold.

Polk led Harold to a nearby cruiser. He pressed him down

into the backseat with a hand on top of his head. As the sergeant turned away he said to the other cop, "You guys have a slam hammer for the trunk?" The cop mumbled something back.

So this was the end, then. They would get him on a stupid outstanding warrant, pop the trunk, find the body, and he'd be gone for life. Why? Because he tried to help someone out. Do a favor. Maybe he could explain all that to them when they booked him for murder. *But Your Honor, it started out with me trying to help someone who was ripped off. One thing led to the next and . . .* He didn't think it would fly.

Harold shifted on the dirty vinyl seat, the cuffs holding his arms behind him and shredding his wrists. He wanted to scream. To pick up something and kill every cop in sight. But he had to hold on. Just maybe they wouldn't find the body.

Christ he hated cops. He'd have to do a book about them. Some how-to about avoiding confrontations with cops and what to do if you're arrested. I wish I'd already written that book, Harold thought, because I have no idea what to do now.

Through the screen mesh he could see Polk talking to Marianna as he wrote on a clipboard. He'd ask her a question, write, then look up at her and ask her another question. She didn't seem the least bit concerned about all this. As he watched, the sergeant took a key off his belt and undid her handcuffs.

The other cop came back and slid in behind the wheel, put it in gear. As they drove past Marianna, he heard her voice through the open window saying to the sergeant: "Come on, what do you think we have in there, a dead body?"

You're really pushing it now, he thought. But then he heard it, the sergeant's laughter, as they drove down the street and off to jail.

Satisfactory, LaBounty thought as he finally released, feeling the pleasure flood through his body like warm milk. Entirely satisfactory. The pleasure lay there glowing in his body as his breathing gradually slowed, the naked woman still lying across his lower body, trying to sense what he wanted next. For a minute or two he wanted nothing, which was extremely rare for him. He wanted just to lie there and think how satisfactory it all was, feel his nerve endings calm for once, nicely played out.

But then the hotel room and the world around it, along with this particular night and its problems, all rushed back to him. He grunted, shifted his massive body, and the woman was dislodged. She kissed his chest, then stood and in the dim light went to her shoulder bag and began dressing.

LaBounty sat naked on the edge of the bed watching her in the gloom.

"Joe take care of you?"

"He pays Dash for the party. Dash pays us."

"I don't know Dash."

"He set this up."

"For a cut. What's he take?"

"Half."

LaBounty snorted. Incredible how people let themselves be exploited. The woman was ready to leave, but didn't. LaBounty knew she wanted to ask him for money. She was afraid to do it directly so she let the awkward silence grow. He reached over and fished his wallet out of the crumpled heap of pants that lay where she had pulled them off him before beginning her work.

He held his wallet open, debating. In the weak light he could see the woman was sad-eyed now, no longer coy and seductive, and he had a rare and disturbing thought. He realized suddenly, and against his will, that she had a life that extended beyond this room, a life as ragged as his own, but in an entirely different way. She had a boss—this Dash—and co-workers, like anyone else. She lived somewhere, had things she wanted to accomplish that were out of her reach. What? Acting, modeling, singing? What was it? He knew it was there but didn't want to know specifically.

Finally she spoke, saying, "I have a little baby. . . . He has this condition where—"

"Okay." LaBounty said in a way that stopped her. He cracked his wallet and took out two one-hundred-dollar bills and handed them to her. She took them, then bent forward and kissed him.

"You gonna see Joe before you go?"

"Probably."

"Don't tell him I gave you that. See what he does." She waited. "Maybe you'll make something extra."

Once she was gone, LaBounty felt restless and impatient to conclude the objective of this trip. He showered and changed, then went out to find Joe. When he got to the banquet room the lights were on full blast, the hotel staff was cleaning up. No Joe.

LaBounty tried Parker's room but found the Do Not Disturb sign on his doorknob. That meant he was still with the other girl. Probably fell asleep on her. The old pump and pass.

Bales was in the lobby bar watching a Lakers game on satellite TV.

"How was she?" Bales said, not looking away from the game, tossing some popcorn into his mouth.

"Satisfactory," LaBounty grunted.

" 'Satisfactory,' " Bales muttered, shaking his head.

"You partake?" LaBounty signaled for the bartender.

"How could I? You and Parker moved right in."

"She might still be around here somewhere. She's looking for Joe."

"No thanks."

LaBounty watched the players running up and down the court, their shoes squeaking on the shiny floor, before asking, "You get it?"

"I'm waiting for Vito now."

"Then the answer is, 'No, I didn't get it.' "

Bales turned to look at LaBounty. LaBounty held his eyes for a moment and then they both looked back in time to see a fast breakaway that ended in a slam dunk. The crowd went nuts.

"When's this Vito gonna show up?"

"He's been gone two hours. He should be back any time."

"Where's Joe?"

"Haven't seen him."

"Haven't seen him?"

"Nope."

"That's not like Joe. He's usually all over us, suckin' up."

"I know."

"Did you talk to Vito?"

"About what?"

"About what we talked about on the plane."

"Yeah."

"Well, what'd he say?"

"He said he'd take care of it."

"*Take care of it.* What's that mean?"

"I don't know. But he said he'd take care of it and meet me here."

"When?"

"He was supposed to be here an hour and a half ago."

"So what happened?"

"I have no idea."

They watched the TV for another five minutes without speaking. Then LaBounty said, "This is bizarre," and left.

"When did you realize he was dead?" the detective was asking Harold, clicking her nails against her coffee mug, the one with a big county sheriff shield on the side.

The detective was about ten years younger than Harold, but she had the most incredible bags under her eyes. The skin was like rotten peaches, but the eyes were steady, probing him for signs of weakness, lies, silently inviting him to come clean.

Harold was willing to admit he left the scene of that stupid fender bender on Euclid. That didn't seem like much at all. The problem was, everything they asked him sounded like they knew about the body in the trunk. But they couldn't know. They just weren't making a big enough deal about it. Still, Harold didn't want to take any chances, so he was keeping his mouth shut.

The detective's partner, a young guy, sharp dresser, Hispanic maybe, had been standing back against the door. Now he leaned down and whispered something in her ear. That was his thing. He didn't say a word. Just whispered to his partner. Harold knew it was a way to keep him off balance. But knowing this didn't help. It *did* keep him off balance and he hated them both for manipulating him.

In this cramped interrogation room, with the institutional desk and chairs, Harold felt like he was in a sales office at a dealership, negotiating for a used car. He thought of his recent encounter with Vito, the one that started all this, but then he panicked, realizing Vito was dead now, and averted his eyes before this detective could read his mind. He found himself staring down at the side of the table, reading gang names carved deep in the wood with ballpoint pens. The same pens used to sign confessions, he thought, and looked back up at his interrogators.

"Harold, you keep saying we've made a mistake. But you won't tell us what happened. Maybe we do have the wrong guy. But how're we gonna find out unless you tell us what happened?"

Harold shifted in the chair; the paper jumpsuit he was wearing rustled loudly, startling him. "I know what you do," he said at last, not being able to keep the hate from his voice.

"And what is that?"

"You've got a crime, you find someone to match it."

She thought that over. "True."

"I.e., you don't care if it's the person who really did it."

"Well why don't you tell us what you really did? That'd be an excellent place to start."

They're just like car salesmen, he thought. They keep repeating the same thing. But instead of sign the contract, they say: Tell us what happened. Tell us what happened. Tell us what happened.

Harold looked away, hoping someone would come to the door and say, "His lawyer's here." And Zorich would come sliding in in that sneaky way of his and make monkeys out of these cops. He never thought he'd want to see that little snake so badly in all his life.

"We know you were on that road. We've got a witness that puts you there."

That road. Which road was she talking about?

"Okay, so we know you were there. We know a man was found dead in that car. How did that happen?"

Harold was silent. Could that old guy in the Tercel really have died? Certainly not from injuries in the accident. But maybe he had a heart attack. Were they trying to pin that on him? If the guy had a bad ticker it could have conked out anytime. Little earthquake, lots of people dropped from fright. No one to blame there.

The partner whispered something to the detective again. She listened, her sharp eyes on Harold, waiting for a reaction. Just keep breathing, he thought. Keep the air moving through his lungs. He wished he had his therapy ball. But he knew if he did he'd shred the thing.

She continued: "We have it that two officers went to your address—which is in fact not your address—seeking to serve this warrant, and you misrepresented yourself to the officers. You said you were not Harold Dodge when in fact you are."

Harold heard footsteps in the hallway outside. He wanted the door to open and to see Zorich come in wearing one of those flashy suits of his. But the footsteps kept going down the hallway. A door slammed. The detective was staring at him, her eyes watery in their bags of rotten peaches.

"Now my partner has determined these two officers are on duty and has suggested we radio for them to come to the station here and ID you. If they make positive ID you know what that means?"

Harold kept looking at her but said nothing.

"It means, Harold, that we're looking at an extra count of making false statements. That, on top of these other charges means you do time. County time at the very least. And you don't want to go to County. Believe me. This place is the Holiday Inn compared to County."

Prison. It was out in the open for the first time. She let the silence grow. Let it all sink in. Then started again on a more reasonable note.

"You don't want us to waste their time and ours over something like this. So why don't you work with us?"

"I am working with you."

"How? Name one way in which you're cooperating."

"Putting up with this shit."

She was disappointed. "Harold, that's not what I wanted to hear."

It was a lot better than what I was thinking, Harold thought.

"As soon as my lawyer comes I'll tell you everything you need to know."

"Fine. So where is he?"

"I'll call him again."

"One call. That's the law. Now we think this is a simple matter and we want to clear it up, get you out of here so that—"

The partner whispered something else to the detective. She leaned back, her eyes still attached to Harold, nodded, and took a new approach.

"Let me put it this way, Harold. When someone holds out like this on us, it makes us wonder what else he's done, to be quite frank."

Harold tried to remain very still, to block all thoughts of Vito dead in the trunk, of Marianna with that stain on the front of her shirt. After all, what had he really done? Driven a car somewhere. What was so wrong with that? He wanted to talk, but he was afraid of words. They always betrayed him.

Still, if he could say what he needed to get out of here—to *get the hell out of here*!—then he'd never come back again. Never. And the longer he waited, the more chance there was Marianna's Matsura would be searched and then it'd be the old throw-away-the-key syndrome. It was worth the risk. But the words had to cooperate. Keep it simple, he thought as he took a deep breath, keep it simple.

"I want to make a deal with you." The two cops waited. "It's simple. Well, not simple exactly, but—" Words! They were already tripping him up. Just say what happened in the accident. Block all the other stuff. He took another breath and started speaking again.

"I have a little business, buying damaged goods, insurance claims and—it's completely legal."

"Sure. Everyone's got a little hustle on the side."

"So I have to work it on my spare time, i.e., after work, lunch hours. Okay, so I made a purchase earlier this week of some radiators."

"Radiators? Harold, what in hell do radiators have to do with this?"

"You'll see in a second. What you have to do is make a bid on these insurance claims from the insurance company, then find a source and resell it. But it costs a bundle to make a bid. Just to make a damn bid."

"Harold . . ."

"I'm getting to the point."

It was working. They were getting confused. Bored.

He continued talking, and as he did, he felt the first slight inkling of hope since he'd been handcuffed and crammed into that patrol car.

Sometime in the middle of the night Vikki became aware that Joe hadn't come home. She woke up and checked the bedside clock. Then went back to sleep. Checked the clock. Went back to sleep. Finally she woke up and stayed awake. Not really worried. But more worried than she should be. It was that unexplained fear that gripped her for no reason from time to time. But it usually turned out to be nothing at all. Evaporated the second she heard the garage door rumbling up. Then she knew he'd be coming through the door soon saying something like, "Shit, what a day."

But the garage door never rumbled up and he never slid into the sheets next to her. Instead, the wind picked up outside and she felt so empty she got out of bed at 4:18 A.M. and went down to the kitchen to make coffee, all the time hoping he'd still walk in the door. She was prepared to be upset but ultimately understanding and forgiving. If he'd just come home.

She knew he was going to be late. Entertaining the big shits from Cincinnati is what he'd said.

"Why can't I come along? Impress them with your sexy young wife."

"Car talk. It'd bore the shit out of you."

"You talk about cars all the time and it doesn't bore me." In fact, she had gone to the library and taken out books on the internal combustion engine and studied them until she knew as much about cross-flow exhaust manifolds as he did. When he wasn't around she read every word of *Road and Track*. She didn't just want to be Joe's trophy wife in the palace on the hill. She wanted to be a part of his life.

"I like listening to you guys talk about cars. I want to come along."

"This is different. These guys're pigs."

"Who is?"

"Bales and LaBounty. You met Tom Bales. And LaBounty, huge guy from the main office. When they come here they want to raise hell."

"So what're you going to do? Go to a strip show or something?"

"Something like that."

"*Something like that*? What're you going to do? Come on, Joe."

"I don't know. I haven't decided. We're gonna start out with dinner, then see what's happening. See a show or something. I don't know."

Vikki remembered smiling that *come-on, you-can-tell-me* smile, and holding it until she thought he would finally start laughing. But he didn't.

"Joe."

"What?"

"What're you going to do? I want to know."

"I told you. I haven't decided. Okay?"

Then he got that *back-off* look he used sometimes. The one that slammed the door in her face and said, "Don't come any closer." And then he walked out the door. To where? To do what? She had no idea.

The first time he used his back-off look she made the mistake of crowding him. Demanding to know what he was doing. And he refused. She threatened to leave him. He laughed. "What're you going to do? Go back to waiting tables? Lemme tell you something. You get the taste of money, you can't go back. So get used to it."

And she had. Once, twice a year, some big shit would come to LA and Joe took them out on the town. Came home at 3:00 A.M. with the smoke and booze seeping out of his skin like poison. But at least he came home.

It was 6:05 now and she could see the sun coming up over Long Beach from the kitchen window. It was a dirty sunrise. The backlit clouds hung like smoke over the horizon. The air was hot and dry. Santa Anas.

She had to move, had to get the hell out of the kitchen. She walked through the silent house, her feet sinking into the thick carpeting, unaware of where she was going until she found herself at his study door. There was a pad of paper on the desk with some writing on it. "Dash" it said in Joe's handwriting. "Four Seasons—7:30." And a telephone number.

Joe's leather chair creaked as Vikki lowered herself into it and picked up the black cordless. She dialed the number next to Dash, and a recorded voice asked her to leave a voice-mail message or enter her number and the page would be returned. She disconnected and sat there, phone in hand, wanting to call someone else to get this answered. Maybe a reasonable explanation was only a phone call away.

She found the Four Seasons number and dialed.

"I'm looking for someone that might be a guest there."

"What is the party's name?"

"Covo. Joseph Covo."

Pause and a slight intake of breath on the other end of the line. "Mr. Covo had a private banquet room last night. But he's not a guest in the hotel. . . ."

She wanted to ask more, but knew she couldn't. She disconnected and sat there in the leather chair, watching the clouds lighting up with the new day and thought that someone at that hotel knew where Joe was. What were the names of those guys from Cincinnati. Tom. Tom something. Something unusual. Short. She ran through the alphabet saying to herself "Tom A . . ." "Tom B . . ." "Tom C . . ." The name wouldn't come.

Until the third time through the alphabet.

When the phone on Tom Bales's hotel bedside table rang he thought it was his wake-up call. Instead he heard a voice that was familiar but strangely altered. Like an old friend played at the wrong speed.

"Tom, hey, it's Vito, man. Were they outrageous or what?"

"Who?"

"The *ladies*. Man, I figured you'd have your hands full for the rest of the night—so to speak. So I left you alone."

"Are you all right?"

"I should be asking you that." Vito's laughter was out of sync, too.

"Where are you?"

"Pay phone. Gettin' a bite on the way to the dealership."

Bales's head was clearing now. He remembered how Vito stood him up the night before. How they needed that book. How LaBounty was pissed when Vito didn't come through, and tried to shit on Bales for the screwup.

"You get what I asked you for?"

"Yeah . . ."

"Well, did you get it or not?"

"Not *literally*. But I took care of the problem."

Bales paused. Since no more information followed this statement, he said, "I don't understand."

"Joe won't be a threat anymore."

"Vito. I'm still not gettin' the gist of this."

"The gist of it is this: Everything is copacetic."

"I think you're confused, Vito. We asked you to get us whatever—"

"My mind is crystal clear, Tom. I've never been sharper. Okay? Now I know what you said and I know what you need. But hey, when you tell a pro to get something done, you don't tell him how to do it—not *literally*. So I, like, made an executive decision."

"Executive decision."

"Right."

"And what was that decision?"

"You don't need to know. Believe me. All you need to know is, I did you guys a huge favor."

"I don't follow you."

"You will. Now relax. And tell John your man Vito's a good soldier. That should count for something. Something big."

They were silent on the phone for a moment, Bales wondering what else to say when he heard an intercom in the background paging Doctor someone. In a restaurant? Why not? The point was, he wasn't getting anything more from Vito. But before he hung up he asked, "You talk to Joe this morning?"

There was a confused pause before Vito answered, "No. Not yet." Then, thinking, he said, "You got a message you want me to give him?"

"Have him call me."

"Might be tough. I think he said he was taking his wife down to Cabo for the weekend."

"Mexico?"

"That's the only Cabo I know. They go there a lot. So if you have anything for him, give me a call. I'll see he gets the message."

When Bales set the phone down it rang again immediately. Someone had been holding.

"Hello."

He heard a woman's voice say: "Uh, hi. I'm trying to reach Tom Bales."

"This is Tom."

"Tom, I'm sorry to bother you this early, but . . ." She hesitated long enough for Bales to think, I *don't care what you want,* I *love the sound of your voice.* "This is Vikki Covo. Joe's wife. I—I feel silly asking you but—Joe didn't come home last night. I was wondering if he was there at the hotel. Or—or if you knew where he is."

Later, when Bales related all this to LaBounty over breakfast, the big man grunted, putting the two calls together immediately.

"So what do you think?" Bales asked him.

"What do *you* think?"

They both laughted a little as they thought the same thing. Then Bales said, "You think he's capable?"

"Who, this Giuseppe?"

"Vito. Vito Fiorre."

"You know him better than I do. What do you think?"

"I'm trying to remember exactly what I said to him. I mean, did I say anything that would make him—you know . . . ?" Bales searched his memory as he watched LaBounty eating eggs so runny they looked like they hadn't even been cooked.

"Well?"

"I told him I wanted the book. I told him Joe was out of the picture and if he got us the book it would look good for him when we picked the next GM. I don't think that's like telling him to, you know, go out and—and do away with someone. Do you?"

"I don't know how the hell this guy thinks. People do screwy things based on no one saying anything. The good thing is Joe's out of the way. The bad thing is we got this Vito character running around out there. We don't know what he's done and if he might tell someone we told him to do it."

Bales thought that over. As usual, LaBounty was right. "So what do we do?"

LaBounty shrugged. "Get Slade out here."

"*Slade*? Why?"

"You want this Vito running to the FBI?"

"No. But, I mean—*Slade*? Jesus."

"I tell you one thing right now, Tom. I'm not going to prison 'cause you wouldn't take care of business."

Bales thought about it. "Maybe it wouldn't be such a bad thing. I mean, he's just going to get the book, right?"

"Right. Exactly. Just get the book."

On another day the courtroom would have seemed cheesy and depressing to Harold with the dusty flags, leatherette chairs, and Formica desktops. But after all those hours in his eight-by-ten jail cell, with two tattooed guys reeking of vomit and screaming obscenities at each other, it seemed gleaming and spacious. It was like being allowed to breathe again after having had your head rammed into a bucket of sewage until you thought you would explode.

The bailiff corralled Harold into a boxed-off area on one side of the courtroom, and he listened as the judge whipped through arraignments with alarming speed: aggravated assault, armed robbery, attempted murder. The charges and circumstances blurred together into an unending stream of mayhem and human misery that, Harold realized with a sinking feeling, he was now a part of. He had finally joined this sad parade of bungled lives, lives so out of control the state caught them in their free falls of destruction.

Harold tried to tune out the judge by searching the faces in the gallery for Marianna. He yearned to see her olive skin, her glossy black hair, and that smile that seemed to say, *We know each other's secrets*. She'd come to get him. She *had* to come. He had helped her and she wouldn't forget it.

After searching the room, Harold saw she wasn't there. Instead he found Zorich, his lawyer, decked out in a flashy suit, sitting next to his father, who looked so defeated it seemed he had collapsed into himself.

"Harold Dodge!"

Electricity shot through Harold as he heard his name called. He rose and stumbled through a narrow door in the box and down onto the courtroom floor, rustling in the ridiculous paper jumpsuit. The bailiff positioned Harold in front of the judge and Zorich slid in beside him saying, "I'll do the talking."

The judge, meanwhile, was reviewing Harold's case—and he didn't like what he saw. He looked down from the bench at Harold with hard little eyes filled with stern disapproval. Harold felt a sense of schoolboy shame and had the urge to apologize for ruining his day. But Zorich, beside him, was mustering an air of injured incredulity.

"Your Honor, I submit that the treatment my client is receiving is disproportionate with the facts of this case. Mr. Dodge is not just a client, he's a family friend I've known for years, with an exemplary character. He's a chemical engineer for Aerodyne, a book author and consumer advocate who—"

The judge's eyes, which had been examining Harold's file, rose up above his half glasses.

"Counsel, I'll remind you Mr. Dodge is charged with leaving the scene of an accident involving a fatality. His occupation is irrelevant in this—"

"Your Honor, I submit that character is relevant in regards to his—"

"—extreme lack of concern for others in a high-speed chase. There is more than adequate reason to be here today. The question instead is why has the defendant felt it necessary to endanger others in this manner?"

Harold squirmed. Zorich was losing ground.

"Your Honor." Zorich softened his approach. "We feel this can be settled to the satisfaction of the state without further incarceration. Mr. Dodge has extenuating family and occupational commitments which he needs to address. Therefore, I urge you to release him on his own recognizance at the conclusion of this hearing."

Harold wasn't sure what that meant. But he loved the

sound of it. He ventured a glance at Zorich, feeling a newfound admiration for the little weasel.

"Your defendant took extreme measures to avoid arrest . . . misrepresented himself . . . endangered the lives of others . . ." The judge sighed loudly and regretfully. "A bond of ten thousand dollars is hereby ordered in lieu of release."

"Jesus." It was out before Harold could stop himself. The room was spinning around him as the judge seemed to be saying *back in your cell, back in your cell*. He could feel the walls closing in on him, smell the tattooed maniacs and hear their screaming.

Zorich caught Harold's arm and steadied him.

"Your Honor, the client's father is present in the courtroom and can post the amount indicated"—Harold's hopes jumped—"so we move for immediate release—"

"See the clerk," the judge said, already turning to another case at his elbow.

Harold felt a new hand on his arm. The bailiff was leading him to a side door, back toward the lockup.

"Hang in there, buddy," Zorich was saying. "We'll have you out in no time."

Harold couldn't make his feet move. Every muscle in his body resisted carrying him through that door. He desperately searched the faces for someone who could save him and saw, instead, a threatening pair of eyes, hauntingly familiar. A woman with a large bulky body and short haircut, her surprised eyes following him keenly, as if trying to place him in the way that he was trying to place her and succeeding a moment before he passed through the door and out of sight as he thought, *Shit, the* DMV *lady*, and pictured the case file he'd borrowed lying in his briefcase like a ticking bomb.

An hour later the jailer was handing Harold his possessions

and having him sign release papers. Harold was in his own clothes again, clothes that didn't crinkle when he moved, clothes that brought back his own smell—funky as it was—his own identity as he put them back on. He took his keys and, as he accepted his wallet, it felt out of shape. He opened it and found the bastards had rifled through everything like burglars ransacking a bedroom looking for jewels. Even his card with inspirational quotes (which he read over and over when he was depressed) was folded the wrong way and stuffed in next to his Mobil credit card where it didn't belong.

"That's it, then," the jailer, a skinny blond deputy, said as he took the signed release from Harold. "You're a free man."

The deputy positioned himself in front of a video camera and signaled to someone on the other end. There was a pause, then the sound of bolts shooting back and a hydraulic sigh. The door opened and, as Harold stepped through, the deputy said, "You be good now."

Harold walked through the door and back out into the free world. There was Zorich coming at him, hand extended, saying, "I told you we'd get you out," and his dad looking old and small, but no one else, not the one person he really wanted to be here, the one who he'd hoped would be right there to say, "We're clear now, Harold. Everything's going to be okay."

The lobby was cramped, tiled in a sick yellow color, the obligatory pay phone in the corner. A stringy-haired kid was talking on it, saying to someone on the other end: "Lies, man. Lies is the worse thing you can give me."

"They treat you okay?" Zorich asked, inspecting Harold as if he was a newly delivered package and a complaint might have to be lodged about its condition.

"What the hell took you so long?" Harold said, slipping on his sport coat. Things were out of place in it, too, he realized as his comb stabbed his hip. He dug it out and slid it back to the inside pocket, found his therapy ball on the left side, and moved it over under his right thumb. It was incredibly reassuring to have that back in his hands. He kneaded it greedily.

"Shift change," Zorich said. "They couldn't find your files at first. I raised holy hell. Didn't I, Sammie?"

Zorich was one of the few people who called his father Sammie. And he never took the hint when anyone else called him Samuel. Harold looked at his father and saw him accept the mangling of his name the same way he accepted all the other things he hated in his life but couldn't control.

"Thanks, Harry," his father said. He could hardly hear him with that kid in the corner screaming into the phone.

"For what?"

"Gettin' rid of Randy and them."

"Look, Dad. I got some voice keys I'm gonna put on your doors. Only you can open the locks. I'll—"

"He'll be back."

"What? No. I'm telling you, I'll get the locks changed. We'll get a—a court—what do you call those things?"

"Restraining order?" Zorich offered.

"Yeah. There's gotta be a way to—"

"He'll be back."

Harold put his hand on his father's shoulder, despising himself for not taking better care of him.

Harold suddenly hated the lobby as much as the lockup itself, the walls seeming to come in on him. He moved for the door on wobbly legs, getting a weird breaking-down feeling like he was just realizing how terrible it was now that it was over.

But halfway to the door Zorich said something that stopped him.

"Turned out some broad from the DMV had it."

"Had what?"

"Your file. She was in there reading your sheet. I reamed her good, didn't I, Sammie?"

It was getting worse. Harold couldn't deal with it in here, not with these greasy tile walls and the kid screaming into the phone, all the people around him with their shredded lives and hard-luck stories. He pushed through the double glass doors, out into a courtyard with jungle landscaping and a fountain that had been turned off sometime in the early seventies. But he was out, breathing real air, listening to the drone of the freeway that had been near him all his life, taking a lot of people someplace, all the time. He dropped onto a bench realizing it was hot—real hot—and breathed deeply, soaking in stimulation from all around him, the smell of rotting vegetation mixing with cigarette smoke and diesel exhaust from a delivery truck idling nearby. He was out. He was finally out. His father sat next to him and Zorich stood nearby, unwrapping a piece of gum. People passed, talking, he heard the intercom inside paging someone, and then a new voice, closer, said, "Harold," and the DMV cop, the Paige-lady, was in front of him.

"Harold Dodge," she said, looking down on him. "That's your name, isn't it?"

Zorich stepped forward protectively, ready to raise holy hell if it was necessary.

"Why'd you leave without saying good-bye?"

Harold ordered himself to speak. "I told you. It was my lunch hour. You were gone awhile so I gave up on you."

Harold didn't like the way she was looking at him. Nostrils flared, breathing hard. Pissed. Really pissed. She was taking this whole thing personally.

"You took my case file."

"Your *what*?" Harold hoped his surprised act was convincing.

"My secretary put it on my desk and you—"

"What's this about?" Zorich was puffing himself up.

"Your client came to me, offering me information on a federal case. He stole the case file."

"That's a helluvan accusation."

"Come on. We're going to my office to settle this."

"No way. Harold, what the hell is this?"

"I went to see her, sure. But I didn't take anything. You think I'm crazy? Stealing from a cop."

"I've got five witnesses say you were carrying a file when you left by the *side* door."

Harold looked at Zorich and said, "Do I have to take this?"

"No."

"Than let's get the hell out of here."

"Harold." She was walking with him across the courtyard toward the parking lot, her tone different. Typical cop move—try everything, see what works. "Let's back up. I just want my file. And I want to know what you know. I really do. Let's get a cup of coffee. Talk about it."

Harold was almost to Zorich's boaty white Cadillac. "I haven't got your damn file."

"Don't make it hard on yourself. Call me." She pushed a card toward him. He ignored it. Zorich appeared next to him and opened the door. She threw the card in after Harold and it landed on his lap. Zorich whirled around and through the glass Harold heard him saying things like, ". . . very unprofessional . . . subpoena my client if you want to interview him . . . constitutes harassment as outlined in state code . . ."

Harold did his best not to look or listen. But the one time

he did glance up she was leaning around Zorich, totally unconcerned about his stream of legal threats, pointing at Harold through the glass and saying, "I know your name."

The blood was going to be the hardest thing to deal with, she could see that right off. Marianna was standing there on a side street near her Sherman Oaks apartment looking down into the Matsura's trunk. A blistering Saturday afternoon whirled around her—motorcycles accelerating, teenage girls in jog bras on Rollerblades, a gardener with a leaf blower across the street—and here she was looking at human blood in her car trunk. There were even fingernail scratches on the underside of the trunk lid. It gave her a satisfied thrill to think of Vito dying in agony in the tight space. His suffering eliminated her pain and humiliation. A feeling of power and control edged through her residual drowsiness.

Last night her free fall into sleep seemed to bring the whole ugly Vito episode to a close. She got home just before dawn, showered, and fell into bed with an exhaustion she had never known before. It was like dropping off a cliff and falling, deliciously, for an eternity or two. She'd wake up every four hours, feel stiff and tired, and go back to sleep.

Meanwhile, the new day was blown into LA by white-hot Santa Anas. The heat radiated in around pulled shades, turning her sleep feverish and troubled. Pancho felt it, too, and paced the floor, clawing the sofa leg. Every time she came to the surface she thought, it's over now. He's dead now. There's nothing more you need to do.

But around three in the afternoon her dominant thought began to change. In between waves of sleep, she thought of

Harold, in handcuffs, being hauled away in the cruiser, and she wondered if he was still in jail. She had assumed Harold's father would bail him out. But looking back on it, his father didn't seem capable of speaking in complete sentences, let alone finding an attorney and making bond.

In one brief episode of consciousness, she actually made it to the phone, picked it up, and began to call Harold's number. Two hours later the phone in her hand rang and woke her out of the narcotic slumber. She clicked the phone on and listened, but no one spoke. Someone was there, breathing, but no one spoke. She could hear background noises and almost said, "Harold?" But something told her to keep quiet.

As she finally woke up she realized she wanted to see Harold. She wanted to listen to him go over the situation with his orderly mind and say, *You did the right thing, i.e., what else could you do*?

After soaking in the shower until the hot water gave out, she put all her clothes from last night into a trash bag and came out to the car and stood there looking down at the gore in the trunk. That's when she found the gun, the one she'd seen earlier under the front seat of Vito's Mercedes. It must have fallen out of his pocket as she dragged him out of the trunk. She put it in her purse along with the thick wad of hundred-dollar bills she found in his pocket before she disposed of him the night before. That had been a real struggle. But he was gone now, and all that remained was to clean up the mess inside the trunk and pick up her Escort parked near Harold's apartment.

The trunk liner went into a dumpster along with the bag of her clothes. Then she used engine cleaner at a car wash to take off the blood. She knew she couldn't get everything out—cops had sneaky lab tests that could find even a speck of blood—but at least it didn't look like someone had cut a pig's throat in there anymore.

When she was done rinsing the trunk she was dripping with sweat, so she headed back to her apartment to soak it all off in the shower. She was spending a lot of time here, she realized. With the water pouring down on her head she knew she had to find Harold and maybe even endure a meal at Denny's. Tease him about his habits and watch him get all embarrassed. Like in the beginning. Before all this. When it was just an exciting lark. Pull someone's strings and see what they did. How did it get so out of control?

When she got out of the shower the phone was ringing again. Her heart started pounding unexpectedly. She debated not answering, then finally picked it up. No voice. But someone was there. She kept the receiver to her ear for a long time, listening to background noises. The only thing she could make out was a woman saying to someone, "Have you done your rooms yet?" She hung up, got dressed, and left.

She took a cab to Harold's apartment and stood there knocking on the door even though it felt deadly quiet and empty inside. Finally, she gave up and headed for home in her Escort, feeling lonely and let down. She brooded as she drove, paying little attention to where she was going, then realized she was heading north on La Cienega, going over the pass through the hills with their grasshopper oil pumps creaking away. Maybe she'd pull off and see if his truck was still where they left it last night. Then she'd know if he was out. She signaled for the turn, and the Escort dropped off the edge of the pavement and onto the rutted dirt road. As she came around the corner she saw his truck there, the chrome gleaming in the afternoon sun. She cut the ignition and stepped out, not knowing what she was looking for.

Being back in this place made her think of her fight with

Vito. Where had she been parked? She found the tire marks in the dust and saw their footprints. Leaning closer she saw dark spots in the dust. Blood. It was here for anyone who wanted to look. What else was there? The hammer. That was somewhere within a stone's throw of this spot. With his blood on it. His hair. Shit. That's enought to put you away for the rest of your life, she thought. For a dirtbag like Vito, too. No thanks.

She was trying to recall which direction she threw the hammer when the sound of a car door slamming made her jump. On the road up above, a big white Cadillac was idling. A man was walking back up La Cienega to the dirt road. As he turned the corner she saw it was Harold.

Marianna waited until Harold rounded the corner and came down the dusty dirt road with his sport coat over his arm, breathing heavily; then she stepped out and planted herself in his path.

He stopped and stared at her, first as if she were a ghost, then with a flicker of relief and happiness passing over his face like a flash of sunlight; then finally anger and resentment moved in and stayed there.

"What the hell're you doing here?"

"You don't sound exactly overjoyed to see me."

"Spending the night in jail can do that to you."

"You just got out? I thought—"

He began walking again, stepping around her and heading for his truck.

"I figured your dad would bail you out."

He didn't answer.

"So what happened?"

Harold kept walking.

"Harold. I called you. I went by your place. You didn't answer."

He was almost to his truck. She hurried to catch up.

"Harold. Where are you going?"

He was reaching for the handle.

"We have to talk. I have to tell you what I did with—"

"I don't want to know! Okay? Nothing more." He spun around as he said this, and she noticed for the first time how flushed his face was.

"But if the cops come after us, you need to be able to—"

"—say I know nothing. 'Cause I don't. I don't know anything."

She could see his hands shaking as he tried to get the key in the lock. Then she was moving, running at him and grabbing his hand, trying to get the keys so he couldn't leave. He tried to wrestle free but she kept at him, trying to get his arm.

"Don't!" he said, throwing an elbow that caught her flat across the face and dumped her into the dust. Looking up, she saw the struggle in his face, the desire to reach down and help her up. Instead he got in the truck. She jumped up and rushed at him again, but he had the door shut and the power locks were slamming home before she could get him.

When the truck started up she realized she was going to lose him unless she did something. She grabbed the wing mirror. The truck started forward. She jumped up, one foot on the front bumper, her hand in a death grip on the mirror, her other hand on the wiper arm. The truck was picking up speed now, bucking on the rutted dirt road. It was hard to hold on.

He was looking at her through the glass yelling, "Get off!" and "I don't want to hurt you." And she was yelling back at him, "You're not going to leave me."

They had reached La Cienega by now, with the Saturday-afternoon traffic speeding by, drivers looking at this woman attached to the hood of a pickup truck, wondering—as they themselves did—what the hell was going on. Harold hesitated, his foot on the gas.

"That's enough now," he yelled through the glass. "I'm gonna pull out!"

"Go ahead," she yelled back. "I'm not letting go."

He revved the engine and nudged the truck forward, hoping she would lose her nerve and jump off. But she clung there with determination that was both ugly and impressive.

He pulled out into traffic. Fast, faster, faster . . . She looked down at the pavement whirling by underneath. The wind was trying to tear her away from the truck. Her hands were slippery. She'd fall now, she thought, onto this hot LA street, and her body would be hit over and over again by the cars behind them until it was nothing but pieces of raw meat cooking on the pavement.

But then she looked up through the glass and saw Harold's face, as frightened and determined as hers, and they exchanged something, something that caused her to know she wouldn't lose him, and caused him to pull to the shoulder, roll down the window, and simply say, "Okay. Get in the damn truck."

She let go and came around the front of the truck hearing the power locks thump off and knew she had won. If raw willpower could accomplish anything at that moment she could have had the world. The passenger door was open when she got there and she slid in and across the bench seat, hugging Harold and putting her head on his chest, feeling him stroke her hair, and thinking at the same time that she fit nicely there. Just right.

Sometime later she felt the truck starting to move and she realized she didn't give a damn where they were going. As long as they went there together.

There was one other person he really had to call. Vito hesitated before he picked up the phone, thinking what to say to Vikki Covo and what she might ask in return. It would be dicey, no question about it. But it had to be done.

While he played the conversation in his mind he picked at the bandages that came down as far as his eyebrows in front, covered his head down to his neck in back. Wasn't that overdoing things a little? It wasn't like they cut his gourd open or anything. Just took a CAT scan and gave him those drugs to make his brain stop bleeding. And sewed his ear back on.

The young doctor had explained all this in great detail with a grave look on his face. Vito didn't understand a word of it, which gave him great admiration for the doctor. It was a real gift to be able to talk all that time and not have people follow you, but at the same time believe you were probably right. This was a bigger racket than car sales.

Finally he said, "Doc, I'm no rocket scientist. So put it to me this way: What's my out-the-door time of departure?"

The doctor frowned and gave him some more mumbo jumbo about follow-up tests. Obviously, this guy was a pro. They get you in here, start billing your insurance company, and it was gravy-train time. So why would they want to release you?

Vito wondered what his head looked like under the bandages. He knew there were cracks in his skull and plenty of nasty-looking stitches on his shaved scalp. Okay, so he'd have to get himself a decent rug to cover all that up. And his bad leg had gotten worse with all that staggering around. But with a toupee and a new cane he could probably make the dealership by Monday. Then he could smooth all this over and get in position for his big promotion. Make that self-promotion. If he could handle Vikki, keep her from calling the cops.

Vikki had come to all the dealership parties for the past few years. Joe wore her like a hunk of expensive jewelry, letting the guys drool over her world-class bod. But over the years she developed an attitude. For starters she was always zinging you with questions about cars. That made him a bit nervous. How was he supposed to know what went on under the hood? The Japs built great cars and that was basically all you needed to know on the subject.

Vikki answered on the first ring. "Hello." The tone of her voice told Vito everything. No one had called her. Here it was late Saturday afternoon and she was worried as hell. And she was dying for some news.

"Vik. It's Vito Fiorre."

"Yes." She was bracing herself for bad news.

"Ah, Joe asked me to call you."

"Where is he?"

"I'll get to that in a sec. First, I got to tell you some unpleasant things."

"Is he all right?"

"Joe?" Vito laughed as if the thought that he was otherwise never crossed his mind. "Physically, Joe's fine. But he's in a jam. That's why he had to take off."

"Take off? Where is he?"

"Vik. Hold on. Okay? I'll get to that."

"But he's all right. Right?"

"I told you. He's fine. But here's the deal. I won't go into detail—I mean it'd be very boring to you basically, but—"

"Tell me everything."

"Frankly, Vik, it's very complicated. There's no point in trying to—"

"Don't patronize me. I want to know everything."

See, this was the problem with her. She looked like a bimbo but acted like a ball buster.

"Vik, I'm sorry, I had no intention of patronizing you. You have to understand, I'm in a delicate position here. I don't know how much Joe told you about what was going on down at the dealership."

"Not very much," she said quietly.

"Okay. So I don't want to violate that husband-wife thing. But at the same time I want to help you out."

"What about Joe?"

"And I want to help Joe too, of course. So you have to go with me on this one, Vik. And when I say there's something I really can't tell you you have to—"

"What happened last night? I know he was entertaining some hotshots from Cincinnati. Tom Bales and LaBounty."

Oh, man, she was really into this. "Yeah," Vito said, feeling his way along. "We bought them dinner and—"

"Who's Dash?"

"Dash is, well, a friend of Joe's that . . ." He scrambled to come up with something more substantial. Maybe he had lost a few brain cells.

"Is he a pimp?"

"Vik, don't be ridiculous."

"I have his number. I'll call him and ask him what he does if you can't remember."

"Let me put this to you in the simplest possible terms."

"That's the only way I'll understand it."

"There you go again, getting defensive. That's not going to help."

"Well, Vito, when Joe didn't come home last night, I

realized I really didn't know anything about his life—what he does down there. He could be a drug dealer for all I know."

Vito laughed until his head hurt. It was from relief really. She guessed, but guessed wrong.

"Vik, Joe's no drug dealer. He's a businessman. A very savvy businessman. But this is a dirty game. If he didn't tell you what was going on it was to protect you. See, to get the premium cars you have to do favors for the guys in Cincinnati. They fly out here and we show them a good time, give them stuff."

"Bribes."

"Gifts. It's how the business is run. But lately the Feds found out about it and started putting pressure on Cincinnati and now it's CYA time."

"CYA?"

"Cover your ass, if you'll excuse the expression."

"But I don't understand. Why are they trying to cover their asses?"

"It's very involved Vikki but, see, the number of cars we can get is controlled by the Feds."

"Why?"

"You know the government—they try to control everything."

"So Joe was breaking the law."

"That's not for me to say. I mean, that's more of an ethical thing."

"Out of your area."

"Right." Wait a second, Vito thought, was that a put-down? He continued anyway, saying, "Last night things didn't go too well and Joe realized he might be in a certain amount of danger."

"Danger of what?"

"In physical danger."

"From who?"

time but hadn't ever let himself. His expression and silence worried her.

"What? What are you thinking?" She was natural and relaxed for the first time.

"I feel—I don't know. I can't describe it." Tears were coming to his eyes and he blinked to hide them, ashamed.

But she was laughing, as happy as the bubbles forming around them, laughing and hugging him with her breasts alive against his chest.

"It's all right, Harold. It's all right to feel good. Don't you see? Our problems are over."

"But this hit-and-run—"

"It doesn't matter—"

"—this DMV lady's on my ass—"

"It will work out."

"How?"

"I don't know right now. But it will. I feel it. Our troubles are over."

At that moment he believed her. And that feeling carried through hours of incredible sex in the spa and more on the king-sized bed.

But sometime in the middle of the night, in that stage when you wake up suddenly sober and realize there isn't a chance in hell you're getting back to sleep, Harold realized that his problems were far from over. They were, in fact, stacking up by the second, like jets in bad weather, waiting to land with ever-increasing urgency. The fact of the matter was that jail was just too real a possibility. It didn't matter whether he landed there for a hit-and-run, stealing federal documents, or a murder he didn't technically commit. He didn't want to be there.

It was at that moment that her voice came to him through the darkness of the motel room, flat and drained, as if she was speaking from the bottom of her soul.

"These guys from Cincinnati."

"You mean they might—?"

"It's conceivable. So he took off. Just for a week or two. He's gonna get himself a good lawyer and figure out how to protect himself."

There was a pause as she thought it over. He couldn't tell whether she was buying it or not.

"What about the dealership?" she finally asked.

"Joe asked me to run it till he gets back."

"You?"

"Yeah. Me."

More silence.

"What does this Dash have to do with it all?"

"He—well—he set up some entertainment for Bales and LaBounty."

"Entertainment."

"Yeah. Couple of girls came in and danced a little."

"Ballet or folk?"

Vito allowed himself a laugh. "It was kind of like those singing telegrams." Except with attachments, he wanted to add. "So the point of all this is Joe wants you not to be worried and not to go to the police or anything."

There it was, out in the open. Now what would she do?

"I want to believe you but—"

"Believe me? Vik, I'm just giving you a message. You can believe it or not."

More silence. This was tougher than he'd thought.

"Look, I know how tight you and Joe are. So for his sake, don't call the cops. And in a few days either he'll get in touch with you or get me a message to give you."

Pause. "Vito, where are you?"

"Home."

"What's your number there?"

"Best way to reach me is my beeper."

"Give me both numbers."

After he did, and hung up, he called his home. The answering machine didn't pick up. That meant he was on call waiting because someone had already dialed in. That meant she didn't buy his story. But it might slow her down long enough for him to do what he had to do.

"I can't believe I did that," Marianna giggled. She was lounging in the huge tiled Jacuzzi in their Spa King room at the Best Western in Costa Mesa. "What did I look like out there hanging on to the side of your truck? No. Don't tell me. I don't want to know."

Harold filled up her glass from the sweating quart bottle of Pete's Wicked Ale they had bought at Von's before checking into the motel. He had a towel wrapped around his waist and he was worried it would fall off. He wasn't as relaxed as she was about being naked. She dropped her clothes the second the door was closed and headed for the spa.

"You looked like one hell of a determined woman," Harold said, dropping the towel just long enough to step into the sudsy water with a satisfied groan. It felt so good. With the beer working in his bloodstream and the world closed out, the universe was reduced to just this hotel room, just this moment. What lay beyond these walls and this night was frightening and uncontrollable. But for this small compartment of time Harold felt he could be happier than ever before.

"Last night it all became clear to me," she said, pausing to taste the beer. She smacked her lips. "Mmmmmm. That's good."

"What became clear?"

"Why we met, why we should be together. That's why I had to stop you back there."

"Why?"

"Remember the story you told me? About how you were in a coma and saw God?"

He nodded, drinking, and wondering with a small corner of his mind if he had bought enough beer.

"You said you worried 'cause you'd said no to God. Remember? Well, I believe God gives you the chance to make up for the bad things you've done. To, like, redeem yourself."

She smiled at him as if it should all be clear now. Her face was incredibly radiant, like there was light coming from just below the surface of her skin. Problem here was, he didn't understand what she was getting at. Liked her energy, didn't get her point. She read his expression.

"Look, I was out of control. I could have gotten pulled down by Vito and all that bad stuff. But you were there to catch me. To save me. And by doing that you redeemed yourself."

"You mean God's not mad at me anymore?"

"Exactly."

"The slate is clear?"

She rose out of the water, bubbles on her glistening shoulders, breasts, and stomach, and made the sign of the cross above him. "Go in peace, my son. Your sins are forgiven," she laughed.

It made him a little nervous to be kidding about God things. Still, her words carried a strange and wonderful weight, echoing cathedral-like in the tiled room above the hum of the Jacuzzi motor. Deep inside he felt the continental plates of his soul shifting. Something huge broke away, tugging him toward somewhere he'd wanted to go for a long

"I threw him over the side of a mountain, Harold. I drove way the hell up to Santa Barbara and—"

"I don't want to know."

"Please."

He waited, knowing he would hear it.

"I stopped in a rest area."

He knew she was seeing this as she was telling him. Seeing it, and enjoying it.

"I dragged him to the edge and threw him over the side. I saw him start rolling and then he disappeared and I could hear him rolling and crashing down there for a long time."

They were both quiet for a while, breathing in the dark side by side. Then she spoke again, her voice as lifeless as the night.

"He's down there, Harold, and he's never coming back. The coyotes are going to get him. Or the maggots. Someday they'll find a skeleton and they'll never know who it is. I'm glad he's down there and I don't give a damn what anybody thinks."

A little while later her breathing became heavy and when he touched her forehead it was warm with sweat, like a baby's, her body getting—or giving off—some strange energy, making him wonder what God thought of them at this moment. He was pretty sure they weren't forgiven—neither of them.

Harold dressed in the unfamiliar light coming through gauzy motel curtains and quietly let himself out. He found the lobby deserted except for an Indian clerk behind the counter watching a Schwarzenegger flick on cable.

"Can't sleep," Harold explained.

"What?" the clerk asked, turning the volume down.

"I have trouble sleeping," Harold said. "I'm just going to sit here awhile."

The clerk turned back to his movie as the screen filled up

with a fireball of an explosion. Harold took out a three-by-five card and his pen. A half hour later he looked at the list he had written out:

"How to Stay Out of Jail"

1. Get a good lawyer and hope you win your trial
2. Represent yourself (not recommended)
3. Plead guilty and hope you get a suspended sentence
4. Trade information on a larger crime
5. Don't show up for court and hope they don't catch you
6. Change your identity

He sat there for a long time, reviewing the list and searching for a seventh option. He liked lists of seven steps because seven was a lucky number. Something told him that if he could find a seventh alternative it would be the one he would choose.

He put the list in his shirt pocket and headed back to the room. When he opened the door the room was too quiet. In the weak light he saw the bed was nothing more than a mess of twisted sheets. Through the curtain he saw a taxi idling and heard its door slam shut.

Harold watched the taxi pull away, then sat on the edge of the cold bed with his head in his hands.

There was a huge stack of requisitions waiting in Marianna's box when she got to work Monday morning. They had piled up at the end of last week when her attendance was less than perfect. Hefting the stack she realized they would take at least two days to finish. Two days of repetitive, mind-numbing work. It gave her a sudden sense of claustrophobic panic to think of being trapped here, buried under the dull work as she had so many times in the past.

With the stack of requisitions in her hand she swung by Harold's office. It was time to say hello, to let him know she wasn't mad at him. Her departure from the motel had more to do with a very practical matter. She didn't think it was wise to leave her Escort parked at La Cienega and Stocker. So she had the cabdriver drop her off there, then drove back to her apartment, thinking how worried Harold had seemed. There was nothing to be concerned about now, she had wanted to tell him. Not even the fact that she had both cars again—though not the Escort's pink slip. But she would handle that somehow, and whatever else might come up.

But Harold wasn't in his office, and the sight of his empty desk cut into her mood like a shadow across the sun. She counted on him always being there when she wanted him. Where was he? Probably running late. Probably swinging one of his little deals for a grand or two. No, I know, she thought, laughing inside, he's at Denny's telling the waitress, "One glass with water and one with just ice, extra napkins, and salsa on the side."

Marianna's phone was ringing when she got back to her desk. She thought of the calls she'd been getting at home and wondered if anyone would be on the other end of this one. Only one way to find out, she thought, picking up the receiver and feeling her system kick up a notch in anticipation of the unknown.

"Marianna Perado speaking."

There was a pause and an intake of breath on the other end of the line.

"Yes, ah, Marianna, this is Joe Covo. At Joe Covo Matsura."

The dial on her adrenaline meter shot up, then settled at the halfway mark. A second or two later she heard herself saying, "Yes, Joe, what can I do for you?"

"Ah, we need to talk."

"We do?"

"Yes, we do." There was an odd quality to his voice. Like it was being put through a shredder or something.

"I see here you purchased a car from us . . . '89 Matsura Accell. Took possession last Wednesday . . ."

Christ, was it just last Wednesday?

". . . and traded a . . . '82 Ford Escort." He said the word distastefully, like it was a piece of junk.

"Not exactly," Marianna said, feeling the old anger rising again, giving her what she needed to deal with this new dirtball. "You see, one of your salesmen, Vito Fiorre, made a mistake—"

"Let me cut you off here for a second, Marianna. Vito told me all about this last week."

"He did?"

"Yes, and, frankly, I expected him to take care of it by now. But, well, I'm embarrassed to admit it, but he hasn't. In fact, I don't know how to say this but, we don't exactly know where he is. So I thought, rather than let this drag on I'd step in and clear it up. And I'll deal with Vito when he turns up."

And that will be when hell freezes over, she thought, feeling back on top again.

"So why don't you stop by, bring in the Matsura, and we'll unwind the deal."

U*nwind*, there was that word again. They all said it.

"And you'll give me the pink slip on the Escort?"

"If you want to buy it back, okay. I mean, I don't see what you're so unhappy about."

"Because you ripped me off. That's why."

"Marianna, please. I don't know exactly what Vito promised you here but, well, sometimes he gets carried away. But with the best of intentions."

Marianna laughed.

"Hey, believe it or not, Vito is one of our top sales guys. Always has been. But if you're dissatisfied I'll take care of you."

"You will?"

"Listen, no one goes away from Joe Covo's unhappy. It's a rule of mine. So when can I expect you?"

"I think I could make it on my lunch hour. Twelve, twelve-fifteen."

"Fine. And, Marianna, Vito made a note that your dad was with you last time."

"He's *not* my dad."

"Whatever. Will he be with you this time?"

"I don't know. Why?"

"There's no need to bring anyone else. This is all cut-and-dried."

She hung up thinking *perfect.* All the loose ends taken care of. Wait till Harold hears about this. Maybe then he'll get that worried look off his face. Maybe he should come with me, she thought, remembering what it was like to be in that tight little salesroom with Vito scribbling figures on his yellow pad, pushing them around and stabbing a finger at the open space for her signature.

She walked by Harold's office again and saw it was still empty. Okay. That was okay. She could take care of this on her own. Just like she took care of Vito.

"Ready to do it, big guy?"

Zorich was crouched next to Harold in the hallway of the courthouse in Long Beach, talking to him like a high school football coach. Harold hated his facing-up-to-the-music tone of voice and wondered if he was going to give him a lecture on his other responsibilities next, like personal hygiene. Zorich had just come out of his meeting with the assistant DA with the exciting news (or so he thought) that they would drop the charges on the police chase if he pleaded to the earlier charge of leaving the scene of an accident. Zorich wanted him to plead. Harold wasn't so sure.

It was almost noon, and Harold had been waiting on the hard wooden bench since 8:00 A.M. At first he had scanned the paper to see if they found the body. When he saw nothing he dully stared out the fifth-floor windows in front of him, out across the metro sprawl of palm trees and flimsy apartment buildings to the dark clouds rolling in from the west, chasing out the Santa Ana winds. An hour later it was coming down like it had been raining his whole life.

Harold's emotional barometer fell with the weather. And, as he looked around him at the shyster lawyers and their scumbag clients, the stringy-haired heavy-metalers and gang-bangers with pants drooping on their skinny asses, he realized that he had fallen face first into a human cesspool. If he kept sinking he'd soon be drinking the filth, eating it, and sleeping in it. He lowered his eyes to the worn tile floor of this overrun hellhole and his heart ached for that sunny life he'd chased all his life: a good woman who loved him, a stable home, and, yes, even a kid. A good kid, interested in kid stuff, science projects, and baseball—not drugged-out killers like the ones around him here. Where was that life he ached for? And would Marianna ever lead him there?

A door nearby banged. He jumped and looked up for Zorich. Instead he saw a woman—a girl really—with the biggest black eye he'd ever seen. The signs of torn lives were all around him and he was going down. Down, down, down. Marianna was all he had to hold on to. She was real. He needed her. And she needed him, too. Why couldn't she see that? If they could just get past this and find their way back onto that road, the road that led to the house on a quiet street, to the family and—

The door opened and Zorich slid out, still chuckling over something someone inside said. He quickly put on his grave face and gave a "so-so" hand gesture as he crossed the hallway and crouched beside Harold, pants hiking up on lizard-skin cowboy boots.

"So, definitely no prison?" Harold had asked after Zorich laid out the deal.

"If the judge wanted to be a complete asshole, he could give you a couple of months. But he won't. The prisons are exploding as it is. You gotta practically kill someone to get in these days." *Why did he have to put it that way*? "So basically, no. No prison."

"Okay then."

"Ready?"

"Yeah. Ready."

Harold stood up and they walked together into a cramped conference room. The walls were yellowed and bare with a single window looking south out over the harbor where jagged cranes loomed over hulking freighters. A dark wood table was set in the middle of the room. On it were case files and Starbucks paper coffee cups. Someone had been smoking, and the air was stale and spent. At the table was the detective who was at the interrogation after his arrest—the sharp Hispanic—and a young assistant DA with sandy hair and a thick mustache he kept pulling on. He looked too young to be in a position of authority, let alone to be sitting in judgment of Harold's life.

As the door closed Harold's heart suddenly began hammering in his chest. They knew all about the body in the trunk, he thought, and they'd lured him here with innocuous babble about a hit-and-run accident. Heart-attack time. It was coming for sure this time. His heart would explode and he'd pitch forward on the table, blood gushing from every pore in his body and then they'd know. Know that he was guilty of far more than a stupid traffic offense.

"This is my client, Harold Dodge," Zorich said.

The cop nodded minimally as the DA said, "Harold, I'm Dennis Parker, the assistant DA. Your counsel has informed us that you would be willing to plead to leaving the scene of a serious-injury accident. Is that correct?"

"Yes."

"You understand that, if convicted, this carries a possible sentence under California law of up to four years in state prison?"

"Yes, I do."

"And you still wish to plead guilty?"

"I will plead guilty, yes."

"Okay then. You will need to enter a formal plea at your court appearance Tuesday morning at ten-thirty in Judge Vollick's courtroom. Is that clear?"

"Yes."

Zorich had his hands on the armrests of the chair, ready to push himself up, when Parker said, "Ah, there's one more matter before us. Detective Torres?"

The Hispanic leaned forward. "Harold, as long as you're here, and your attorney is here too, we have a few questions concerning another matter."

Harold's heartbeat accelerated wildly. It was so loud he could barely hear Zorich as he sputtered, "Wait a second—"

"Counsel, it'll only take a moment, and it'll save us picking him up at his workplace or home. Don't you agree it's easier this way?"

"Why don't you just tell me what the hell this is all about?"

Torres was moving around the table to the door as he said, "I'll let Detective Gammon tell you."

Here it comes, Harold thought as Torres opened the door and motioned to someone in the hallway. It's starting now. They're going to find the body and I'll spend the rest of my life in prison, my teeth rotting, hair falling out.

The doorway was filled by an enormous man who seemed to have to duck to keep from bumping his head on the doorframe. He had bushy brown hair and a wild beard out of which came a long thin black cigarette. Somewhere inside all that hair and whiskers and smoke were two little black eyes that seemed both angry and frightened at the same time. High on his hip, in a leather holster worn shiny in spots, was a gigantic silver automatic handgun.

"Thanks, chief," Gammon said to Torres. He pointed at Parker by way of greeting and his eyes finally met Harold. "I'm Detective Gammon," he said in a voice that sounded like broken glass being poured from a truck. Then he added a word that went through Harold like a bullet: "Homicide."

"I'm Bill Zorich. Mr. Dodge's attorney."

"I knew that," Gammon said, smiling, small sharp animal teeth appearing in the darkness of his beard. He gestured at Zorich. "Nice suit, chief."

"Listen, I want to know what this is about," Zorich huffed.

"Of course you do."

Gammon took a seat across from Harold and sat there looking at him. The room seemed to be filling up with his presence. Finally he spoke: "Someone doesn't like you."

Harold waited a long time for more, then looked at Zorich for instructions.

"You don't have to say anything."

Gammon sighed. Then, almost sympathetically, he said, "Someone's trying to tell us you were involved in a homicide."

All Harold's systems were in chaos—heart, lungs, brain. But somehow he managed to say, with just the right tone of annoyance, "The hell's that supposed to mean?"

"Someone called the bureau, gave us your name and said you'd killed a man."

"You gonna tell me who said that?"

"I would if I could. It's what the newspapers call an anonymous tip." He grinned at Harold, watching him closely, enjoying putting him on the spot and seeing him sweat. But wouldn't anyone sweat in this position? Harold was sure they would.

The room was suddenly very still except for the rain on the window. Harold sensed the other men around him breathing, wondering who was going to speak next, who knew what and what would be said. He concentrated on keeping his mouth shut and returning Gammon's stare, pretending he was in a selling room at the dealership with a prospect and negotiations had broken down.

"Whoever it is calling us knows a lot about you, Harold. Knows about this little deal with the Lakewood cops, knows they never sprung the trunk on that Matsura you were driving. Knows you were up in the oil fields at La Cienega and Stoker before you started playing Mario Andretti. Who's saying these things about you, Harold?"

Harold was silent.

"What're you into?"

Harold looked at Zorich. Zorich shook his head almost imperceptibly. *Don't say anything.*

Gammon's voice was so soft it was almost inaudible as he asked, "Why did they tell us to look for a hammer up there? Up at La Cienega and Stoker? A hammer with blood on it."

Marianna. The name flashed into Harold's brain like a message on a billboard. It could have only been Marianna. Anger and sadness rolled through his system like a tidal wave, destroying the house in the suburbs, his sunny life with her, and the kid. All gone. It was all gone.

Harold couldn't keep his emotions off his face and Gammon saw it. He leaned toward Harold, smelling the truth rising to the surface like a hungry dog.

Harold couldn't trust himself to speak. He let his eyes wander past Gammon and out the window to the rain falling on his world, washing the pieces of his life down the storm drain and out into the harbor with all the rest of the garbage. He knew then that no one cared about him, not a single person on the face of the entire earth.

"We can spend all day looking for that hammer," Gammon was saying. "We can look all week. But my hunch is that you can tell us everything we need to know. And I'll tell you something else, chief, my gut tells me you're clean. Whoever's calling us is the one we want. Help yourself, Harold. What the hell's going on here?"

Harold knew this gorilla didn't give a damn about him. It was a job for Gammon. He just wanted to clear a case, make his job easier. But for Harold, his whole existence was at stake. But he couldn't help reacting to the friendly tone, the simple request. He wanted to unburden himself. To be done with this mess.

Yes, he'd talk. But only after he made a little trip to Santa Barbara. The only way he'd be ever be convicted of murder was if the cops found a body. Until then, it was all talk. And everyone knew talk was cheap.

It wasn't what Marianna had expected at all. When she asked the receptionist to see Joe Covo she thought she'd be led into a gaudy office where the fabled salesman was waiting in plaid pants, pinky rings gleaming and girlie calendars on the walls. Instead she was shown down a long dark hallway to a heavy wood door that swung open on an exotic lair.

It was dark in here, very dark, especially with the rain hammering down outside, and a whisper of FM music oozed into the room from various hidden sources. A single chair sat in front of an enormous desk centered on an Oriental rug. There was nothing on the desk, not even, she thought, a single speck of dust. The only sign of the person who occupied this office was a row of pictures on the shelf behind the leather executive chair. Wedding pictures. Embarrassingly personal in this stark setting.

"He's with a customer right now. But he'll be right with you," the receptionist said, retreating from the room even as she was still talking. Was it Marianna's imagination, or was she acting nervous, like she was in on something she didn't want to be part of?

Marianna took the chair and readjusted it to an off-center position in front of the formidable desk, hoping to throw him off balance. Let him turn to see me, she thought, let him get a stiff neck.

As the tomblike door closed behind her, she heard the music more clearly and, in the distance, the harsh call of a PA paging some poor schmuck of a car salesman. Harold had once worked here, she remembered, trying to picture him as young and slim and hungry. He probably stood before this desk, or sat in this hot seat. She shuddered, thinking how nice it would be to have Harold here with her now. He'd know how to handle this joker. Know how to deal with anything the guy throws at her. He'd just sit there with his unblinking gray eyes and stare the guy down. Why was it she felt so good about Harold when he wasn't around?

The door opened behind her with a whoosh of cool air. She heard footsteps on the Oriental rug, uneven footsteps,

Then we got the fat asses of a bunch of guys in the national office. All that's riding on the book."

"The book?"

"The little black book in my briefcase. What's in it will put those guys away."

"LaBounty, Bales?"

Vito smiled. "You never cease to amaze me. How'd you know that?"

"I've been working on this whole thing from another angle," she said, remembering the case file Harold stole from the DMV. "Vito, you really think they'll let a little twerp like you push them around, just because you've got this book."

"I can handle LaBounty."

"And the guy he sends after you?"

"No one's gonna touch me as long as I have that book. I control the book, I control the dealership. That's a couple million bucks a year easy. You get me the book, I get the dealership. I make it worth your while—big-time."

He let it hang there in the air for a minute before finishing. "Where's the book?"

She needed time to see all the options here. So she said, "You already called it, Vito. He's got it."

"Dad-boy?"

"Harold."

He studied her expression, his damaged face straining painfully.

"What is it with you and that guy?"

"Who said there was anything there?"

"I say 'Dad-boy,' you say Harold. With this, like, *tone*. This tone that tells me there's something going on. But I can't figure it. Belly hanging over his belt. Makes me sick to think of you and him."

"Of course it does. If it isn't about you, you don't give a damn."

she realized, suddenly stabbed by uneasiness, although she couldn't exactly say why. She was trying to find the source of her anxiety when a figure brushed her arm heading around the edge of the enormous desk.

Don't look around. Don't seem too eager. She forced herself not to look up, preparing an opening line, wondering if she should rise and shake his hand or let him make the first move, set the tone of the meeting.

Oddly, this man seemed to be keeping his back to her, his white shirt and black hair suggesting a younger man than she expected, suggesting, in fact, a familiar person, one she had put out of her mind with complete finality. And so, even as it was somehow beginning to dawn on her who this was, he was turning and thrusting his face toward her, saying in a loud voice, "Hi, Marianna!"

Vito! It looked like Vito! But it couldn't be!

"You look a little surprised to see me!" he was saying, laughing at what he saw on her face, laughing hoarsely in that crushed-windpipe voice with dark circles under his eyes and a skewed look to his face as if it had been reassembled with missing pieces.

Vito. She had beaten Vito to death then thrown him away. To be eaten by coyotes or rot in the sun on a mountainside.

Vito was dead.

Vito was standing in front of her.

Marianna fought her body. It wanted to shove back in the chair. To run from the room. To hide somewhere until she could reorder reality and figure out what in holy hell had gone wrong.

"You look like you've seen a ghost," he was saying, laughing maniacally, practically in tears.

"Shut up, Vito," she heard herself say, hoping the words sounded better than the raging storm in her head.

"I'm not Vito. I'm Joe Covo," he said, spreading his arms and gesturing at the office. "See? I'm in Joe Covo's office. I must be Joe Covo."

"You'll never be anything more than what you are, Vito. Now stop laughing and tell me what you're doing here."

Vito came around the desk and sat right in front of her, making her want to shrink back in revulsion as if he was cold, cold as a corpse. He didn't look well, she was pleased to see. So she had hurt him. But she hadn't finished him off. He had returned.

"You see, Vito couldn't be here today. Vito has disappeared," he said, echoing the words he'd told her on the phone. "Strange as it may sound, we think that someone killed Vito. Now who the hell would do that?"

"Vito, you're not scaring me with this stupid act."

"No?" He reached out toward her face to stroke her cheek. She batted his arm away, the fire suddenly flaring up inside her again as she realized that, whatever happened to bring him back, the real tragedy was that he wasn't dead. All her feelings of control disappeared and left her furious, impatient to deal with him again.

He was seeing the rage in her eyes and was impressed. "I gotta admit. I thought you'd run screaming into the street."

"Hoped I would. That's why you got me down here."

"Not exactly," he said, returning to the black leather chair behind the desk.

Her mind was accepting it now. He was alive. But she had thrown *someone* down that mountainside. Someone who was cold and lifeless and covered with blood. She remembered wrestling the body out of the trunk and thinking it felt heavy for a skinny shit like Vito. Her eyes moved from Vito to the row of pictures behind him on the sideboard. Wedding pictures of a middle-aged man and a stunning wife. Joe Covo.

She remembered gripping the bloody arm, slippery in her grasp, and feeling the ring. A *wedding ring*.

"Why'd you kill Covo?" She was guessing, but she watched as his face clouded and darkness filled his eyes.

And she knew then her guess was right. She didn't know how or why he'd killed Covo. But she knew he had. And that shared knowledge pulled them together in that dark room with the rain falling outside.

"I'm not gonna bore you, Marianna. Suffice it to say, it's a long sad chain of events. And we need to do something about it." Vito's eyes slid off her and wandered out the window.

"We? You killed him. It's your problem."

"They come looking for Joe and find me. I give them you. Who are you gonna give them?"

"You, of course."

"Of course. But why? I mean, it's pointless, when you think of it. We're birds of a feather, you and me."

"I'm not following you."

"I heard an old saying somewhere: 'There's only one way three people can keep a secret.' " He paused, moving back around the desk. " 'And that's if one of them is dead.' "

"I heard it was if two of them are dead."

"Whatever. What I'm proposing here is, let's join forces." He was leaning in close now, and his voice hissed as he added, "Let's get Dad-boy. He's the one we should have been after since the beginning."

"Keep going," Marianna said, buying time as she turned it over in her mind. She thought she saw a way.

"Got your attention, huh?" He was an eager salesman with a prospect that was finally warming up.

"You gotta understand. There's a hell of a lot more going on here than just you and me. We got a dealership at stake.

"That's where you're wrong. I'm a very bighearted guy. Ask anyone."

"Like Joe Covo."

Vito stood up and turned away. She continued.

"Or maybe I should ask Joe Covo's pretty little wife waiting for him to come home."

"Yes, well . . . Like I said, that was a very sad chain of events, Marianna. One in which you played a significant role. I'm here now asking you to help me find some good in all the shit that's happened. Get me Dad-boy—and I'll get the book."

"One more thing," she said, seeing how she could wrap all this up for good. "Bring me the pink slip."

"The pink slip?"

"On my Escort."

"You're joking. Right?"

"Do I look like I'm joking?"

"Fine. Whatever you say. When do we meet?"

She was quiet for a moment, thinking of her options. There were several now. Several very viable options. She wasn't sure which one she'd take. So for now she just said, "Tonight. Let's do it tonight."

"Time and place?"

"To be arranged. I mean, I better talk to Dad-boy first. Right?"

Vito smiled.

Slade could hear the doorbell echo inside the apartment. It felt empty. The whole damn building felt empty and silent, pasted up against the Hollywood Hills on a dead-end street. It couldn't be a better location for what he had to do. He took out the pick and slid it in and over the tumblers, feeling it slip and grab, slip and fit until, yes, the knob was turning. Whoever lived here thought a key lock would stop someone like him. Either that or he didn't give a damn about his things. That was clear to Slade as the door swung open.

It was neglected, undecorated, and careless. He was in a hallway with a kitchen to his right and the living room straight ahead. It was silent and gloomy; the only noise was the rain spatting against the sliding-glass door leading out on a balcony where a mountain bike stood rusting in the acidic rain falling from a lead sky.

It had been a while since Slade did a job like this. But he was pleased to find that all his senses were reliably feeding him information. For two months he'd been building his body back up, lifting cases of beer in a liquor-store cooler. But the eleven years he'd spent in prison hadn't dulled his senses. He could feel the stale dampness, the silence of the rooms, the stillness of the walls around him. Empty, he thought. It feels empty.

Rustle.

He spun around and met the unblinking eyes of an iguana in a glass tank. It had outgrown its cage, was bigger than the ones that looked down on him from tree limbs in El Salvador. It was undernourished and neglected. Slade hated anyone who would do this to another living thing. It gratefully scrambled over the top of the tank when he took the glass lid off. He'd find some food for it later.

His customary visual inspection took only a few minutes to confirm that he was alone here (no one in the bedroom) and that someone had been here as recently as this morning (the shower stall was still wet). Only one person lived here (one of everything and no sign of recent visitors).

He also had the sense he wouldn't find what he was looking for. Whoever lived here was disorganized and careless. Too scattered to systematically collect and hide incriminating documents. In fact, Slade saw little that told him what this man did, except for the Ferrari poster on the living-room wall.

There was only one place of affection in this loveless apartment. The TV. It was as if the entire apartment was created for its existence. Wide screen and huge speakers, VCR, leather armchair and footstool, coaster on the glass side table next to the cordless phone and answering machine. The TV would take you away from this loveless empty box in this plastic city. Give me the desert anytime, Slade thought, or the jungle. Give me nothing, and I'll have something.

The makeshift office area had nothing of interest and looked like it was never used. One locked filing drawer opened easily with a twist of Slade's commando knife blade, but there was little in it. The mortgage on the condo. Some car insurance papers for a Mercedes 560 SEL. The phone messages contained nothing but more evidence of a worthless life, one spent in meaningless detail.

B*oom*.

Slade felt and heard the downstairs entrance door slam, shaking the flimsy building. He took up a position behind the front door, the place he'd decided on when he first entered. The footsteps were coming. And he felt his body preparing, a feeling he had last experienced in a prison fight, but not since he'd been paroled. He looked down and saw the iguana waiting too, looking up at him and feeling the movement with a flick of his dry tongue. Someone was coming . . . Coming . . . Coming . . .

But now Slade could tell they were short steps, and the heels were hard on the stairs. A woman. There was a pause in the hallway outside, a jingle of keys, and the door across the hallway opened, then slammed shut. Silence, then the sound of a TV. Good. He could move freely again.

The false alarm showed him he would respond. He felt no

fear. Only a certainty that he could handle whoever was coming through the door. That was the most important thing. To *know* that you would be victorious. It didn't matter that his senses weren't fully attuned to the outside world, or that his body was that of a sixty-eight-year-old man. His mind was still fit.

The leather armchair complained as Slade lowered himself into it and picked up the phone from the glass side table. As he waited for an answer he saw his reflection in the empty glass eye of the blank TV screen, hairless and nearly toothless, a frightening figure of justice. He was, as one of his employers once said, "a man you couldn't lie to."

"Yeah." It was how LaBounty answered the phone.

"I'm in," Slade said, noticing the iguana next to his right leg.

"And . . ."

"Nothing."

"Nothing?"

"No briefcase. No book. No papers."

LaBounty thought about that. "Then he has it with him."

"If he has it."

"He has it. He said he has it."

"That doesn't mean he has it. He could be lying."

LaBounty thought about that. "We'll assume he's not."

"There is another way to find out."

"What's that?"

"Let me talk to him. Find out if he's lying."

"How do you do that? I mean, how do you know for sure."

"There's a point at which you can tell."

"What do you mean?"

"I'll give him a religious experience."

"Okay," LaBounty said suddenly. Then: "So talk to him."

"I will."

Slade set the phone down, wondering about something

he'd read somewhere. *You can't be honest with others until you learn to tell yourself the truth.* Who said that? He'd have to look it up next time he was in the library. He looked across at his reflection in the TV screen and saw he was reaching into his pocket and pulling out the small book. He had first read the Koran when he was head-hunting in the Middle East. It made sense in context, in the desert where he was sent to kill men, one on one, life or death. And it made sense when he reread it for eleven years in his cell at Pelican Bay, serving time for killing two men with his bare hands.

Those Arabs got it right, Slade thought, feeling the familiar delicate paper under his rough fingertips. Out there in the desert. In their tents. They felt God. The desert didn't lie to you. Los Angeles was a desert once. To him, it still was.

Boom.

The front door slammed, shaking the building. Footsteps coming up the steps with urgency. Slade saw his reflection tuck away the book and glide from the chair and to his feet, standing in the gloom next to the front door.

A man you couldn't lie to.

Harold had been driving north on Highway 101 for about an hour, battling traffic through the Valley, when he realized the rain was good. Good for what he had to do. He had the rope and the plastic tarp in the truck bed. No one would be out in this weather nosing around. No cops eager to get out of their cruisers and ask what the hell he was hauling. Thinking this, he felt his mood lighten slightly as he pushed onward, the rain steady on the pickup's roof, fogging the edges of the windshield until he felt like he was getting tunnel vision.

The 101 finally climbed out of the Valley and, for the first time, he found himself free of the LA sprawl. Glimpses of mountains on the left with dark shapes he knew were live oaks. And farmland to his right. Neat rows of low plants stretching across the rain-soaked field.

The radio poured chaos into his ears. Rising rivers, flooded houses, mud slides, children washed into swollen creeks and out to sea. Traffic accidents everywhere. Overturned trucks. Now, as he came over the pass and started down into Simi Valley, the reception began to break up. He snapped off the radio and was left with the therapy ball in his palm and his own thoughts, dark thoughts of Marianna. Another bright hope reduced to ashes. His life was a long string of broken relationships and disappointment. Why did he even try anymore? But he did. And he knew he would do it again.

Of course, how could he blame himself? There was something between them they both could feel. Chemistry? Christ, he didn't even know what that was. But he did know he was inexplicably pulled toward her again and again, even when her actions would make anyone else think she was a psycho. But he understood her. That was the scary part. Because, if she was a psycho, and he understood her, what did that make him? He didn't want to know.

And now it looked like she was getting ready to slip the old knife in his back, giving him to the cops for Vito's murder. Why? Maybe the cops had found her and were already starting to squeeze the story out of her. But the way they told it she was volunteering information. And Harold knew that he was the one with his dick on the chopping block. He was going to have to take steps before the ax fell. Once he had moved the only real evidence that a murder had been committed, he could relax. Then he would find out why Marianna had blown the whistle on him.

Santa Barbara County. The green sign flashed at him between wiper blades.

I *threw him over the side of a mountain,* Harold. I *drove way the hell up to* Santa *Barbara.*

He was getting close.

The ocean appeared on his left with a pier reaching out into the water. The surf was huge. Not a soul on the beach. Good. That meant no one would be where he was going either.

The rest area would be coming up anytime now. He clicked the wipers on high and strained through the foggy windshield and the sheets of rain. Man, it was coming down like it'd never stop.

The road climbed inland now, away from the ocean. Did he miss it? Damn. He'd have to circle back and—

"Rest area one and a half miles." Okay. This must be it. This had to be it.

I *stopped in a rest area.* I *dragged him to the edge and threw him over the side.*

He turned off the highway and braked hard as the road narrowed and twisted downhill. He strained forward in his seat, watching the rest area appear in front of him, and eased the pickup under dark trees, blurry in the rain, their branches reaching out overhead, dead leaves swirling in the wind. The parking lot was empty except for a bobtail truck parked at the end near the railing. The truck was dark and quiet, the driver probably sacked out in the bunk behind the seats now that he'd dropped off his trailer. Shouldn't be a problem.

Now, thought Harold, if I was Marianna, where would I go? He imagined her pulling in in the dark and tried to guess where the easiest spot was for her to unload it. He settled on a spot beyond the guardrail near a steep drop-off slanting away further down the mountainside.

He killed the engine and reached for the cheap raincoat he bought as he was leaving town. As he struggled into it, he heard the wind picking up and oak leaves, like huge paws, smacked onto the windshield and stuck like glue. The rain rose to a roar on the pickup's roof, then suddenly stopped. As he stepped outside, he saw bright patches of sky between fast-moving clouds, coming in over the tops of the mountains. The storm was breaking up. He'd been counting on the rain to hide him. Now, as he moved across the wet parking lot, he began to feel exposed. He eyed the parked bobtail, but it was still and dark. Maybe it was broken down and no one was home. Hard to tell. He had to be careful.

I *dragged him to the edge and threw him over the side.*

Harold walked the perimeter of the rest of the area, looking over the guardrail and down the mountainside. The steep slope was covered with low brush and leaves turned to mush in the rain. Water was draining from the highway and parking lot and roaring down the slope, washing branches and trash with it. But he couldn't see anything yet. Not what he was looking for.

I *threw him over the side.* I *saw him start rolling and then he disappeared and* I *could hear him rolling and crashing down there for a long time.*

The rain had stopped completely now. He shot a look at the bobtail and started down. Damn, he was stiff after that long drive. Stiff and—the running water made him realize his bladder was bursting. He unzipped his fly, thinking, if anyone's watching they'll think I'm just out here to take a leak. Relieved, he watched his fluid mix with the runoff and swirl away down the mountainside. He started down the slope again.

The leaves were slick underfoot, and he grabbed at bushes and trees to keep his balance. The mud sucked at his feet, and he wished he'd changed out of his work clothes. But somehow, he felt this would make it look more real if someone stopped him. "I was on my way up to San Luis and I stopped to take a leak, looked down and there it was."

He'd reached the bottom of the slope now and found all the runoff collecting in a creek that had swollen to an angry river, tanned by the mud it carried and choked with logs, branches, Styrofoam cups, an old shopping cart, and a wooden cane. He looked back up toward the rest area but found he was now hidden by the trees and brush. Good. He began moving downstream, walking uncertainly along the bank, slipping and catching himself, his hands cold and raw.

Suddenly, startlingly, the sun came out. A shaft of light fell between trees and he felt its warmth on his back and saw his shadow on the ground in front of him as if caught in a spotlight. He stood there breathing hard, frozen by that light, seeing the events that led him there replayed in his mind. At each turn was Marianna's face, her red lips, her dark eyes full of violence and secrets. She was leading him into darkness. Slowly, certainly. Revenge. Then murder. Then deception and lies. He hated lies. He wanted to find his way back. But he wanted to take her with him. He would take her with him, back into the light.

The sunlight faded as if it was never there. Rain started falling again. Harold was about to start walking again when he jumped back, grasping. He had been standing right next to it.

A human hand, indecently white and wrinkled, was rising from a tangle of debris by the edge of the roaring stream. Then he realized he was seeing the whole body; the force of the floodwater had been so strong the torso was cracked backwards, U-shaped, so that the ankles were beside the ears, the face hanging upside down. A white shirt still covered the chest, the suit coat partially torn away, the disfigured face twisted toward him, open-mouthed, eye sockets empty and dark, hair hanging limply and moving in the wind.

He's down there, Harold, and he's never coming back. The coyotes are going to eat him. Or the maggots. Someday maybe they'll find a skeleton and they'll never know who it is. I'm glad he's down there and I *don't give a damn what anybody thinks.*

Harold tried to turn away from the sight, but couldn't. He became aware that he was making a strange low hissing as if he were trying to hyperventilate with his mouth closed. He felt depressed, oddly sad, for this thing that was once inhabited by a person, a person who loved it and fed it and cared for it. Now it was washed up here unloved and neglected. It should be underground. Or burned to ashes. Not treated like garbage. No one deserved to end up like this. Not even a car salesman.

The first step was to get this thing free from the logjam of debris. He forced himself to grab the soaked pants leg and pull. He had to pull it toward him since it was driven up against a tree trunk fallen across the stream. To get a good hold Harold had to stand close to the face, which seemed now to be smiling at him. He noticed he was holding his breath, afraid to inhale the stench of decomposition. He ordered himself to breathe normally. His body wouldn't obey.

With a good handhold on the pants leg, Harold threw his weight against it. Unexpectedly it came free and fell toward him, rolling up against his leg, as if lonely and seeking some contact with the living. Harold scrambled backward, losing his footing and falling in the muck, the body landing across his legs. He savagely kicked it away, but it seemed to keep coming. He scrambled out from underneath it and got to his feet, ran a few steps still making those strange breathing noises before he stopped and looked back.

It was facedown now. Good. Now he could deal with it better. He would get the rope and the tarp and get it up to the truck. Then if Marianna tried to give Harold to the cops, there was no evidence. But first, Harold approached the body and turned out the pockets. A dime fell out onto the ground. Some soggy paper with blurred letters. And a sticky mess that was once a roll of breath mints. No wallet. He slid the ring off the bony white finger and put it in his pocket. As he was standing to leave, he saw purple markings on the skin above the ankle. He lifted the pants leg slightly and saw a tattoo of a long thin dagger.

It was much harder going back up the mountainside than it was coming down. He pulled himself up with handholds of roots and brush going from tree to tree, his feet shooting out from under him. He fell repeatedly, his suit pants muddy and pasted to his legs. His shirt and suit jacket under the plastic raincoat were soaked with sweat.

Harold was planning his next move as he scrambled the last twenty feet to level ground. As he approached the parking lot he gradually became aware of a new sound. But he didn't react quickly enough to it and walked right out of the trees and directly across the path of a highway patrolman. The cop was talking to a man near the open door of the bobtail cab. The noise he had heard was one he'd been hearing all too much of recently: a police radio with the lifeless female voice of a dispatcher.

It took a moment to sink in. And in that moment Harold was still walking across the parking lot, as if his legs refused to react to what his eyes had seen. As he continued walking, the highway patrolman and the trucker kept watching him, this bearded middle-aged man in a business suit, stumbling out of the brush, covered with mud, pretending nothing was wrong.

Several alternatives whirled through Harold's mind; maybe he would, if he reached his truck, get in and just get the hell out of there, come back later and remove the body. But what if the cop pulled him over a mile up the highway, brought him back here? Then it would be far worse. No, things were going to unfold here very quickly and he had no idea what he was going to do.

"Sir?" The cop's voice came to him across the parking lot. "Sir? Are you all right?"

Harold turned, almost to his truck. The cop was coming now, black boots crunching on the sand-covered asphalt. Harold saw himself from the cop's point of view—soaked hair and mud-spattered suit—and felt the old just-stopped-to-take-a-leak excuse wouldn't fly.

The cop was crisp in his khaki uniform, his chest bulky with a flak jacket underneath and thick forearms covered with freckles. The boundaries of his hairline were intact, but it was thinning alarmingly. Harold could see light through his hair, silhouetting individual hairs on a greasy scalp. Another time, he might have pitied this man. Now he only felt general terror as he found his eye going to the automatic in the leather holster on the cop's hip.

The trucker hung back a few steps as Harold tried to form an answer. He must have seen me down there in the woods and flagged down the cop, Harold thought. Nosy bastard. Now he thinks that gives him the right to find out what the hell is going on.

"Sir? Is something wrong?"

The cop and the trucker were still waiting for Harold to speak, their expressions caught between concern and suspicion, and Harold felt something rising in him, a way out of this, at least for now.

"I—I don't know," Harold said. "It's such a shock."

"What is?" the cop asked.

"When I saw him down there."

"Who?"

Harold was at the point of no return now. So he said it: "My brother."

The cop shifted his weight. "Sir. Can you tell me what's going on? From the beginning. What is your brother doing down there?"

"I'm sorry. I'm not thinking clearly. It's a, well, a shock, you know?" Harold breathed hard. It was coming together now. All the pieces he needed.

"My brother, he's been depressed a real long time. He can't find a job, and, well—last week some friends he was staying with, they said he was acting strange. One of them was driving up to San Luis and Randy, my brother, wanted to go along. They got this far and he wanted out."

Harold stopped. His mind was racing ahead to possible questions, problems. The cop respectfully allowed some silence, then prompted him again. "Have you located your brother?"

"Yes."

"Is he all right?"

"No. He's—"

"Is he injured? Does he need medical assistance?"

"No."

The cop paused, trying to frame other questions, but finally just said: "Would you show me where he is, please?"

A few minutes later the cop and Harold were standing above the body beside the running stream. Harold noticed the cop started breathing hard as he took in the sight of the twisted corpse, the torn clothes, and white wrinkled skin. The silence between them was heavy as Harold wondered what this other man was thinking about life and death and all those questions that are always there below the surface but are never resolved. For Harold's part, he was thinking how we can speculate all we want to about death, but it's quietly waiting there, knowing nothing will keep us from it in the end.

"This is your brother?"

"Yes."

"You're sure?"

"Yes."

"It's—he's in pretty bad shape. Are there identifying marks that—"

"The tattoo on his left leg," Harold pulled up the pant leg and revealed the faded purple dagger. "I was with him when he got that."

They were both quiet for a while; then the cop turned toward Harold. "Well, I'm very sorry."

Harold nodded. "Like I said, he was depressed a lot lately. We were worried he might . . ."

The cop waited, but Harold couldn't finish. He was surprised to find that he was supplying residual emotion collected over the years about his own brother. His brother, although he never actually died, was lost along the way, and this scene allowed Harold to set aside his anger and grieve for him. So, as he stood there, feeling the waste of his brother's life and his own role in it, the tears that made his eyes hot and unsteady were quite real and very convincing.

"Are you suggesting he took his own life?" the cop finally asked.

"I don't know," Harold said quickly. Then, "We were afraid he would do something like this for a while now. He talked about it some too, but . . ."

"I'll radio for the coroner. You'll have to come back to the station with me. Fill out a report. Make a formal identification."

Harold nodded. They were both still looking at the body as if expecting it to do something, to answer some question. But the corpse didn't speak or move. The only movement was the wind's riffling the hair.

"Are you ready to go, sir?"

Harold hesitated.

"I'm very sorry," the cop repeated. "I lost a brother too. Once."

Harold nodded. He was sorry for so many things. For all the things he couldn't change, the people he couldn't help, the problems he couldn't fix. And, as he turned away, he was aware that the resolution he felt over his brother's imagined death was temporary. Eventually his brother would be located and the records reversed. But by then, this body would be cremated, beyond retrieval and accurate identification, and Harold would have tied up the other threads of his life that were now hopelessly snarled and out of control.

Harold felt that some kind of control was now within reach. All he needed was more time, a few more good ideas, and a little luck. Then his life would be back in order. But, as he climbed the hill beside the highway patrolman, he had to admit that he had often felt control was within reach. In fact, he'd felt that way for the better part of his life.

Vito opened the door of his condo and saw the big man standing there for a split second before the man's fist slammed into his solar plexus. He doubled over and heard someone—himself probably—making desperate sucking noises, trying to draw air into his lungs despite the collapsed diaphragm. In that strange state of mind that occurs during intense pain, which Vito had experienced several times recently, he was aware of the big man stepping around him and calmly closing the condo door. Then he was back standing over him. He heard him breathing heavily for a moment. Then the serious damage began.

Vito was knocked to the kitchen floor and heard distant thuds as he felt himself being violently jarred, his head slamming against the bottom of the dishwasher. The man's boot smashed into his kidneys, stomach, thighs, back. And with each blow he could hear the tearing of his internal organs and muscles.

Then everything was quiet again and he was finally able to pull some air into his lungs and it felt so good, like water after the desert, and he was just beginning to feel all right when—*crash*!—his stomach caved in again. And the beating continued. He was suffocating, choking, dying, being torn in a thousand pieces. A hot fluid he'd never tasted before filled his mouth and trickled wet and pink across his cheek and onto the floor.

Darkness. Then he was moving. Being slid across the floor and down the hallway. He was being sat up in a chair, his favorite chair in front of the tube. He opened his eyes. His vision took a long time to clear. The man was sitting in front of him on the leather footstool holding a bloody towel. He raised a glass of water to Vito's lips. Vito sipped, washing down the bitter taste of whatever had risen from his stomach and spilled across his shirtfront.

"Now," the man said. He breathed through his nose, which was sharp and beaklike. His eyebrows flared at the corners, making him look like an old hawk.

"LaBounty," Vito said. "He sent you."

"That's not important," the man said. "What's important is that we get this all straightened out. So we don't have problems in the future."

Vito listened to the man breathing sharply through his nose and stared into his dark eyes, eyes that seemed to be sucking the truth from him.

"The book," Vito finally said.

"Yes."

"I told him I didn't have it."

"This isn't about what you don't have and can't do. It's about reaching a complete understanding of the truth so we can mutually solve this problem. Are you willing to do that?"

Vito felt himself nodding eagerly. He hated himself for his weakness. But the pain had been too great. And the threat of pain was filling the room. What he had to do was think of a way to use all this for his own good. Then he wouldn't be lying. And, more importantly, he wouldn't *look* like he was lying.

"Here's the deal," Vito started.

"I don't make deals. I'm just a simple soldier, doing a job."

"Figure of speech. Lemme start again. Since I talked to John—to LaBounty—I've been working on this—this problem."

"And?"

"And I've got it all set up."

The man was so close to Vito he could smell cigarette smoke on his clothes. The only sound in the room was his breathing, sharp predatory snatches of air through that long nose. That and the rain tapping on the picture window onto the balcony where the day outside was dissolving into gray darkness.

"The bitch that stole the book, I saw her today. She's bringing me the person that has the book."

"There are two others?"

"Yes."

"Are they together?"

"Not anymore. That's part of what I was telling you. See, I split them up, so they'd—"

The man spoke slowly, to be absolutely clear. "Who has the book?"

"His name is Harold Dodge."

"What's he think he can do with it?"

Vito had to figure out how to answer that. The man saw motion behind Vito's eyes and said, "Don't think. Talk."

"Basically he thought he could push Covo into a deal."

"Covo."

"My boss. He owns the dealership. LaBounty's his boss."

"What kind of deal?"

"To unwind the sale of a car."

The man drew back slightly. "A car? One car?"

"That's right."

"That's what this is all about?"

"In a way, yeah."

"Shit." The man breathed out the word in utter disgust. Then he turned his bird-of-prey eyes back on Vito. "Where do I find Dodge?"

"He's got a dump in West LA. Near the airport. But he's never there."

Vito ran out of words and, at the end of them, found the man still staring at him, his eyes still asking the same question. What the hell, Vito thought, he'll help me get the book. This time I'll be ready for him—for all of them. This'll work out just right.

"I've got a meeting set up. Tonight. I can get the book and turn it over to you."

"This Dodge. He'll be there?"

"Yes."

"And the other person?"

"Yes. She'll be there."

The man sat back a little, as if willing to watch Vito from a distance, give him a little leeway now that he controlled him completely. A hawk circling above as a mouse scrambled for cover.

"What I just did to you, that was three on a scale of ten. I can make you feel ten without killing you. Understand?"

Vito nodded, his mind trying, but unwilling, to comprehend what was being said.

The man leaned back into Vito. "Where's the meeting?"

Before Marianna opened her apartment door she could hear him on the other side. His cries sounded so accusatory to her. She hadn't been home much for the past week and Pancho was telling her all about it.

The door swung in on the apartment, and a stale blast of air hit her in the face. It had been hot the last time she was here, just after she thought she killed and dumped Vito. Now it was rainy and cold and Vito was alive. It was, in other words, a very different world.

In the dark kitchen she could hear Pancho's claws raking the rattan covering on the cabinet doors. She scooped up the cat and held him as she dialed Mrs. Gustin, the manager across the courtyard. Yes, she'd be happy to take care of the cat for a few days. Hanging up, Marianna thought how the old lady would fall in love with Pancho and keep him, even after Marianna failed to come back for him and mysteriously disappeared.

She went into her bedroom and pulled open the top drawer. She reached in back and found the gun she took from the Matsura trunk. She dropped that in her purse next to the wad of bills she had taken from Covo's pocket before dumping him. Then she started packing. Not much left in the way of clean underwear. Not many clothes worth taking, really. It was a pretty sad statement about your life when leaving only means clearing out a few old clothes and finding a new home for your cat.

It was time to try something new, leave for parts unknown. Actually, she knew where she was going—San Antonio—but that was just another stop along the way. Along the way to the perfect place she hoped she'd find someday, somewhere. She could live with her cousin Tina and walk along the river and drink coffee all day while things cooled off here. Or while she figured out what the hell to do with the rest of her life.

It helped to think of being on the road to Texas. That way her mind wouldn't keep going over what she had to do tonight, in just a few hours. She had gone over it a bunch of times and it was really very simple. Now it was time to put it aside, just wait for the right moment. And do it. Too much planning sometimes screwed things up. So she kept her mind on the things at hand, folding her favorite blouse and setting that in the bottom of the suitcase, sorting through the dresses in her closet, deciding which shoes to take and which to leave behind.

Points unknown. She had the ten grand she took off Covo's body, and that gave her a little breathing room. More than she'd had before, so her mind played with possibilities. Unexpectedly, she found her thoughts in Guatemala, the village where she was raised, where her parents were killed by a death squad the night she left by the back door and ran out into the mountains. She long ago put all that out of her mind. Or thought she did. But now she had the time, and the bucks, so the memories were exhumed and began to haunt her. The courtyard in the village, the fountain, the music on Saturday nights with lights strung between the trees, the smells of the market. The past was suddenly around her, as fresh as yesterday.

There was Mrs. Gustin knocking at the door. Right on time. She scooped up Pancho, feeling the furry bulk in her arms, and opened the door.

Harold stood there covered with mud, his face the color of ashes, hair tangled. He looked like he'd been dragged through a field behind a tractor. Anger hung around him like a bitter smell.

"Harold."

"That's right." He was watching her closely, the gray eyes not letting her go, making her as uncomfortable as possible. "I thought it was time we got a few things straight. Can I come in?"

She hesitated, thinking of Mrs. Gustin, thinking of her suitcase with the money and the gun in the other room. Harold's breathing suddenly accelerated. He was a bomb ready to blow up and cover her walls with his rage.

"Of course, come on in." She turned away and he entered, closing the door behind him. They were in her kitchen. He stood on one side of the table facing her. She leaned against the refrigerator with Pancho still in her arms.

"Are you going to tell me why you look like that?"

"Eventually."

"Harold." She said his name again in her special way, filled with knowledge and playfulness, trying to soften him up, get him ready to hear about the latest episode in this saga of woe. But as she searched for a way to tell him about Vito, she saw his anger growing and knew he had come for a reason.

"You want a beer?" She turned and opened the refrigerator door and began exploring. "I think there's one lurking about somewhere in the back here . . ."

"No. We'll just talk. Then I'll go."

She closed the refrigerator door and they both sat at the table. In the silence she could hear the hand on her battery-operated clock jerking forward through time. She wondered if she'd take that with her. She loved it when she first bought it, just after she landed the job at Aerodyne and the money started coming in. No, she realized, that would be left behind and wind up in Mrs. Gustin's next yard sale. She saw her things spread out on the front lawn and heard the old woman explaining how one of her tenants took off. Left all her things. Her cat, too.

Harold had seen her eyes wandering, thinking of the future without him, and it made him break the silence.

"I don't get it," was all he finally said.

"That makes two of us, Harold. You show up here, looking like the wrath of God and you just stare at me. Why don't you just say it? Whatever it is? I'm a big girl. I can take it."

"Wrath of God," he mumbled. "Maybe I am the wrath of God. You know, my ex-wife, we were married fifteen years. One day she said, 'I despise you.' Just like that. 'I despise you.' "

Marianna was suddenly tired. Very tired. "That's got nothing to do with me."

"I think it does."

"What?"

"You came to *me* for help. I helped you. Then you do *this* to me? Why?" For a moment his anger was replaced by pain.

"Okay. Is it about the hotel? Leaving like that?"

"Shit, no. You left. Big deal. What I don't get is why you're putting this on me? Okay, you want out—fine. But why put it on me?"

"What am I putting on you?"

Harold rolled his eyes. "I went to court this morning, okay? On this traffic thing. They were all done—or I thought they were—and this cop comes in. Guy the size of a gorilla. *A homicide cop.* You hear what I'm saying? Said someone was calling him, saying I killed someone."

Marianna wasn't tired anymore. Suddenly Harold's anger made sense.

"Harold, Jesus. Who would do that?"

"I have no idea," he said sarcastically, his eyes still accusing, filled with pain.

And then she knew, knew what was behind this. Harold thought she turned him in to the cops when it was actually Vito. She laughed, about to tell him what had happened. But then she stopped. There was still that mud all over his suit. What had he done?

Harold leaned forward now that it was all spilling out. "The cops *knew* he was in the damn trunk. You told them. Didn't you?"

She shook her head. "Why would I—?"

"You figure they're gonna find out eventually. It's gonna be me or you. You figure it better be me. That's natural."

"Harold. I can explain all this. Listen to what happened." She tried to touch his hand, which was on the table in front of him. He pulled back.

"You're the only one who knew, for Christ's sake!"

"No, I'm not." She said it quietly. But her voice stopped him. She was still catching up with herself, remembering Vito that afternoon saying, *Let's get Dad-boy*. He had already started.

"Harold, look. I'm sorry. I should have said something before. I mean, like, even at the hotel. I just thought, what am I doing to your life? It's between Vito and me, not you. And now, this afternoon, I found out it still is between me and Vito."

"But he's dead."

"Well . . ." She laughed again.

"Is this funny?"

"I don't know. Wait till you hear." Pause. "Covo called me this morning."

"Covo?"

"Actually, someone claiming to be Covo. I went to your office but you weren't in."

"I was getting the third degree—because of you."

"Will you forget about yourself for a second, Harold? I'm trying to explain something." Harold clamped his mouth shut. "Covo said to come in and he'd unwind the deal. I knew it had to be done eventually. So I said yes. When I got there I found it wasn't Covo. It was Vito. Vito Fiorre."

"Vito's dead."

"No, he's not. He was sitting behind Joe's desk like he owned the place."

Harold stood up. "This is a load of crap, okay? I'm just here to tell you your games ain't gonna work."

"Sit down, Harold, please."

"What I'm telling you is, I took care of the problem. Now I'm out of here, done with you."

"Took care of what problem?"

"Just remember, next time you talk to the cops, they can't nail me without evidence."

"Evidence. What evidence?"

"Vito's body."

"I *told* you. Vito's alive."

"He didn't look that way to me."

"Oh, Jesus. What did you do?"

He didn't answer. So her eyes went to his mud-covered suit and she began to understand, even though part of her was saying, I*t can't be*. Harold was smiling now, proud of himself, yet still hurt and defensive, like a little boy trying to save his pride, trying to act tough.

"You see? You can talk to the cops all you want. There ain't no way they can touch me."

"You moved it, didn't you? You found the body and you moved it."

He smiled his little-boy smile again. "I did more than that. I got it taken to a damn mortuary. They're gonna cremate it as soon as I get back up there with the money."

"How the hell did you do that?"

"Positive ID from next of kin. I told them it was my brother."

The exhaustion suddenly came back and swept over her like hot, humid air. It had all gotten so confused.

"Harold. That was Covo you moved. You realize that, don't you?"

"It couldn't have been."

"It was. It really was."

He stared at her a long time before murmuring: "But how . . ."

"I don't know. I guess I didn't hurt Vito as much as I thought. He killed Covo and put him in the trunk. When we came back to move the car, Covo was in there. Not Vito."

Harold's anger and suspicion were finally gone. "Jesus," was all he said.

"Yeah. Jesus is right."

The silence was suddenly heavy in the kitchen. Harold looked at her a long time, his mind spinning, putting the new pieces in place, evaluating the situation from this completely different angle.

Harold was about to speak when there was a knock at the door. And they both jumped.

"That's my landlady," Marianna said, crossing the room and noticing as she did that Harold was stepping back out of sight.

She pushed the door open and the breath caught in her throat. A big blond guy was standing there with a "remember me?" grin on his face.

"Well?" he said.

"Well, well," she said, flipping through snapshots of faces in her head, knowing there was a match here somewhere.

"I'm Tony Polk. Sergeant Polk, from Garden Grove? I stopped you—"

"Last week, sure. I didn't recognize you—"

"Out of uniform. No one does." He hesitated, looking around the inside of her kitchen. She could feel movement behind her and realized Harold had stepped into the rear hallway, near the top of the back stairs. The cop caught the motion, too.

"Sorry. You got company?" he asked.

"Just my roommate."

Polk left a little pause during which she was supposed to invite him in. She didn't.

"I feel like an insurance salesman out here. You mind if—"

"I was just leaving," she said.

"But you just got here."

Bad news, she thought. He's been watching the place.

Polk glanced past her at the bag on the floor of her bedroom.

"Going on a trip?"

She was noncommittal. "Friend of mine's picking me up in a few minutes so . . ." She stood her ground in the doorway.

Polk's expression seemed to darken as he took a breath and began. "Listen, if it ever comes up, I'm not here."

"You're not?"

"Not officially. I need a favor."

"A favor."

"I want you to back me up on something. Just a little thing really."

"Little enough for you to come up here, stake out my apartment."

He didn't like that. It meant she was one step ahead of his sneaky cop tricks.

"Let me explain something to you," he said, shifting his

weight, reminding Marianna of a cop leaning in her car window, giving a lecture instead of writing her up. "In police work, man, you gotta dot your i's and cross all your t's. All the way. Otherwise some slick lawyer'll get the whole thing thrown out of court. On a technicality. Okay, so I didn't open the trunk. You said you didn't have the key. I looked for my slam hammer, we got to talking, it slipped my mind."

He paused as if it should be clear to her now.

"So what's the favor?"

"Say you opened the trunk for me and I did a visual."

"But you didn't."

"That's the favor."

Marianna stood there in the doorway, aware of Harold just out of sight, hoping he could hear all this and enjoy how she had this cop over a barrel.

"I don't know," she finally said. "It seems like a silly little thing."

"It is. It is."

"Why would it ever even come up?"

"It's highly unlikely it ever would."

"Still, you're asking me to lie."

"I wouldn't really call it a lie."

"Than what would you call it?"

He sighed impatiently, his eyes sliding to the side. He didn't seem to like putting up with this kind of shit.

"Look, can I come in and talk about it?" he asked, flashing his big white teeth. "I'm sure we can work something out."

Like what? she wondered. I get to fondle your gun? She used to go for cops. The uniform thing, probably. But lately they were losing their appeal.

"I've really got to go."

"So what do you say? Ya gonna help me out?"

"It's a pretty big favor. And I don't see what I get for it."

He looked at her for a long time in silence, trying to make her as uncomfortable as possible. When she didn't look away he said, "Everyone's a whore. Is that it? Never give something for nothing."

"Something like that."

"All right. Here's what you get. A little heads up: Someone's trying to put you away."

"Excuse me?"

"Someone's telling homicide you killed a guy." He was watching her very closely now. "And you had him in your trunk when I stopped you."

"So you told them you inspected the trunk and there was nothing in there."

"No. I didn't *tell* them that. I put it in my report."

It was finally out in the open. Telling lies was one thing. Putting them in print was another.

"Who would tell homicide such a thing?" he asked, swinging the conversation back against her.

"I have no idea."

"Where is your car now?"

He had been watching her apartment. So he probably knew the Matsura was parked outside. Still, he was trying to catch her in a lie. Make her dirty just like him.

"Out front."

"Mind if I look in the trunk?"

"Now?"

"Yeah."

"Why would I mind? Just let me get my things."

She went into the bedroom and got her bags. On the way back to the front door she saw that Harold had disappeared, probably slipped out the back door and down the back steps while they were talking. How much had he heard?

She picked up her bag, turned out the lights, and shut the

Vito heard a rasping noise and realized it was his own breath. He was hyperventilating. His heart was beating like a trapped bird in his chest.

"You shouldn't have said that, John."

"Oh, no?"

"You need me."

"Like a case of the clap." He started to walk back to the hotel.

"John. You want the book or not?"

LaBounty paused. "Look, whatever your name is. I'm not gonna kiss your ass, or whatever you want me to do."

"No. You'll just send your man after me instead. Then think I'll bend over and do anything you want. Doesn't work that way, John."

LaBounty paused, apparently realizing what this was really about.

"I didn't like that, John."

"Fuck with me, that's what happens. Now, you got it or not?"

"In the trunk. Open it."

Vito could see him thinking it over, suspicious. Finally he sighed, disgustedly, and walked to the rear of the Mercedes. As he was opening the trunk Vito reached into the passenger door. LaBounty looked up, saying, "I don't see it," and saw Vito pointing the assault rifle at him. Vito had never seen so much knowledge go through another man's face in such a short time. Two seconds later, Vito said, "You shouldn't have sent him, John."

"Who?"

"Your man. He came into my house. He hurt me in my own house. You should have trusted me."

LaBounty's eyes lost their usual apathy, and his big chest began rising and falling under the tan trench coat.

door. Mrs. Gustin had the keys. She'd come and get Poncho. Eventually she'd have one of her yard sales with Marianna's things. With any luck, she'd make enough money to keep Pancho in cat food for a while. A couple of weeks at least.

As Vito waited in the parking lot behind the hotel, he thought what a great city LA was. A quick visit with Neto (he was always hangin' by the dumpsters behind the dealership) and two hours later he delivered the goods. Where else could you get this kind of hardware on such short notice? And Neto even threw in some tweakers, too. He'd need that 'cause he was popping the painkillers like breath mints. That way he could be in two places at once: up and down.

He angled his watch so it caught the rays of a nearby streetlight: nine o'clock straight up. By midnight he'd have all this taken care of. Then he'd go home and crash. Maybe throw a few beers down and let the painkillers take over. In the morning he'd be Joe Covo again and no one would be able to say he wasn't. Till then, he was gonna have some fun. He'd wanted to do something like this for a long time. Some days he felt like he'd just explode, self-destruct. But something always held him back. Tonight it wouldn't.

Time to make the call.

Leaning against his Mercedes, Vito slid the cell phone out of his suit pocket. LaBounty was on top of the phone, had it off the hook in 1.5 rings once the hotel operator connected them.

"John?"

"Yeah."

"Vito."

"Who?"

"Vito. Vito Fiorre. Got what you need."

"Oh. Bring it up. I'm in room—"

"No. Meet me at a place called Barney's. It's on Holloway at La Cienega. See you in ten minutes."

Vito disconnected before LaBounty could start bitching. That felt good. From here on in, he'd set the agenda. No more eating shit for this boy. Besides, it was important that LaBounty be near his car when Vito met him. That was part of the plan.

Looking up at the hotel, black against the sky, only a few lights on, he wondered which room was LaBounty's. Which room was Tom Bales's? Parker's? Were they still in town? He'd like to pay them a visit when he was done with LaBounty. But that wasn't necessary. LaBounty was the one.

Vito had the Mercedes fired up and idling when he saw a huge figure fill the back doorway of the hotel and walk out into the night. Vito slowly glided toward him as LaBounty cut through the rows of parked cars like a destroyer lumbering through heavy surf.

Watching the other man, Vito felt like God. He knew the future, while LaBounty, the dumb shit, had no idea what was headed his way. He was smart enough to make all that money, control all those dealerships, push all those people around, but he didn't know what was going to happen to him five minutes from now.

LaBounty found his rented Lincoln Town Car and opened the door. Vito pulled his Mercedes in behind him, blocking his car, and called out.

"John!"

LaBounty was half in the car. He turned and straightened, looking at Vito with mild annoyance. He was wearing a tan London Fog trench coat that probably cost a million bucks.

"Decided to meet you here. Restaurants are so noisy, ya know?"

"You got it?"

"I do indeed."

"Let's have it."

"Not so fast, John." Vito slowly climbed out of his car an stood facing LaBounty. It hurt when he moved. The pain wa distant because of the drugs, smothered on its way from hi torn body to his brain. Still it was there, reminding him of the damage, of the humiliation of lying on his kitchen floor eating the bottom of his dishwasher while that animal kicked the shit out of him.

He lit a cigarette and leaned against the Mercedes, savoring the moment.

"Tom told me what the deal was on Friday night—the FBI investigation and all that," Vito said at last. "I told him I took care of the problem. You understand what I'm saying?"

"He told me you said that, yeah."

"When I said I took care of the problem, that means I took care of the problem."

Vito realized LaBounty was watching him with a certain wariness, as if he was over the top. He didn't really know how over the top he could get.

"You took care of the problem. How was I supposed to know what that meant?"

"You were supposed to trust me, John. But you didn't. Did you?"

"No I didn't—" He paused, confused. "Your name again?"

Unbelievable. The big bastard didn't even know his name.

"Vito. Vito Fiorre."

"Right. Okay."

"Say my name."

"W*hat*?"

"Say my name. I want you to say my name."

"Fuck you."

"Look, ah, Vito . . . Don't be stupid. Anything happens to me, who's gonna call him off?"

Vito smiled. "Already thought of that, John. We're gonna go talk to him now. Get in your car."

"I don't know where he is."

"Let's find him. Get in your car."

LaBounty slowly pulled his car keys out of his pocket. He opened the car door and Vito shot him, bullets ripping up the back of the tan trench coat. Christ, Vito thought, thing's jumpin' like a jackhammer, trying to get away. But when he was done, and the gunshots had stopped echoing through the neighborhood, the effect was just what Vito had hoped for: LaBounty lay across the front seat of the rented Lincoln, his car keys on the ground next to him. Another pointless car-jacking. And they didn't even get the car. What a waste. But they did have time to grab his wallet before they took off.

As Vito drove away he thought, man, crime's really on the rise in this godless city. It's really gettin' out of hand.

It was one thing to die. It was another thing to die stupidly.

Slade woke up from his nap with that thought in his mind. He looked at the alarm clock on the hotel-room bedside table—nine o'clock. Two hours till the meeting. Get there early and survey the lay of the land. See the area through the enemy's eyes. Then there would be no surprises.

As Slade packed, alone in the stark room, he remembered how, when he was younger, he trained constantly. When he trained forces in Zaire and later in Guatemala, he told them: If you train sixteen hours a day, and you meet a man who has been training seventeen hours a day, you will die.

As he got older Slade trained his body less and his mind

more. That's where it counted. In most cases all you needed to do was outthink your enemy. Most mistakes were made by laziness. And tonight, like all nights, he would avoid that. He would avoid a stupid death.

He looked down at his clothes, neatly packed in the suitcase on the bed. It had been just like this on so many jobs in so many cities. But now it felt different. He felt an odd stirring. Memories from the different parts of his life, Korea, Africa, Central America, overwhelmed him and left him disoriented. He looked up, reminding himself where he was, what he was doing, where he was going.

Slade left the room at 9:35 and climbed into his rented Chevy Corsica. He drove south on Lincoln, a strip of chain stores and seafood restaurants. In Venice, the street narrowed and beach bungalows pressed in on either side. Then he cut down toward the ocean on Culver and ran along the beach on Vista Del Mar. Without looking he could sense the ocean to his right now, enormous and dark, wild and frightening.

A power plant appeared in the distance, the stack ringed by lights that blinked at an unnatural intensity. A scenic turnoff appeared in his headlights, and Slade was tempted to pull into the lot, walk down to the pounding surf in the darkness, and let the waves carry his mind across the water to places he'd rather be. But he had business tonight. He would push on. Survey the land. It was his rule and he couldn't break it.

A jet came in low overhead, gear down, engines whistling. He knew he was close and soon hit Imperial, turned left and climbed back through the dunes on the west side of LAX. The road flanked the runways, then rose to a grassy ridge overlooking the airport. He pulled into a long narrow parking lot and stepped out into the heavy night air, smelling the ocean so close and wondering, *Why here*? A meeting could be set anywhere. *Why here*?

It was a long open parking lot, deserted except for a carload of Mexican punks drinking and throwing beer bottles down the hillside. Another few cars held couples clinched together, ignoring the scenery they supposedly came here for. Below, the blue runway lights lured jets out of the sky, guiding them in over the mountains outside San Bernadino.

Why here? He asked himself once more, as he reached under the front seat of the car and took out the 9mm automatic. It wasn't his weapon of choice, but, since he was still on parole, he had to take what he could get on the streets. He checked the clip, then shoved the gun into his waistband above his left hip pocket. The big gun dug into his side, but it gave him a feeling of security as he climbed back into the Chevy and moved the car up onto a side street.

From here he would see them arrive. And be ready.

Harold sat in the dark in his truck watching the light in Marianna's apartment window and feeling happiness flooding his body. She hadn't turned him in! It was Vito. He was still alive. And he was trying to turn them both in—and split them up in the process. He had heard the cop say so just before he crept down the back stairs and out to the truck. *Someone's trying to set you up*. Just the way the homicide cop said it to him that morning.

This changed everything, Harold thought. It made it all worthwhile. They were in it together, instead of fighting each other. He felt ridiculously happy, like a teenager finding a love letter in his locker in high school. It also showed him, once and for all, what an utter mess he was. Out of control. Way out of control. He was like a car weaving from one side of the road to the other, threatening to kill first other people, then himself. But what could he do? He loved her. And he had promised he'd help her.

He'd have to find a way to get rid of this cop for her. But it would be tough. While his newfound love was calling him to action, his long-standing terror of the police still held him back. So he just sat there, torn in two, and slid in a CD of Amazon rain-forest sounds, hoping it would soothe him. The sounds of thunder filled the truck cab like a cue in a bad horror film as he saw Marianna's apartment light go out.

The cop and Marianna emerged from the front door and walked to the sidewalk, turned down the street, and stopped at her parked Matsura. They stood at the rear of the car talking, the cop gesturing, a little pissed about something. Marianna was doing her I-don't-know-why-you're-so-upset routine as she reached into her purse. He stepped back and stood spread legged as she unlocked the trunk. Typical cop pose. Power. Domination.

Then it was like he was seeing a replay of a scene from his life. He remembered being in the back in the cruiser on his way to jail, handcuffs slicing into his wrists, and seeing Marianna with this cop. Only now the trunk was opening and this cop was looking down into it. A wave of acid sweat, cold and oily, seeped out of Harold as he watched the cop leaning forward, reaching into the trunk, turning to speak to Marianna, then turning back and suddenly taking something out, holding it out for her to see.

Shut the trunk and walk away, Harold thought. *Shut the damn trunk*!

Marianna took whatever it was the cop had found and looked at it as the cop stepped closer. Marianna stepped back, shaking her head.

What the hell did he find?

Harold couldn't stop himself. He saw his hand reaching for the keys and felt the V-8 rumble to life. He dropped it in gear and drove toward them, their faces flashing white in the headlights as he pulled up alongside. The passenger-side power window whirred down and Harold yelled out, "Let's get going."

"Just a second," she said, turning back to the cop.

But the cop wasn't interested in her anymore. He was trying to see through the open window.

"Come on. Get in the truck," Harold said.

The cop was almost to the truck now, saying, "Maybe she doesn't want to get in the truck."

"Maybe you should let her decide, asshole," Harold said, seeing that Marianna was finally moving, shoving in front of the cop and opening the door, sliding in.

Harold hit the gas as her door closed; his last image of the cop was his mouth moving, saying, "Hey! You're the guy from—" and then his words were torn away as the truck took off and he disappeared, then reappeared in the rearview mirror, standing in the middle of the dark street, hands on hips, legs spread.

"What did he find in there?" Harold said, trying to calm himself.

"What?"

"In the trunk. What did he find?"

"Oh. This." Harold looked down at her hand as it opened and he saw the small brass shell casing gleaming in the weak light. His stomach shrunk to the size of a walnut.

"Where did that come from?" His voice sounded like someone just jumped on his throat.

"From the gun, I guess."

"I figured that out. What was it doing there? I mean, you cleaned the trunk, didn't you?" This was putting a major dent in his good mood. This was supposed to be a happy reunion, he thought, finding himself on Ventura Boulevard, heading toward the 405.

"Okay," he said after a few deep breaths, "I can handle that. I mean, now that I know, I can handle that."

She was quiet, pondering that word and coming up empty. "Know? Know what?"

"I heard what that cop said." He glanced at her, smiling, hoping that was enough.

"Yeah?"

"What I said before, about you turning me in. It isn't true."

He wanted her to agree. She was silent.

"It was Vito gave the cops my name. Now that I know that I can deal with these other things."

He felt that he had thrown a glass ball she hadn't caught, one that was still in the air but falling fast, ready to shatter on the floor.

She looked around as if suddenly realizing where she was. "Where're we going?"

"My place." She didn't answer. That ball was falling fast. "That okay?"

"Look, Harold," she finally said, her voice edged with impatience. "This whole thing's coming unraveled fast."

"What's happening?"

"Why should I tell you? The world you live in, you can make up something better on your own."

It stung. And he realized she wanted it to sting. Still, he couldn't help say, "What's that supposed to mean?"

"You always see what you want."

"Wait a second. You came to me, i.e., you asked me for help."

"For help. Not a lifetime commitment."

"I never pressured you."

"You didn't have to. Your attitude said it all."

"Really? And what did my attitude say?"

"You really want to know?"

Harold's masochistic forces were fully operational. He wanted it all now, and wanted it to be just as bad as possible.

"You're like this old dog following me everywhere."

Old. He always knew she thought that. "Go on."

"It's like you're looking at me all the time, hoping I'll scratch you or say something nice. But you know I might give you a kick too, and you're attitude is like, 'That's okay, everyone kicks me.' "

Her harsh words sunk in, connecting with things he'd suspected all along, and he could feel the knives inside him, slashing himself to pieces. He started to signal for the exit toward his apartment.

"Keep going," she said. "You're dropping me off."

"Where?"

"Down by LAX."

"What's going on?"

"That's it, Harold. You drop me off and we're done."

"Done?" There it was. All out in the open. "What's going on?"

"I'm meeting Vito."

"But he's setting us up."

"You should have known better than to believe a cop. Take Imperial."

Harold swung onto the connector ramp, driving automatically, feeling removed now, knowing he'd have plenty of time to rehash it later, use every word against himself.

"It's you and him then?"

"Something like that," she said laughing. She was hardly looking at him, staring out the window like she was a million miles away.

"I don't believe it."

"You don't?"

She slowly turned to him. "You don't listen so good, Harold. So I'll make it all real clear. I don't want you hanging around anymore. You make me sick. You and your plans, your little deals. Always talking about your stupid car books all the time. I got news for you, Harold, no one even reads your damn books."

"That's not true. They're in all the chains."

"Okay. Let me make this very clear. You're old. Used up. I'm still young. And I want someone young. So drop me off and get out of my life."

They were going faster and faster, hurtling along the elevated freeway beside the runways of LAX. Harold saw he was pushing a hundred. At this speed he could put the truck into an abutment, never feel a thing. Put an end to all this pain.

"The freeway's ending. Slow down before you kill us both."

He silently obeyed.

"Straight ahead, then left."

He had no more words. None that worked. All he'd do is drop her off and see what this pickup could do. Then find the nearest fixed object.

"Right here."

He U-turned and climbed to a ridge overlooking the sprawl of LAX with the patterns of mysterious colored lights. How far would he have to go to forget the things she had said to him?

"Pull over here." She pointed to the cars angle-parked into the curb, facing a grassy park that fell away and revealed a view of the airport. The truck idled as he waited for her to leave. In the distance he could hear shouts and whistles. Across the parking lot a car load of gangbangers were cheering two boys sparring in the headlights.

"Why don't you say something, Harold? Call me a bitch or a slut or something. Do something mean."

He said nothing.

"Jesus, you piss me off. I called you old. Doesn't that make you hate me?"

"I'll never hate you."

She gave a disgusted laugh. "I unload and you just take it. That's so typical. You know what's really bizarre? You have this everyone-kicks-poor-old-me attitude. But you walk away without a scratch. That's the thing you don't see. And that's what pisses me off the most."

There seemed to be something more she wanted to say, maybe even to take it all back. Harold waited, feeling numb. As she gathered up her things he noticed her hands were shaking.

"I'm getting out and you're going to leave now," she said, making it almost sound like a question.

"If that's what you want."

Her face went through a range of emotions, none of which he understood, then became hard and set again. She gripped her purse as she said, "Yeah, get out of here." She pushed open the door and stepped out.

Harold slowly pulled away. He cruised past the long line of parked cars. At the end he saw the Mercedes, a figure—probably Vito—leaning against the car smoking a cigarette, turning to look at him with a smug expression. Harold turned right up the hill and happened to notice, inside a parked car, a tall hairless man staring intently down at Marianna. As he continued down the street he glanced in his mirror and saw the tall man get out of the car and head down the hill toward the park.

The truck door closing behind her made it so final. She was cut off, on her own, moving toward Vito with a gun in her purse. She heard the truck drive away and forced herself to walk along the edge of the park toward him under the limbs of a big cypress tree. Everything was telling her to turn back, to flag Harold down and just leave with him. They could blow the ten grand on a pretty amazing trip. Then settle down somewhere else and get shit jobs.

But something was moving her feet toward Vito. It was the same thing that, years ago, turned her back from the jungle, back to the room where her parents lay dead at their executioner's feet, where she surprised him, swinging the machete she got in the woodshed and seeing the plume of blood spurt from his throat and spattered hot across her face as she swung it again and again. Only with the satisfaction that their deaths had been avenged had she been able to leave for the border with a clear heart.

Here was that same need for revenge, carrying her toward the Mercedes parked by itself at the end of the lot. He was leaning against the car, watching a jet barrel down the runway and lumber into the sky. When the noise died he sensed her there and turned.

"It's the little killer," Vito said, flicking his cigarette away in a shower of sparks. "That Dad-boy that dropped you off?"

"No. It was Harold."

"'It was Harold,'" he echoed, his laughter barking out, then stopping abruptly. "I thought we had a deal."

"What was that, Vito?" Being here, talking to him face-to-face, calmed her. She could handle this dirtball.

"Put all this on him."

"No need for that. I got what you want." She pulled the book out of her purse and waved it at him. "We can wrap it up here. If you got what I asked for."

"Refresh my memory."

"The pink slip on my Escort."

As he studied her in the weak light, she saw his eyes, crazy and bloodshot, and knew he was up in the jet stream somewhere.

"You were serious about that?"

He laughed, throwing his head back and braying at the sky. "That's what all this has been about?"

"It's mine. I want it back."

"I love it." He wagged a finger at her as he said, "Ya know, it's too bad we got cross-threaded, you and me. We could have had some fun."

"Is that a yes?"

"Actually, killer, I don't have the old pink slip with me. But I have to say, it doesn't matter much either."

"Why's that?"

"I'm not negotiating with you anymore." He was moving toward the trunk of his car.

She realized she was breathing hard, her hand straying toward the purse, part of her saying, "Now! Now!" But part of her was enjoying the moment, the control, the anticipation, wanting to push it all the way to the last second.

"Vito." She had the gun out now. "This look familiar to you?"

He turned, saw the gun—his gun—and licked his lips quickly, that little lizard tongue flicking out, hesitating as he stood next to the Mercedes trunk.

"Tell you what. I'll throw that in with your Escort. That and the car for the book."

"So we are negotiating?"

"I'd be a fool not to. I mean, you're kind of forcing the issue."

She was standing there with the book in one hand, the gun in the other, when she heard a voice she didn't recognize from her left, saying, "I'll take that."

Marianna turned and saw the tall man step out of the darkness holding a large silver gun and had no idea who he was, except that he was trouble. In that moment, Vito opened the trunk, and when she looked back he was lifting out the big rifle, so she fired and punched a hole in the Mercedes rear window, fired again and caught Vito in the right side. He caved in on the side, propped himself with the rifle under his arm, then, steadying himself as she continued firing, leveled the barrel toward her.

Then the world exploded.

Fire and noise enveloped her. She felt like it picked her up and threw her to the ground where she felt a sick wetness in her legs and became utterly helpless. No legs to keep her standing, to take her where she wanted to go. It was like they never existed. And so she lay there on the grass of the park waiting to die. Waiting for Vito to come and bring her complete darkness.

Slade had known the guy might be armed. But he never figured the girl would. As he came out of the trees it surprised him to see her with the gun and slowed him with a moment of indecision. Who should he go for?

And then he saw the damn assault rifle come out of the trunk and knew he'd been outgunned. It was like being back in the jungle with bullets cutting the trees to shreds around terrified, as Vito slowly began toward her in that step-drag, step-drag rhythm on the bad leg, keeping the rifle level and ready.

Harold found himself running back uphill and almost tearing his truck door from its hinges, jumping into the cab and shoving the stubborn little key into the tiny ignition. The truck roared to life and bucked forward, charging down the hill and across the intersection and up over the curb into the park. Harold yanked the lights on and hit the high beams, leaning on the horn to distract Vito, who was seeing the truck but continuing toward Marianna, faster now.

The truck engine was roaring, tires slipping and grabbing on the wet grass and picking up speed. But not fast enough. Not fast enough. Vito had stopped and was leveling the rifle at Marianna, fifty feet away, as Harold gave it everything, jamming his foot through the floorboards. As the gun started firing the pickup caught Vito from behind, a dull thud shuddering through the steel frame, throwing the body through the air, sailing in a high arc, the rifle lighting up the sky with bursts of flame like fireworks, and falling in a heap next to Marianna.

Harold slammed on the brakes and fishtailed to a stop beside the two bodies. He jumped out and gathered Marianna up in his arms, feeling the legs bend where they shouldn't. But he could feel her breathing. She was still alive. As he lay her across the front seat of the pickup he found the black book still in her hand and took it from her. He picked up her purse and threw that in on the truck floor.

Vito's body had been wrenched around so the feet were pointing down, the torso faceup, the toupee lying nearby. Harold searched Vito's pockets and took his wallet. There was the pink slip for the Escort. He'd shove that into Marianna's purse.

him, twigs raining down on his shoulders and head as he crouched low and moved down the ridge for cover. He found the wide trunk of a eucalyptus and steadied his gun hand against it as he looked back up the ridge for a clear shot.

Now gunshots were coming from a new direction. The Mexicans at the other end of the park were returning fire. He saw Vito, silhouetted against the orange streetlights, turn slowly like the turret of a tank and pour fire out in their direction. Screams and the sound of breaking glass blended with Vito's hoarse laughter. Then it was quiet and he heard a woman crying, "God, no! No!" Vito turned away, satisfied.

Slade could see the girl lying in the grass a hundred feet away. She was shot in the legs, and the delayed pain was hitting her now. He could hear her crying, saying something over and over again, calling a name he didn't recognize.

A jet thundered down the runway for takeoff and Slade hoped it would mask his fire. He leaned out and squeezed once, twice, three times, the gun bucking in his hand. Too hard to hit him with a sidearm in the dark at a hundred feet. All it did was draw fire. Vito turned and leveled the rifle as Slade pulled back behind the tree, feeling the bullets thudding into the other side. He was firing wildly, wasting ammunition. This was good. But it made Slade wonder: Did he have another clip on him?

Slade looked out across the park and saw Vito hunched over the gun, aiming at the woman. He braced for another fusillade. But nothing came. Was he dry? Maybe. He was staggering toward the car. Maybe he had his ammo there? He'd try drawing fire again and see what happened. He leaned out, aimed, and fired. The bullets kicked dirt at Vito's feet. He seemed to be fighting with the gun. Slade could hear metal-on-metal noises and tried to recall the reload sequence on the AK-47.

A siren wailed in the distance, getting closer. Another siren took up the call like coyotes in an urban wilderness. They were coming. There still might be time to scoop up the book and head out.

Check your weapon, soldier, it's time to go.

Slade started up the ridge, moving from tree to tree, none of them big enough to shield him completely. He was only thirty feet away when he stopped for a last check. Vito was swearing and jacking the lever back and forth. He'd only need another ten feet before he'd be in range, before he could take him. Go for the chest to knock him down. Then one in the head.

He started moving. The figure on the crest of the ridge was backlit in an orange glow, jerking the weapon and swearing, then looking up and seeing the man coming and swinging the rifle into position. Slade raised the automatic, hurrying the shot, as the AK-47 began firing again. Bullets tore his right arm away, only the material of the jacket holding it to his body. He looked at the arm, willing it to do what he said, and was trying to pick up the pistol with his left hand when the next burst caught him in the right lung, instantly filling his mouth with blood that tasted hot and young.

As he fell back he thought: *And that was how this simple soldier died.*

When the shooting started, Harold had been on his way down the side street from his parked truck. He didn't know what he was going to do, but he had to find out where the man was going and what Marianna was up to. He saw her talking to Vito, the body language hostile and the sound of their voices charged. It didn't look like they were going to

take off together. Then there were the three pops from the small gun and a moment later the terrible explosions of the assault rifle. As he dove behind a parked car he caught a movement that sickened him. The dim form of Marianna crumpling to the grass and lying still. A second later bullets were everywhere. The car window above him was blown out and hailstones of glass showered down on his head and neck.

It was over, he thought, feeling the agony growing in his chest. She was dead. Alone out there. And he had let her walk into it. Unprotected, helpless. She had insulted him like that because she knew what was coming and wanted him out of the line of fire.

The gunshots had stopped now and so had the rumble of jets on takeoff. A hole of silence filled the night in which he heard it.

His name.

He looked down through the darkness of the park and saw Marianna trying to get up, reaching out for help, her mouth open, black hair falling across her pale face. The face he loved. She seemed to know he was out there waiting to help.

Harold felt a surge of incredible strength. He would help her. He would run through bullets or fire to reach her. He could do anything.

He was about to charge blindly. But then the shooting started again and he watched the tall man, so frightening and strong and certain, rush Vito and, in the strobe of the muzzle flash, saw him jump and thrash, and then fall spinning to the ground. He knew then that it wasn't enough to make a gallant rush and die by her side. He had to do something else.

As he watched, Vito leaned over the fallen man and fired a single bullet into the still shape, making it jump up and fall back. Then Marianna's voice came to him again, and he realized that Vito was hearing it too, and he watched,

The sirens were closer now, coming fast. But he had to do one more thing.

Harold took the black book and tucked it into Vito's inside suit-coat pocket, his hand feeling the stillness of the body, no heartbeat, no breathing. As he ran back toward the truck he saw the toupee and scooped it up, an idea beginning to form.

Harold slid in behind the wheel, gently raising Marianna's head and settling it on his lap. She murmured softly as he slammed the door and pulled out. The truck bumped over the curb and headed down Imperial as the first cop car flew past him in the opposite direction and continued up the hill.

Marianna was shaking, so Harold dug his sport coat out of the jump seat and laid it over her. He saw then that her jeans above the knees were soaked black. She stirred, then woke with a start, coming back from a great distance. She looked around, confused, then her eyes came alive, looked up at him, dark in the night, yet intense as if backlit.

"Harold," she said. It was only a memory of her normal voice, which was strong and playful, filled with sensuality. She weakly reached for his face and he caught her hand. He hated how cold it was.

"Parts unknown," she said.

"What?"

"That's where I'm headed. Parts unknown."

He glanced down at the face in his lap as it filled with pain and sadness. She looked so pale and helpless, and emotions began rising in him he couldn't control, a desire to stop something unstoppable. But how do you stop a wave from breaking? He felt an enveloping tenderness for her, as if she was not his lover but his child instead. His little girl. A poor sick child with no will of her own, no understanding of the danger she faced. Here only for a moment, then gone.

"Who was the other guy there?" he asked her.

"Some leg breaker they sent after Vito."

"LaBounty?"

"They didn't know Covo was dead so they were trying to make sure—"

Something jumped into her mind and she tried to rise.

"My purse!" she was looking around wildly.

"It's okay. It's on the floor."

She fell back, exhausted. "Oh. Okay. There's something in there for you. Ten grand. I took it off Covo before I dumped him." She searched Harold for a reaction. "Nice, huh? That's what you're dealing with." Then with disgust. "But you know that by now."

"That's not what I think."

He slowed for the light at Hawthorne, then floored it through the red, turning left and heading north.

She laughed as if realizing something for the first time. "You pretend to be so tough. So cynical. But you really care about people. Those damn books of yours. You do it to help people."

"And make a buck."

"Sure, Harold." She was suddenly crying, a lost child. "I didn't want it to be like this. But it got all fucked up. Why?"

Centinela Hospital loomed at the end of the block. If she could just hold on. He looked down. The seat under her legs was black.

"Almost there," he said. "Hang on."

"Stay with me, Harold." Tears were streaming down her face. "If you don't I'll die there."

She suddenly grabbed his face and held it, hard. "Take me to Chile with you."

He could feel the end coming, like night too quickly closing a good day. He swung the truck past a lighted sign pointing toward the emergency room. It was dark and quiet now. No paramedic vans. No cops. This might work.

"Promise me, Harold." She was still holding him.

He looked down and saw her eyes, like a terrified animal, clawing at the world, trying to hold it before her but losing it, the pieces breaking up, sliding out of sequence.

"I promise," he said.

She closed her eyes.

The emergency-room loading dock came into Harold's headlights. A black orderly in scrubs was leaning against the wall smoking a cigarette.

Harold jumped out and ran around to the passenger-side door as he called to the orderly.

"I've got a woman in here's been shot!"

The orderly looked at the bullet holes in the truck door and said, "Oh, okay," and tossed his cigarette aside.

Harold lifted Marianna out of the cab, her legs hanging limply. As he turned the orderly was there with a gurney and he laid her down. Her eyes opened and she looked up at him and deep into his heart, in a way he'd remember for the rest of his life.

"You promised. Remember?"

"I remember."

The gurney was moving away from him now, down the loading dock toward the double doors of the ER. A team of doctors was coming toward them, coats flying open as they hurried down the hallway. And behind them, a security officer was approaching, looking beyond the gurney and the doctors, out into the night at Harold.

He watched as the gurney was pushed through the double doors. The last thing he saw was Marianna's hand rising, fingers closing, as if reaching for something. But she was moving. She was alive.

"Sir!" It was the security guard. "Sir!" He was coming out

onto the loading dock, motioning to Harold. "I want to talk to you."

"Of course," Harold said. "Let me just get my truck out of the way."

He slid in behind the wheel, backed up, and drove away.

At some point in the middle of her dance Kim became aware that he was standing along the back wall of the bar, watching her through a haze of smoke and pounding music. He was standing there alone, with an injured look on his face. Problem was, she had the foursome from Riverside on the runner (worth $110 so far) and the little old guy in the flashy suit and gold rings. He'd pay off handsomely before the night was over. If she worked him right.

And now Harold walks in, looking like a ten-year-old who got beaten up by the neighborhood bully. She kicked her dance up a notch, thrusting deeper, harder, punishing him somehow for not coming here sooner, for not taking her away from all this.

When her dance ended the hands shot up holding bills. Hands wanting to touch her, get a piece of her body. She collected what she could as she snake-hipped through the crowd, until she reached him ready with an angry word. But then she stopped. A tear was forming in his eye. It ran down his cheek and disappeared into his beard.

"You never learn, do you?"

He waited for more.

"You fucking idiot."

He took that, knowing it was true.

"You had to take it to some little whore who rips you up, then you come crying to me. You make me sick."

He took that, too. Then said, "Why're you so mad?"

"'Cause you're not crying for me."

As she turned away she heard him say, "Kim, I need a favor . . ."

She watched him coldly as they pushed more bills at her, and she let their greedy hands stay on her longer than usual, taking more than usual. He was still there when they were done. She knew he'd be there at closing time. And she knew she'd probably do whatever it was he wanted.

Marianna remembered being in his arms. Then she was falling. Falling and reaching up, trying to catch his hand once more. But he was gone and she was landing on something hard and cold that moved through darkness and into sudden bright lights. Then she was being touched by strange hands, clothes torn away, things pushed into her mouth and arms. And the hands on her legs. Cutting, tearing, pulling. She wanted to get up and walk away. But she knew that was impossible. So she lay there and let them touch her while she came loose from the thing someone had long ago named Marianna.

Yes, this was much better. Now she could go anywhere and do anything. All her life her thinking took place around her body. She was always conscious of where her body was and what it was doing. But now she was floating around the room as these people worried down below. Occasionally she went back to herself, but she felt scraping and clicking as they removed bone chips and cleaned the shredded area, cauterizing severed vessels. And she went back to floating.

Then there was a long dark period during which she drifted far away and heard music and could feel herself moving. Her body was completely gone now and she had a new one, a young one. She was a girl again in her village in Guatemala and she was dancing. She was clean again, too. Cleaner than she'd been in many years, before she moved to LA and became covered with the filth of the city. Her long white dress was moving around her and she was floating. Turning and drifting between the notes of the music and the breeze of a spring morning.

Someone was watching her dance now. She could feel a man's eyes on her. And it felt like love. Across the square, sitting alone in the café, was Harold. He was watching her and smiling sadly, with all the wisdom of the world in his eyes. She danced toward him and saw he was dressed up, a white shirt and dark tie, and he looked clean, too. So clean and handsome, younger than before, yet somehow not changed either. And she felt love all around her, connecting them, and everything. But his eyes were infinitely sad, and as she got close she saw, at his feet, a suitcase. And in his hand was a ticket.

The floating stopped and she was in a cold room. Shivering uncontrollably while someone held something wet in her mouth. She touched it with her tongue. It was a washcloth with an ice cube inside. Two nurses were talking. Talking about going horseback riding over the weekend in Griffith Park. She was back in LA. She was back in her body. And, between convulsions, she began to feel the pain in her legs.

"Harold!"

He turned and saw Zorich coming down the courthouse hallway, slipping as he hurried in his cowboy boots. The tone of his voice, the look on his flushed face, said it all. They were coming to get him. And the fragile hope that Harold had built up overnight, sleepless in his truck parked by the beach, thinking he could simply enter his guilty plea for the hit-and-run and then walk away, was dynamited into oblivion.

"What the hell have you been doing?" Zorich asked, noting Harold's rumpled suit and haggard face.

"You know, same old shit," Harold said, trying to pass it off.

"That's not what I mean, and you know it," Zorich hissed, leaning close. "Listen, we've got to get something straight. If you expect me to help you, you're gonna have to—"

Zorich stopped, seeing someone behind Harold. Harold tried to stop himself from turning—but failed. Jesus, his nerves were just about shot. Coming down the hallway, looking like a runaway truck, was Gammon, the thin black cigarette leading the way, trailing smoke into his beard. In his wake was that DA, Parker, lugging a heavy briefcase of legal documents.

Gammon stood in front of Harold staring at him silently and breathing hard until Parker finally arrived and said, "Mr. Dodge, the people will no longer consider your offer to plead due to circumstances which have arisen since our last—"

Gammon cut him off. "We gotta talk. Come on." He turned into a conference room and Parker followed. Harold looked at Zorich hoping he could stop this, but he solemnly gestured to follow them into the room.

As he entered the cramped room, with its tinted windows looking north over the parking lot and police station, Harold saw that Detective Torres was already in the room. They were ganging up on him. Gammon whispered something to Torres and they both laughed. But when the big cop sat down and faced Harold he wasn't laughing anymore. He looked irritated and disappointed with Harold. Then suddenly he smiled, briefly exposing his small sharp teeth.

The room became so quiet Harold could hear voices through the wall and the chirp of a car alarm out in the parking lot. Gammon looked like he was searching for a way to express his disappointment.

Finally he spoke: "You get around, don't you, chief?"

"What's that mean?" Harold asked, letting his resentment show. He figured that was a response that might indicate his innocence.

"I got three homicides. Actually two homicides and a missing person. And you're the central figure in all these dramas. Now, you gonna help me out?"

Harold recalled asking customers on the car lot: "If I give you a great deal on a used car, are you ready to buy today?" You had to get them saying yes. In his books he told readers to agree—conditionally.

"I'll help you any way I can. But I don't know anything about any homicides."

"You might be surprised, chief. You might be surprised. Item one. We have a John LaBounty. Multiple gunshot wounds. Found behind the Four Seasons on Doheny at twenty-one hundred. What do you know about that?"

Zorich leaned forward slowly. "If you're trying to connect my client to a homicide . . ."

"Did I say he'd killed anyone? I merely asked what he *knew* about the untimely death of one John LaBounty. Look, your client has agreed to answer these questions so you can relax."

Zorich slumped back and turned his eyes away. Harold was glad Zorich was there, though. The interruption gave him time to think. He was beginning to see that these encounters with cops were just negotiation sessions. The stakes were much higher—i.e., his freedom—but it was a negotiation nonetheless.

"Now," Gammon said, turning back to Harold. "What do you know about this?"

"Nothing," Harold answered. Out of the corner of his eye he saw Torres light a cigarette and lean back.

"Nothing? Then why was your name on a pad of paper in the victim's car?"

"I have no idea."

"But you heard the name before."

"LaBounty? I been hearing that name for years."

"Why?"

"He used to be the LA rep for Matsura."

"Do you know what he does now?"

"I heard he was kicked up to the national level somewhere. But that was years ago."

"You hear a lot of things."

"It's my business."

"I thought you were a tech guy for Aerodyne."

"I still do the car thing. Keep current for my books. *How to Buy a Cream Puff*—ever heard of it?"

Gammon ignored the question. "If you're current on car things, then you know Joe Covo."

"Sure. He owns a dealership in the South Bay."

"Exactly. Anything else you want to tell us about Joe?"

"What do you want to know?"

"Oh, I don't know. Like, why his car's been parked up on La Cienega in the oil fields for three days. A patrol car tagged it Saturday morning; we towed it into the crime lab this morning."

Harold knew Gammon wanted to give him a jolt with this revelation, try to get a reaction.

"I mean, that's not normal behavior now, is it, Harold?"

"People do a lot of strange things."

"Indeed they do. Twenty-seven years being a cop has

taught me that. And it's taught me something else too. Know what that is?''

''I can't guess.''

''When you find an individual's car, and it's been parked in an out-of-the-way place for a length of time, that individual is probably deceased.''

A picture of Covo's battered face, which he'd seen yesterday, washed up beside the stream in the Santa Barbara mountains, flashed into his mind. He pushed it back, hoping his expression wouldn't reflect his thoughts.

Gammon's voice was soft, almost inaudible as he asked, ''Where is he?''

''I have no idea.''

''Okay, chief. Then let me put it to you this way: You know anyone would want Covo dead?''

''Dead? I thought you said he was missing?'' Harold felt proud he sidestepped that one. Cops tried to be so sneaky.

''Like I told you, anyone disappeared that long is probably dead. So if you didn't kill him, who did?''

''Take your pick.''

''How's that?''

''He's ripped off a couple thousand people over the years. Anyone might have killed him.''

''He rip you off?''

''Not exactly.''

''Not exactly,'' Gammon echoed. He paused, then said, ''How about Vikki Covo? Know her?''

''No.''

''Never met her?''

''Never.''

''She thinks Vito Fiorre killed her husband. What do you think of that?''

Harold pretended he was trying to place the name. ''Vito Fiorre . . .''

"Come on, chief. You know Vito. You were in Covo's dealership last week, talking to him."

Harold looked at the others in the room, then back to Gammon. "You know, this is a real waste of time. I mean, you talked to this Vikki Covo, this Vito Fiorre already. So what's it matter what I say?"

"Chief, it's none of your damn business who I've talked to or what they said. Now I'm gonna make this real simple for you. What matters is exactly what you know. Got it?"

Harold hated Gammon. But he knew his hatred wouldn't help him now, so he answered by saying, "Got it, chief."

"Good. Now why would this Vito Fiorre tell Mrs. Covo her husband was in trouble with his bosses? I mean, since you still do the car thing and are current in the business."

"I heard there was some kind of investigation. If they were going after LaBounty, he might figure Covo was gonna tell the DMV or the Feds what he knew."

"Was Vito afraid they would come after him?"

Harold hesitated again. It would only be believable if Gammon pulled it out of him. In the silence he heard a tap tap tap on the window, looked up, and saw it was raining again. He hoped it would be a hard rain. There was still a lot of garbage in this city that needed to be washed out to the ocean.

"Vito and I didn't have the kind of relationship where he told me a lot of secrets." He paused, looking at the others. "I.e., he hated my guts."

"Why?"

"I was trying to help a friend of mine unwind a deal he put together."

"Would that friend be Marianna Perado?"

"It would."

"And what was your relationship with Covo like?"

"I had no relationship with Covo."

"Really?"

"Yes."

"Isn't it true you used to work for Covo? You were his Bird Dog. Find suckers and send them in to him. He'd rape them."

"That was years ago."

"And he fired you."

Harold felt his anger rising. "Yes."

"Why?"

"'Cause I tried to give a customer a good deal. Scratch that—a fair deal. A little old lady, for Christ's sake. When Joe found out he fired me—in front of everyone on the lot."

"So you really hated Joe."

"Yes, I did."

"And you hated this Vito Fiorre too."

"Not really. I didn't know him."

"But you said he hated you."

"Okay. Look, Vito thought the guys in Cincinnati had sent someone out to kill him and Joe." Harold was playing it by ear, amazed by how the pieces were fitting together.

"Why did he think this?"

"Because he said he thought someone had killed Joe. And he was next on the list."

Gammon sat back in his chair and turned toward Torres. A look was exchanged that Harold couldn't interpret. Gammon turned back to Harold and leaned in close.

"You wouldn't happen to have the name of the guy in Cincinnati."

"As a matter of fact, I do."

"Would you please share it with us?"

"It was John LaBounty."

"But LaBounty's dead."

Harold shrugged. "You told me to tell you what I know."

Gammon looked at Torres, and he wrote something down on a piece of paper. Harold hoped they were going to check LaBounty's hotel messages. They would find the call Harold made from a pay phone shortly after he left Marianna at the hospital. It was just what a hit man would do if LaBounty had sent one.

"LaBounty put a hit on Covo and Fiorre. But someone got him first. That's a pretty story, Harold. I mean, it's always convenient when you can blame something on a dead guy."

Gammon stubbed his cigarette out, folded his arms, and stared at Harold. Finally he said, "You probably think that puts you in the clear, don't you?"

"In the clear? Of what?"

"The little deal you pulled up on Imperial last night."

Harold looked at Zorich. He blankly stared back as if he had given up hope.

"Come on, Harold. We found two bodies up there just after midnight. Fiorre looked like he got hit by a freight train. You did that to him?"

"No."

"Then why did our witnesses say they saw a pickup truck run him down?"

"I don't know."

"You drive a pickup, don't you Harold?"

"Me and three million other people in LA."

"A red-and-white GMC pickup?"

"It's not exactly red. They call it cranberry—"

"Is your truck out there in the parking lot?"

Harold glanced out the window. It was really coming down. He didn't think they'd go looking around for his truck. If they did they probably wouldn't find it where he parked, two blocks away. It was for just this kind of reason he had always preferred street parking.

"I took a cab."

Gammon leaned forward hungrily. "If we impound your truck would we find front-end damage?"

"You might. I don't know."

"You don't know?"

"I don't know if it's fixed yet. I had that fender bender last week. Remember the alleged hit-and-run?"

"Is there front-end damage to your truck?"

"Front and rear. It's in the shop now."

"When'd you take it in?"

"Yesterday."

"And the shop will verify that?"

"It's what happened. Why wouldn't they?"

Harold could feel Gammon's disappointment. "Chief, I think you're full of shit. I think you and your truck and your girlfriend were up there last night. And when Fiorre pulled out that fucking assault rifle you turned him into a hood ornament. Now what do you say to that?"

"It wasn't me. I wasn't there."

"Okay. Where were you?"

Harold sighed. This couldn't come out too easily.

"I'd rather not say."

"Chief, you can tell us now, or you can tell Assistant District Attorney Parker after he books you for murder one. Take your choice."

Harold looked at Zorich. Zorich nodded.

"I was with a friend."

"This friend have a name?"

"Kim. Kim DuPuis."

"Where can we find Kim DuPuis?"

"She works at a bar at Century and La Cienega."

"Nude Nudes?" Gammon laughed.

"Yeah."

"She a hooker?"

"No."

"Of course not, Harold. She's a kindergarten teacher."

Gammon let the silence build while he searched Harold's eyes, boring into his brain, rummaging around for answers. Harold kept everything blank.

"What's your caper, Harold?"

"What?"

"Come on. What's a techno-geek like you doing mixed up with a slut like Perado."

"I told you, I was trying to help her," Harold said, noticing how good it felt to tell the truth. "And she's not a slut."

"But Fiorre thought she was. And when you found out he fucked her you went after him. Right?"

Harold felt Gammon was guessing, pulling his chain to see what happened. So he kept the anger at a distance. He could take it out later and hate Gammon for it, and even fantasize about ways to get even with him. But for now he just said, "I know it'd be convenient for you if I said I killed him. But I didn't. So I'm not going to say I did."

"You kill Covo?"

That was easy. Harold laughed as if it was absurd. "No."

"We'll see about that, chief."

Gammon looked at Torres and he made another note. Parker shifted in his chair and looked up at the clock on the wall. Harold could feel the tension going out of the room. That was all they had against him. And it wasn't enough. Not this time. They hadn't checked with Santa Barbara yet. Either that or his fake ID trick worked. But if they learned he'd been up there in the coroner's office and found he had Covo's body moved to a mortuary, he was sunk.

Zorich sensed his chance and rose, his chair screeching on the linoleum. "I think my client's been more than patient with all this."

"You're client's a fuckin' saint," Gammon said, leaning

back and shaking out a new cigarette. "I liked the part about buying the little old lady a good used car. That was inspired."

Everyone stood up. Gammon looked down at Harold from his enormous height. "I seen guys like you before. You think you can bend the rules and still go home for dinner with the folks. But you can't, Harold. You broke the law, and I'm gonna prove it."

Zorich nudged Harold toward the door saying, "You don't have to listen to this."

"Not now he doesn't. But I'll be in touch again real soon." Gammon smiled broadly and pointed his unlit cigarette at Harold, "You're my number one, chief."

Marianna's desk was empty, of course, the coffee cup rinsed out and set in place next to the sign that said, "Just because you're paranoid doesn't mean they're not watching you." The pencils were sharpened and set alongside a square block of Post-it notes. It all looked so sad and empty that Harold felt like crying.

He had arrived in the office after his court appearance ready with an excuse to explain his absence. But no one seemed to care. People were clustered around the coffee machine by the window, talking and looking frightened. Something was up. Harold went into his office and was setting down his briefcase when Jerry spoke to him from behind.

"Harold."

Harold turned, saying, "Sorry I'm late, Jerr. You get my message?"

"Harrington just made the announcement."

"What?" Harold was having trouble focusing on this. He was still thinking of Gammon and all those questions.

"He met with Wilson."

"Yeah. And?"

"It's over."

"We're going to Dallas?"

"No. It's over. Go home and work on your résumé."

The phone on Harold's desk started ringing.

"You mean—"

"The whole damn division is closed. Four hundred and fifty of us on the streets. And more layoffs coming after the first of the year. Go home, Harold."

"Jesus."

"Jesus is right. I heard a lot of people are going to be leaving LA." He looked at Harold resentfully. "At least you don't have a wife and three kids to feed." He felt bad about that as soon as he said it, so he added: "Sorry. I know it's hard for all of us. Good luck."

After Jerry left, Harold became aware that his phone was still ringing. Out of reflex he answered it.

"Harold. Thank God you're there." It was Zorich. The tone of his voice caused a light sweat to break out around Harold's collar.

"What's up?"

"I called a buddy of mine, a cop up in the Valley. He told me they got the car."

"What car?"

"The car. The Matsura you were driving when they picked you up that night."

"Okay."

"Okay? Shit, Harold. They're taking it to the lab. They're gonna pull the thing apart."

"Why?"

"For samples. Hair, fiber, blood. If Covo or Fiorre was ever in it Gammon's gonna nail you."

"Of course they were in it. They owned the damned thing before they sold it to Marianna."

"Yeah, well. It gets worse. They talked to your friend Kim DuPuis. She says you were there, but said she doesn't remember the exact time you arrived."

Harold's voice felt choked and small as he asked, "So they actually think it was me that ran down Fiorre?"

"Let me put it to you this way. They're coming after your truck next."

Harold sat behind his desk. The seat felt oddly cold. "What should I do?"

"I'm not talking to you as counsel now, okay?"

"Okay."

"If they ever ask you, your attorney never said this."

"I understand."

"Unless you're ready for them to go over your truck with a fuckin' electron microscope, you better do something about it. You know what I'm saying?"

"I got you."

"And Harold?"

"Yeah?"

"Is there something you want to tell me?"

"What do you mean?"

"It's getting very bad now."

"How bad?"

"Gammon asked for your passport."

"My passport?"

"They know about your trips to Chile."

Harold wanted to innocently say "So what?" But the words stuck in his throat. It was like they were trying to slam the last exit door shut on him.

"Can they do that? Take my passport?"

"They can ask. And frankly, I think you should give it to them."

"You do?"

"Sign of good faith. Show them you don't have anything to hide." When Harold didn't immediately answer, Zorich added, "You don't, do you, Harold? Have anything to hide?"

"Well, I mean . . . shit. Everyone's done something they don't—"

"Harold, maybe it's time you and me had a very candid talk."

Harold was quiet for a long time. Then he said, "I'll call you when I'm on my way."

"Okay. And Harold? Look, there's still a chance we can beat this. Okay, big guy?"

"Sure."

After he set down the phone he took out the list he'd written labeled "How to Stay Out of Jail" and filled in number seven. When he was finished he felt that Zorich was right, there was still a chance for him. But what he had in mind didn't involve Zorich or Marianna, or anyone he knew. He looked at what he had written once more, then packed up his things and left his office for the last time.

Cao Tran was so glad to see him, bowing across the desk in the cramped office of his radiator shop and taking Harold's hand in both of his. These Asians really know how to give customer service, Harold thought. No wonder they're kicking the shit out of Detroit.

"We just talking golf," Tran said, gesturing to another Asian in the room, holding a putter and stroking a ball into a tin can. The man bowed, briefly exposing a bald spot.

"This gentleman, very big hitter," Tran said proudly.

The man added nervously, "But short game, very poor. Remember what they say, 'The woods are full of big hitters.'"

Harold thought that might apply to his current situation, too.

"Play golf, Harold?" Tran asked.

"I got enough aggravation without that." The men roared with laughter. Harold waited, then: "Can I talk to you outside, Tran?"

In the parking lot, surrounded by dismembered cars, a light rain falling on them, Tran said, "Sorry, Harold. I not sell radiators. Not yet. But I will. Very high-quality metal."

"I know, Tran," Harold said. "That's not why I'm here."

"Okay, my friend. What's up?"

"Tran, I need a big favor."

"What you need, Harold?"

"We were chatting once, about the war, and about your home country." Harold watched his words' effect on Tran; he kept smiling and listening, but there was a lot behind it now. Memories and pain.

"You mentioned your uncle got out first, then helped your family escape. You said he owned a print shop, knew how to falsify documents, passports or something . . ."

"Yes."

"I need your help with something like that."

"Where you escaping from?"

"LA."

"We fought to get here. Why you going?"

"I'm in trouble. For something I didn't do. Well, I did some of the things, but it's not as bad as it looks." He paused, confused. "Hell, I don't want to go to prison."

Tran nodded gravely. "Very bad place."

Harold drew the envelope out of his coat pocket along with his passport. He let Tran see them both, then said: "I'm thinking maybe your uncle could help me out. I can't be Harold Dodge anymore."

Harold was holding out the passport and the envelope. Tran looked at them but wouldn't accept them.

"Here's the deal," Harold said. "I give you my truck. It needs some bodywork but it's practically brand new. You loan me a car—any old junker you got around—just for a few hours. You can pick it up at the airport."

Tran still hadn't taken the envelope and passport.

"I don't know, Harold. Very risky."

"Tell you what. When you sell the radiators, you keep all the money." Tran was softening. "Truck's worth eighteen grand, wholesale."

"You got pink slip?"

"I'll sign it over to you right now. You get yourself a cream puff and a couple grand for an hour's work. Not bad."

"You got yourself a deal." Tran took the envelope and turned back inside. "I'll talk to my uncle now."

"He's here?"

"Yes, you met him. The big hitter."

As Harold watched Tran disappear into the office, he jumped, feeling the beeper on his hip vibrate. It was like a nerve was connected from the beeper to his heart—when it went off his pulse went through the roof. He checked the number and found it was Zorich calling. Third time in an hour. No sense calling back. He knew what he had to do. And no lawyer in the world could help him now.

Marianna knew something was up when she saw the cop arrive. It must have been late afternoon because she had been looking out her window, watching the glow behind the buildings on Century slowly fade into night. The cop looked in on her, then stood silently by the door. Were they afraid she'd try to escape on two mangled legs? The doctor said he didn't even know if she could walk again. And if she could, she gathered by his tone, it wouldn't be a pretty sight.

All this news would have depressed Marianna if it hadn't been for one thing. Vito was dead. That was the most important thing. She'd seen him fly through the air and land next to her, the dead look all over his face. No doubt about it this time. Harold finally did what she wanted. Now, if she got away with it, that was the icing on the cake. The main thing was, Vito was dead.

She was thinking about this—or dreaming about it maybe—when she opened her eyes and found an enormous man straddling a chair next to her bed. He patted his breast pocket and shook out a long thin black cigarette. Then he seemed to remember where he was and tucked his lighter away, the cigarette still dangling from his lips. There was a sense of style and drama about this man she found amusing, even before he spoke.

A nurse came in to check Marianna's chart, and when she saw the man's cigarette, she said, "I'm sorry, Detective, there's no smoking in here."

"Am I smoking?" he said, the cigarette bobbing as he spoke in his deep rumbling voice.

"No. But I thought you might—"

"All right then."

The nurse left and the man sat there looking at Marianna, and she might have smiled back at him, when he finally spoke, his voice tinged with sadness: "Sweetheart, this is the end of the line."

She giggled at that. It was so much like an old movie.

"I'm Detective Gammon. Homicide. We got your Matsura. There's blood all over the trunk. We got a very unhappy sergeant from Garden Grove ready to testify he found a shell casing in the trunk. We've got witnesses saw you up on

Imperial last night talking to Fiorre. And in my pocket, I've got a warrant for your arrest."

He waited for her to speak. She smiled at him, and was careful to use a voice that was nonconfrontational. "That Matsura doesn't belong to me. I hate Japanese cars. I drive a Ford Escort."

"Is that so?" He seemed to be reevaluating her, gaining a better understanding of where she was coming from. Maybe he could sense how good she felt right now, lying in the bed. Rested. Peaceful. She felt like she was floating in a big bubble. And now it was pleasant having this man to listen to. It almost seemed like he was talking to someone else.

"Sweetheart, the Matsura is registered to you."

"That doesn't make it mine."

"In the eyes of the law it does."

"I drive a Ford Escort," she said again, being as pleasant as possible under the circumstances.

"So be it. The fact of the matter is, we've put together a scenario that includes you committing a number of serious crimes. Now I know that you didn't do these things alone. It would have been impossible for you to. You did them with Harold Dodge. Is that right?"

"Well, Harold's quite a guy," she admitted, an image of Harold suddenly jumping into her mind. She could see him smiling and laughing in that half-embarrassed way of his, the way she learned was mostly an act, to get people to do what he wanted them to do. Several Harolds floated across the screen of her mind, amusing her, as he always did, but finally leaving her feeling lonely and let down.

"Where's Harold?" she asked. She suddenly felt close to tears. Her emotions were all over the place.

"We don't know. That's why I'm here. I want you to help us find him."

"So you can arrest him?"

"Yes." He paused and explained, "You see, we think he may try to leave the country. If he does, do you know what that means for you?"

"Why don't you go ahead and tell me."

"You take a big fall. For Covo, for Fiorre, for LaBounty—the whole crowd."

"Detective, I don't recognize those names."

This brought a tired sigh from Gammon. "We're way beyond that now, don't you think?"

Marianna didn't answer.

"Now here's the deal. We got two 747s leaving for Chile in about an hour. Customs is a zoo. We miss him there we got seven-hundred-odd faces to check while the jet's sitting on the runway."

"Why are you telling me all this?"

"I think you know." His voice contained a measured degree of regret when he added, "So you ready to help us now?"

"Come on, Detective. Why do you think I'd help you?"

He looked at her a long time, the unlit cigarette still in his mouth, and timed his line beautifully: "Sweetheart, you ever spent any time in prison?"

Harold saw the detective as he was about to dial Zorich's number on a pay phone at the airport. He was tired of feeling the beeper jump on his hip all afternoon and decided maybe Zorich would tell him something that would help. No matter how much it hurt to hear it. But Torres, the detective, was there in front of him, scanning the faces with his sneaky little cop eyes. He decided to delay the call to Zorich until after a detour to the men's room.

Moments later he stepped back into the terminal feeling

very changed. He had hoped he would be able to keep the beard. He'd had it for over ten years, and without it his face felt exposed, as if he had scraped the flesh off. To complete the effect he stopped in a gift store and bought a pair of tinted glasses. Looking at himself in the store mirror he was shocked by what he saw.

The pager went off again and he checked the return phone number. Zorich's office. No doubt he was calling to tell him there was a warrant for his arrest. He already knew that by the cop's presence, so he discarded the idea of returning the call.

There was an incredibly long line at customs. People shoving and jostling, moving huge bags of presents and bulky carry-on luggage. The line stretched across the brightly lit room with the long row of counters and back into the international terminal.

They know about your trips to Chile, Zorich had said. That was about the only useful piece of information the little bastard had given him.

Torres was beside the counter talking to a customs supervisor, gesturing threateningly and looking over his shoulder as if expecting someone to arrive at any second. Harold couldn't help looking in that direction. But all he saw were more families, tourists, and tired businessmen, lumbering along with huge carry-on bags.

Spanish crackled in the air in staccato bursts as a fashionably dressed woman chattered about returning to see relatives and friends again. Harold picked out phrases here and there. He'd have to get serious about learning Spanish now that he had more time. That would go on the list with all the other things he had wanted to accomplish and never had time for. If he got away.

The line surged forward as one agent waved through a group of businessmen without checking their bags. Harold was perhaps only three people away. But he couldn't keep his eyes off Torres. The customs agent had given him a list and the cop was reviewing it carefully. He took out a cellular phone and dialed. When someone answered he spoke while looking at the list, shaking his head.

"Next in line!"

Harold saw he was being summoned by a young woman with black hair and bored, sleepy eyes. He moved toward her feeling his heart begin to pound, but trying not to think as Harold Dodge. Right now he needed to be another person, a person who at this moment wouldn't be nervous at all. Thinking that calmed him slightly.

"Good evening, sir," she said with a trace of an accent. Now that Harold was closer he could see how pretty she was in the tight blue uniform pants and the crisp white blouse, lingerie dimly visible underneath. Her name tag read "T. Santos."

"How's it going?" Harold asked, having the odd sensation his voice was different, his choice of words unnatural.

"Passport."

He drew his passport out and handed it to her.

"Are you traveling for business or pleasure?"

"I do everything for pleasure," he said, surprised again by his answer.

She raised her sleepy eyes toward him with a give-me-a-break expression.

"Pleasure," he said. "Just a vacation."

T. Santos was examining his passport now.

"Ever been to Chile before?"

"No. Have you?"

She was looking closely at the photo on the passport. She ran her finger over the seal imprinted across the picture, the seal Tran's uncle said was the hardest part of the forgery.

"I was born there. What line of work are you in?" She

looked up at him again, no longer bored, her sleepy eyes inspecting him.

"I'm general manager of a car dealership. Joe Covo Matsura, in Torrance. Heard of it?"

"No."

"Lemme give you my card." He opened his wallet, letting her see the driver's license and array of credit cards, and pulled out a business card. "Ever need a car, call me—personally. I'll give you a superlow price."

She took the business card and looked at it, then back at the passport. She was still bothered by something. Harold removed the tinted glasses.

"It's the glasses," he explained, smiling.

She nodded and handed the passport back to him.

"Don't forget now. Call me. I'll take care of you."

"I won't. Have a nice trip, Mr. Fiorre."

As Harold passed Torres the beeper on his hip was vibrating again. He took it off, dropped it in a trash can by the door, and walked down the jetway to the plane.

The doors closed and the cabin was pressurized. Moments later Harold felt a slight bump as the Air Chile jet was towed back from the jetway. He looked out the window and saw they were moving. Very slowly. One engine started, then another. He settled back into his seat and began breathing deeply, letting all the pressure fall away from him.

"Pillow? Blanket?" a flight attendant was asking.

The little old lady sitting next to Harold took the pillow, and Harold helped her get it settled behind her head.

"How about you, sir?" the flight attendant asked, smiling, touched by his kindness to the old lady. "Pillow? Blanket?"

"No," Harold said. "But I would like some water. One glass with water, another glass with just ice."

"Certainly, sir. As soon as we take off." The flight attendant was tall and blond but had a slight Spanish accent. Probably descended from those Germans that went to Chile after the war. Aryan looks, Latin passion—not a bad combination.

They were on the taxiway when the jet suddenly stopped, the turbines whining down as they were shut off. Harold looked out the window. Several cars were pulling up beside the jet. Harold's ears thumped as the cabin depressurized and he had the sense of outside air filling the cabin, ocean air, LA air he thought he'd never have to breathe again.

"Ladies and gentleman." The captain's voice filled the cabin. "We're going to have a slight delay here . . ." There was bumping and the sound of new voices at the front of the plane. "There's been a mix-up with customs that we need to get straightened out. We'll probably be on our way in just a few minutes."

Harold strained to look between the seats to see what was happening. Several figures were moving toward him, pushing something in front of them. Then he saw Gammon's head, rising above everyone else's. They were slowly coming down the aisle, pushing something, talking, searching the passengers' faces.

"Your first time flying?" the old lady next to Harold asked.

"What?"

She pointed at his hands gripping the armrest. The knuckles were white. He tried to smile at her.

"It'll be okay. You'll see. We'll get there safely."

"I hope so," Harold said. "I really hope so."

Gammon was finished now with the first-class section and was moving into the main cabin trailed by Torres and an airport supervisor speaking nervously into a radio. In front of them was a paramedic pushing something. Between the rows of seats, Harold saw Marianna's pale face. She was strapped to an upright gurney of some sort so she could see the faces of the people in all the seats.

The airport guy heard something over his radio and said to Gammon, "Detective, we have a seven-minute window here. Miss that and this flight'll get bumped back to midnight."

Gammon ignored him. "Take your time, sweetheart," he said to Marianna, watching her face closely.

Marianna's beautiful dark eyes were roving the cabin, searching the faces, moving on, stopping, moving on.

Harold had to look at her, even though he knew this is what Gammon wanted. They were using her as bait, trying to flush him out of hiding. And it might even work because all his feelings were rushing to the surface again, making him feel dizzy and unstable. He desperately wanted to reach out and touch her. She looked so frail and helpless now. He wanted to take her with him, as he had promised, to take care of her, make her feel special. He imagined her small and delicate in his arms, feeling her heartbeat against his chest, remembering their time together in the hotel room. She made him feel all those emotions he thought he'd left behind as he grew older and life seemed to dim a little more each day.

But none of that had worked. Part of her had always been somewhere else, a place he'd never be allowed to go. And now, here they were, with a cop between them, and his freedom as a growing question hanging in the still cabin air.

Marianna's eyes moved past him, then came back, probing his eyes behind the tinted glasses. Suddenly a light came into her eyes, and they filled with a secret understanding. Harold's body tightened, but he forced himself to look at her wondering, Is *she seeing her own freedom*? He felt his whole life turning around the look in her eyes, this silent exchange. The cabin closed in around him and there was a tunnel between them through which something was given and something understood.

"What?" Gammon looked at Marianna, trying to see who she was looking at. "What is it?" The detective scanned the rows of men and women, partially hidden behind seats backs, slumped in rest or obscured by newspapers.

Harold felt the tunnel was still there between them and through it he sent her one word: "Please."

She seemed to hear him and looked away, her laughter building as she appreciated the spectacle of Harold wearing the black wig, the one he took off Vito, his smooth-shaven face and tinted glasses.

"What?" Gammon asked her again. "You see him?"

"I was just thinking," she said. "You're after the wrong guy."

"W*hat*?"

"Harold's no killer. He helps people. He helped me."

"Helped you spend the rest of your life in prison."

"No. He helped me do what I had to do. That's all you can ask for."

The airport guy was on the radio again. "Detective, the tower's trying to push us back. Unless this is a major emergency we really need to—"

Gammon looked at Marianna's changed expression and saw she'd no longer be any help. "Let's get out of here," he growled. Then, under his breath, he muttered, "Fuckin' waste of time."

And then Marianna was leaving him again, going back down the aisle and out the door, making Harold feel his entire life had been nothing more than a few brief moments of happiness connected by, and inevitably leading back to, separation, isolation, and despair.

Harold had been listening to the maids chattering in the kitchen when he first spotted the car coming down the long dirt road from the village. His Spanish had improved more than the maids realized. He could basically make out what they were saying about him. *Flojo,* they said. Lazy. All he did was move his chair on the patio to stay in the sunlight as he stared out at the ocean. They thought he was running from tax problems *en los Estados Unidos.* He smiled as he heard that one.

When Tina came out to check on him again, he made his expression as blank as possible, to hide the fact that he'd been listening to them. Then he added, "*Más café, por favor. Por el extranjero,*" he added, pointing at the car that was now stopping near the stand of pine trees at the end of the driveway. As he rose and headed down the walk toward the car, he felt that sense of panic he had lived with before, a feeling he thought he'd left back in LA with all his other problems.

It was a big Buick, the kind they rented at the airport in Santiago. The kind he had rented when he first arrived four months ago and needed to find a place to live. Too bad he hadn't been able to bring his pickup here. It would be worth a fortune. Instead he drove a *deux cheveaux*—two horses—he'd traded for an old tractor he found on the property. Once he rebuilt the engine it got him into town and back. And at this point there wasn't much more he needed.

Harold watched as a woman got out of the Buick, still holding a map. Good, she was alone. But that didn't mean anything for sure. He had to be careful. Friendly, open, but careful. Yeah, that was the best approach.

"Hello! Can I help you?"

"I'm looking for Harold Dodge," she called, squinting into the sun and revealing how age would someday overtake this face. She was tall, blond, probably American judging from her accent and the way she dressed in tight jeans with a flannel shirt.

"I'm Harold. What can I do for you?"

Her face filled with eagerness, and he could see color come into her cheeks.

"I need to talk to you. Can I come in?"

Harold hesitated. He had known someone would come for a long time. First there had been the letters from the detective agency. Then the international telexes (which he told Tina not to sign for so they would be returned). Yes, he knew someone would come eventually and he'd often wondered what he would tell them.

Now this woman stood in front of him, looking up the flagstone walk at him, her young face filled with questions and a beautiful air of controlled anger. This might be a trick, though. He'd have to stay on guard. She could have brought a detective with her. He might be in the village at this moment, making inquiries about the eccentric Yankee who lived by the ocean.

"Please," she said, worried by his hesitation, "I just want to talk to you."

He waved her up. "Sure, I'm just putting on some coffee." They began walking up the steps to the patio beside the villa. "It took me a second because I'm not used to hearing American—ah, English." Christ, he was so nervous the words were getting mixed up again. Either that or it was because she was such a knockout. He'd always been flustered around beautiful women. And now he was finding that hadn't changed.

"Have a seat." Harold gestured at a chair across the patio,

the one he'd strung with cane. It was nice to have the time to do things like that. He was also practicing casting with a fly rod he bought through a catalog from an outfitter in Montana. A trout stream flowed through the edge of his property and he could see the speckled fish darting in the shadows of the icy clear water. He practiced casting for hours, the rhythm of the rod hypnotizing him as it flashed back and forth like a single strand of a spider's web. What a life he had down here. And now she'd come to take it all away from him.

Out of the corner of his eye he saw Tina watching them from the kitchen.

"My name is Vikki Pearlman."

"Hi, Vikki, I'm—I guess you know who I am." God that was stupid, he thought, laughing at his mistake.

"Yes. I came all the way from LA to see you. I hope you can help me."

"Well, I'll try," he said, trying to look like he had no idea what she wanted.

"I was—I am married to Joe Covo."

"Uh-huh."

"About four months ago, he disappeared. At first I was told he had left for business reasons."

Harold kept the confused look on his face, as if this was all new to him.

"It's a long involved story. But, the point is, for the last four months really, I've been looking for him. I even sent you some letters. Didn't you get them?"

"Me?"

"Yes."

"I've been traveling a lot. And the postal service down here—forget it."

She let the silence build, examining him, then continued.

"Anyway, all along I've had this feeling—this feeling of, like, dread, that Joe is—that he may be—dead."

Tina appeared with a tray and two espresso cups. She nervously smiled at Vikki and then set the tray on a nearby table. Vikki took the small cup and put two sugars in the thick black coffee.

"I've spent a lot of money trying to find him. I've hired several detectives and they keep turning up the same things. First it looks like Joe might have been killed by an executive from the national office in Cincinnati. Then it all begins to point back to this guy that worked at Joe's dealership—Vito Fiorre. But Vito was killed in a hit-and-run accident a few days after Joe disappeared."

Harold nodded politely, still keeping the confusion in his expression, as if it wasn't really gelling yet.

"One detective was sure a woman named Marianna Perado might have killed him."

"Did you talk to her? Marianna Perado?" Harold asked, trying to keep what he felt out of his voice.

Vikki frowned at the memory. "Yeah, I talked to her. Right after Joe disappeared. She was in the county jail for a week but they didn't have enough to hold her."

"What'd she say?"

Vikki laughed, disgusted. "What a bitch. She just seemed to be—to be like laughing inside. She had a real *attitude*, you know, like she knew everything but wasn't going to give me a clue. Not a clue. I've tried to find her again but she's gone."

She began stirring the coffee, staring into it as if she might find an answer there. Then she looked up, her eyes sharp, and an intelligence showing behind them that surprised him.

"You knew Joe," she said, suddenly.

"I—well, yes. A long time ago. I worked for Joe."

"Salesman?"

"I started as a guy who found people who might want to buy a car and—"

"A Bird Dog."

"Yes."

"Joe fired you."

"Yeah. I tried to stop someone from getting screwed." Harold paused and added: "Sorry, but that's the way I saw it."

"That's okay. I knew a little about what went on down there. And I didn't like it. But at that time I was—well, I've changed in the last few years." She laughed sadly. "In the last few months, really. That's why I changed my name back, to Pearlman. I'm trying to put all that behind me."

"What you've gone through," Harold said, "it must be a hell of a shock."

Resentment flashed across her face, which she quickly suppressed.

"Your life goes along smoothly, so smoothly, for so long. It makes you think it will always be that way. What you don't realize is, you're always just one step away from everything going to hell."

"I know what you mean," Harold said, thinking of his life in LA, how crazy it seemed from here.

A brief silence settled between them, and Harold realized he had to start talking now. He had to appear helpful, voluntary, if he wanted to get rid of her. The last thing he wanted was to see her come back tomorrow with a detective. Or the local cops. They could raise all sorts of hell with him. Pull him in for questioning and that would be the last anyone saw of him.

"I guess you know I was involved with Marianna."

Vikki nodded. She looked suddenly hopeful, like something might follow to cancel the months of darkness and frustration she had lived with.

"Maybe involved is too big a word," he said. "I tried to help her unwind a deal she got at Joe's dealership. Vito Fiorre put her in a bad contract and she wanted out. I tried to help, but one thing led to another and I realized I was in way over my head. So I tried to put as much distance between me and them as I could."

"But they had a warrant for you—for killing Vito."

"You see what happens when you try to help someone? I had nothing to do with that."

"Then why did you leave? I assumed—"

"Combination of a lot of things. I'd just got laid off. On the side I have this business—a little publishing company. Taxes were killing me so . . ." He opened his hands to show the end result of those factors. "Tell you the truth, I'm glad I got the hell out of LA. I got a great place. And only three hundred a month—with a maid and a cook. I mean, you can't beat that."

Vikki looked around as if to inspect the place. But she seemed to see nothing. Her eyes returned to Harold, the hope draining from them as they became cold and harsh.

"I'm sorry, but I can't believe she never said something to you—something to tell you what they did with Joe."

"Who?"

"Marianna Perado."

"I don't think she had anything to do with him."

"Come on. She knew Vito. Vito must have told her what he did."

Harold shook his head. "Sorry," he said, feeling vaguely sick; he didn't like the way she was looking at him. He had no idea what she would do next.

"Maybe he said something to her that didn't seem like anything at the time. But now if you told me I could put it together and it would . . ."

Harold looked like he was thinking it over. But he finally shook his head. "I really can't think of anything."

She leaned forward desperately. "Listen, I came all the way from LA to talk to you."

"I wish I could help. But I don't know anything more. Really."

"The hell you don't."

She suddenly sounded exhausted. And disgusted. She stood up and turned her back on Harold.

"Maybe it'd help if I told you why I'm really here. I'm not really the grieving widow. I knew what Joe was like. He could be a real pig. I don't know how I took it. But it's just that—without knowing for sure that he's dead—without having an actual *body*—the will can't be executed."

She stared at Harold, holding her breath and waiting for his reaction. But before he could speak she hurried on.

"See, the way Joe had things set up, I had access to only a certain amount of money. And that's gone now. No money, and the insurance won't even pay. They're going to foreclose on the house. I can't sell it because the market is shit. Things're really falling apart in LA now.

"So you see why I'm here now. If the phone rings tomorrow and they say, 'We found your husband and he's dead'—because I'm sure he is—I'd have to pretend I was the grieving widow. But it would be very hard to pretend because I'd be looking at about a million and a half dollars—and another two hundred grand on the insurance."

Her speech left her depressed and spent. She looked at Harold with raw hatred. "But you'll just sit there knowing what you know and you won't say anything, will you?"

"I think you misunderstand."

"I do?"

"I was just a guy who tried to help someone who'd been taken to the cleaners. In return for that—I, well, you could say I got taken pretty bad myself."

She leaned closer. "*How*? Maybe we could work this out together."

"I would if I could," Harold said, thinking how much he'd like to work anything out with this woman. His mind was spinning, tossing up things he might offer her. But then he remembered the DMV cop, the predatory Gammon, the night he'd spent in the stinking jail back in LA. It's not worth it, he told himself.

"I don't know what happened to Joe," he finally said. "And Marianna never confided in me. We didn't have that kind of relationship. I really didn't get to know her at all. Like I said, she was someone I thought I could help. And look where it got me."

Vikki nodded. "So that's it then? I come all the way from LA and that's all you'll tell me."

"It's all I know."

For a moment it looked like she might cry. She turned her face away as she said, "You're the last one. The very last. I kept thinking, if I could just, just talk with you, I would finally *know*, you know? Finally find out what happened. Because it's not knowing that really sucks."

She turned back to him, letting him see the tears. He looked at her as sympathetically as he could without giving anything away.

"Sorry," he said. "I'm real sorry."

She stood up and started down the walk to her car. Harold rose and followed her.

"Are you staying in La Serena?" he said to her back.

"Tonight. In the morning I'll fly back."

As they were passing Harold's car, she suddenly stopped and looked at it curiously.

"It's a French car," he said. "*Deux cheveaux*. It means—"

"Two horses. I haven't seen one of those since Joe and I were in Le Mans."

She turned and faced him, controlling her anger and disappointment.

"If I think of anything that might help, I'll call you," Harold said.

"You do that." Then softer, as if ashamed of her desperation, she added, "I'm staying in a hotel called Las Palmas."

When Harold got back to the patio there was only a small square of sunlight left. He set his chair in the light and listened as the familiar *squeak squeak* of the wheelchair came down the hallway and stopped at the doorway.

"You haven't lost your touch."

Harold turned to Marianna sitting in the wheelchair and smiled. "For what?"

"Lying. I was listening to the whole thing through the window."

"I don't think of it as lying."

"That's why you're so convincing."

She rolled out onto the patio. "I'm ready," she said.

Harold gathered her up in his arms. Feeling her weight and warmth against his chest filled him with happiness. He brought her back to his chair, sitting carefully with her on his lap. She settled into the familiar position; they often sat this way for hours in complete peace.

But this afternoon his mind started to work. He couldn't help thinking about all that money from Joe's will and the insurance. There must be a way to make a deal with Vikki. He could tell her what happened to Joe's body and then just take a percentage. Say fifteen. No, maybe twenty percent. That would be fair. More than fair, really.

With that money he could afford the surgery Marianna needed. She was scheduled for the operation when he sent Tran the money to bond her out of jail and put her on a flight to Chile. That pretty much finished off the ten grand she'd taken off Covo. But with surgery, she might walk again—if he wanted her to. Feeling her in his arms like this, he wondered if that was such a bright idea.

Harold smiled, planning it all out in his mind. Step one: He'd check and make sure Vikki didn't have a detective with her. Step two: He'd call her in the morning and say he'd "remembered a few things that might shed some light on what happened." Step three: Negotiate a percentage. A very fair percentage. Step four . . .

Harold continued daydreaming, picturing Vikki becoming relaxed and even friendly. And he pictured himself sharing with her something that he had only recently discovered: In a way that's almost impossible to see, you always get what you want from life. Four months ago he was stressed out in LA, wondering how the hell he would escape. Who could have guessed that this was his ticket out of there? Now he was free to enjoy every moment of each day.

Vikki had thought Joe was a pig but couldn't get out of the marriage. Now he was dead and she was gonna collect—big-time. If she just hung in there and waited. That was the tough part. Waiting to get what you wanted—and realizing this was it when it finally arrived.

Tina appeared and asked if they wanted anything before she left for the day.

Marianna shook her head no.

Harold said, "Yes. Bring me a beer, please."

"Sorry, Señor, but we don't have any cold."

Harold paused, thinking how perfectly this fit in with what he had just been thinking. You could get whatever you wanted in life, as long as you accepted that, when it arrived, it wasn't always exactly like you thought it would be.

"Bring me one anyway."

"Warm?"

"Yes."

Moments later, she set the bottle and a glass next to him, then disappeared, leaving the house quiet and Marianna drowsy against him. As he enjoyed the last few rays of sunlight he took a swallow of beer. Yes, it was true what they said: It even tasted great when it was warm.

About the Author

PHILIP REED was born in the Midwest and raised in New England. He began his writing career as a night police reporter for the City News Bureau of Chicago and later for the *Rocky Mountain News* in Denver. In 1982 he continued west to Los Angeles, where he directed his first play, *True Blues*. His plays have been staged in Los Angeles, San Francisco, Chicago, and New York. Phil has also written several nonfiction books, including the recently released *Free Throw*. He now lives in Long Beach, California, with his wife, Vivian Blackwell, a poet, and their two sons, Andrew and Tony.